Readers love the bestselling Enhanced series

The Strength of...

"Victoria Sue did it once again. She wrote another incredible book in the Enhanced series."

—Gay Book Reviews

"...this series is very well written and grabs you by the heart strings...."

—Scattered Thoughts and Rogue Words

Guarding His Melody

"All in all, this was a very smooth read, with quirky but relatable characters, a suspenseful and moving story and a stimulating peep into another world."

—Love Bytes

"I know I can always count on Victoria Sue for a great book every time and *Guarding His Melody* is no exception."

—Kimmers' Erotic Book Banter

Beneath This Mask

"I'm a huge fan of this series. It has hot men with superpowers, action, love, and some nice steam... what more does a girl need."

—Dirty Books Obsession

"...fans of the series will love this and love Jake and Gael as a couple...."

—Open Skye Book Reviews

By VICTORIA SUE

In Safe Hands

ENHANCED WORLD
Five Minutes Longer
Who We Truly Are
Beneath This Mask
The Strength of His Heart
Guarding His Melody

Published by DREAMSPINNER PRESS
www.dreamspinnerpress.com

IN
SAFE
HANDS

VICT♡RIA SUE

Published by
DREAMSPINNER PRESS

5032 Capital Circle SW, Suite 2, PMB# 279,
Tallahassee, FL 32305-7886 USA
www.dreamspinnerpress.com

This is a work of fiction. Names, characters, places, and incidents either
are the product of author imagination or are used fictitiously, and any
resemblance to actual persons, living or dead, business establishments,
events, or locales is entirely coincidental.

In Safe Hands
© 2019 Victoria Sue.

Cover Art
© 2019 Jay Aheer.
www.simplydefinedart.com
Cover content is for illustrative purposes only and any person depicted
on the cover is a model.

Mass Market Paperback ISBN: 978-1-64108-175-7
Trade Paperback ISBN: 978-1-64405-230-3
Digital ISBN: 978-1-64405-229-7
Library of Congress Control Number: 2018961344
Mass Market Paperback published June 2019
v. 1.0

Printed in the United States of America
∞
This paper meets the requirements of
ANSI/NISO Z39.48-1992 (Permanence of Paper).

IN
SAFE
HANDS

VICT♡RIA SUE

CHAPTER ONE

HE WAS going to die.

"Breathe, Mav. Come on," the familiar voice cajoled. "In through your nose, out through your mouth."

He was burning. Flames licked their fiery path to his heart.

"Count with me. In and hold. One… two…. Out for one and two."

Blackened faces.

Dead eyes.

"Mav, Mav, let me go, honey. Mav, you're hurting me."

The chopper in flames.

"*Mav!*"

The pained cry pierced the dust cloud rolling in over the desert, and the smell of coffee—*wait, what, coffee?*—tickled his nose. The deep breath his lungs screamed for flooded his system, and Mav opened his eyes. He saw his sister's living room, the stone fireplace with the pictures of his niece from a baby all the way up to junior year. And the new photo. The one he hadn't noticed before. The one of him walking across the tarmac five or so years ago. All of them in flight suits. Cass and him laughing at some joke Charlie had told. In the oppressive Somalian desert they'd have been happier in board shorts, but he doubted Uncle Sam would be. His sister must have found it and innocently thought to display it, and it had been enough to set him off. Dumped him in the rabbit hole that was his life. Some days were harder to climb out than others.

He didn't realize the TV was blaring until he focused on it, and he looked up into Jamie's worried face as she muted it. No, her *pained* face as she rubbed her arm. *Shit.* "Jamie, I'm sorry." The angry marks, where his fingers had been crushing her wrist, were livid even on her already dark skin. "Shit." He said it out loud this time and tried to sit up.

Her gentle hand on his shoulder slowed him down, and she smiled, brown eyes full of worry. "My fault for trying to wake you up suddenly." Her eyes slid to the half-empty bottle of Jack and the dregs of some in a tumbler. He didn't hear the defeated sigh, but he knew it would have left her lungs.

He swallowed the disgusting taste of old liquor and fear down his dry throat and reached for the coffee she had put on the small coffee table. He didn't bother saying sorry again, as those words were getting older than the whiskey.

"I need a favor, Mav," Jamie said, and sudden shame burned through him. He'd been crashing at his older sister's for a month—no, make that three—since he'd given up on the therapy and the good intentions that would never get him back to what he was meant for, never make him whole. She'd never criticized. Never asked him for anything except to keep his whiskey away from Melanie, his seventeen-year-old niece. Not that Melanie ever seemed to venture anywhere near him.

Sensible kid.

Like her mom.

But Jamie and Melanie were both struggling since his no-good brother-in-law decided a wife and family weren't enough for him and went off to have a midlife crisis in Aruba, or some such place with sun, sand, and a twenty-four-year-old named Traci, or Terry, or *turd* as he had heard Melanie call her.

His brain processed Jamie's request as he practically inhaled the coffee. Not that he could do much, and if the favor involved him going to an appointment or an Alcoholics Anonymous meeting—he wasn't quite there yet, but give him another month—Jamie was shit out of luck.

Caffeine flooded his system. Not enough to chase the alcohol away completely, but he wasn't seeing sand anymore. Or bodies….

"I need a favor, little brother," Jamie repeated, and Mav groaned inaudibly. Really? She was gonna bring out the *brother* card?

"So long as you don't need me to run errands." The sarcasm shot out deadlier than a round from his service 9mm Beretta, and even he winced at the look on Jamie's face when it hit.

"That's not fair," Jamie retorted, and Mav watched in detached interest as his sister finally lost her temper the way he'd been goading her into doing for what seemed all their lives. "I need you to do *one* thing."

He'd been here three months, and this was the first time she had asked him for anything. He had to know. "What do you need?"

"I need you to look competent and go sit behind the desk in the office for me."

"No." The refusal left Mav's lips before he'd even thought about it.

"No one cares, Mav." Jamie's immediate retort was blunt.

I do. He'd seen the averted eyes and the rush of words people stumbled over as they tried not to look him in the face—or not look *at* his scarred face—as they spoke to him. Even the doctors always seemed to want to race through the bad news. Some couldn't look him in the eye. But none of it was Jamie's fault.

"Why do I need to look competent?" Shame burned through every nerve until his guilt was ash in the back of his throat. He'd never needed to *look* competent before; as a US Air Force pilot, competence had been his middle name.

Now it was just *cripple.*

"Because I have papers to serve, and Aaron Malloy is in town. I am reliably told he will stop to visit his on-again, off-again girlfriend at the Blue Room, and it's gonna be my only chance."

It was Mav's turn to frown as he glanced at the time on his phone. It was already after five. He hated Jamie being a process server, but seeing as how Simon—his no-good former brother-in-law—had abandoned his family and the small agency they ran, she had no choice. Unfortunately, the bastard had emptied their joint bank accounts, including Melanie's college money, on his way to the airport. And while they might not have a mortgage anymore, his sister still had to live and his niece still had to go to school.

"Can't you just rearrange it?"

Jamie answered him with her trademark "Mom till I die" look and sat down on the couch. It squeaked alarmingly. The back room had been an area for Melanie to hang out with her friends when Jamie didn't want them to go upstairs into Melanie's room, but since Mav descended on them, he had commandeered it as his. Melanie didn't care, as she wanted the excuse for her friends to be upstairs with her, and now her mom couldn't object. And it was opposite the downstairs bathroom and small shower, which Mav didn't use as much as he should.

As if Jamie heard his thoughts, she wrinkled her nose. "You need to look like a grown-up. I've been recommended to a possible new client, and if I'm going to get the agency started, I need all the help I can get, and even I can't do two things at once."

Mav let the comment slide. "Who is it?"

Jamie looked over at the TV she had muted, clicked through the TV menu, and increased the volume. He glanced at her in surprise. The program was a repeat of a much earlier news item. "Do you know who that is?"

He watched the old clip of the interview they'd shown right after a group he recognized playing in some concert. He rolled his eyes. "The whole world knows who Six Sundays are. *Were*," he added.

The screen panned to the lead singer, Deacon Daniels—which had to be a made-up name—and Mav vaguely remembered the story detailing his career implosion and the demise of the band. Good-looking, obviously, but Mav would bet the blue of Daniels's eyes was helped with contact lenses. And his skin was so white, it had to be helped with makeup. *Airhead.* Mav dismissed him. "What's he done now?"

"According to his publicist—Shirley Maplin, one of my closest friends—he actually hasn't done anything."

"I thought he had an accident or—"

"No, it was his stalker, or that was what they thought at the time. The problems go back to about a year ago, not long after their first hit single. They'd signed a deal with Sony, and Nickelodeon had a show in the works for them. Then this reporter did a big exposé on Deacon and found out that his brother—five years older than him—recently died of a drug overdose. Sony dropped them, and the Nickelodeon show was canceled. Sued the band members for breach of contract—"

"Why?" Mav interrupted. This was getting way too complicated for just coffee, and his eyes strayed to the bottle of Jack.

"Because the reporter implied a connection with Deacon and drug use. Small print, essentially. If they do something to damage the band's image within two years of signing, they get sued personally for all the promo money lost. Between that and the legal fees, which ran into tens of thousands, they are all broke. The band members all blamed Deacon, hoping if they distanced themselves, Sony might reconsider, but apparently, Deacon was the main draw."

Mav shook his head. "Whatever happened to sex, drugs, and rock and roll?" Fuck, he felt old.

"Tweenagers," Jamie said with a straight face. "Or basically, the new biggest spender in the music industry, but because it's essentially their parents who are coughing up the cash, any group aimed at the adolescent market has to be squeaky clean."

"And the stalker?"

"His fool agent—*apparently*—made up an elaborate stalker plot to try and garner public sympathy, hoping to resurrect the Sony deal, and it got way out of hand when a woman handed herself in to the cops."

"How long ago was all this?"

"Last year but the whole thing blew up again around Thanksgiving when this woman 'confessed' and had the press chasing her everywhere."

"And she ran the car off a road?" Mav tried to remember, but seven months ago he hadn't been in a state to remember much of anything.

"With her one-year-old son in it, yes." Jamie looked woefully at the TV. "They both died when the car went up in flames. Anyway, the networks tried to crucify Daniels, saying the hoax had resulted in this woman's death."

"And what has any of this got to do with us?"

"*You know.* We have a friend out in Oregon who started a similar business serving papers like us but progressed to other things. Protection, even bond enforcement. He's ex-military and has loads of contacts. Anyway, he told Simon last year he could easily give him some tips—"

"But you don't have any ex—" *Shit.* It had been him. He'd forgotten that had been their original intention and vaguely seemed to remember a drunken talk one night when he had been home on leave. He'd been eager and listed a few of his buddies he knew would help. Of course, it was before his own world had imploded. The plan had been to incorporate protection into their agency, and while Mav had no intention of chasing shoplifters, it had been an area he was going to be involved in when he finished his twenty and left the Air Force in any other way than the manner he had been forced to.

"I'm confused." *And thirsty.* He glanced at the empty glass on the table. "I must be missing something. He doesn't need papers served, and he doesn't need protection. He might need a better attorney if it isn't too late, but why has he got an appointment in the first place?"

"Daniels went to the cops last week and reported what he believes might be another stalker." Jamie wrinkled her nose to show what she thought of his decision.

"And the cops are saying, what?"

"The cops laughed him out of the precinct." Jamie sighed. "Everyone thinks Daniels is trying to pull the same stunt he did before."

"But wouldn't that be incredibly stupid?"

Jamie nodded. "Exactly, and from what Shirley tells me—"

"Do you trust her?"

"She has some narration work lined up for him— audiobooks are a big thing. If that works out, he may do voice-over commercial work. Apparently his spoken voice is as good as his singing one. It's a really good chance for him, but if he's to have any chance of resurrecting his career, this needs to be resolved quickly, so he needs to stay out of the limelight."

"When you say 'resolved quickly,' what do you mean? You're not running a detective agency, sis." Mav let a little amusement creep into his voice.

Jamie rolled her eyes. "Shirley thinks the stress might be getting to him."

And the penny dropped. "She thinks he's making this whole thing up too?" *Wonderful.* Daniels was some diva who wanted the attention for fuck knew why.

"She wants us to hold his hand for a couple of days. I know we're not officially protecting anyone yet, but she needs someone discreet."

It made some sense. Jamie had been a cop for six years before Melanie was born and twelve years after. Running a home and an office never stopped her from going to the range or running the marathons she favored. "And there's no way this is for real? It's been a long time since you had to protect and serve, sis."

Jamie grinned. "I know. They only need someone to look good. No chasing down suspects or anything."

"As if I can do either," Mav muttered.

Jamie met his gaze unflinchingly. "Don't you think you've hosted this one-man pity party long enough?" She smirked. "Besides which, I think it makes you look badass."

More like Freddy Krueger, Mav thought, and forced himself not to finger the burn scars that twisted the skin on his neck and jaw.

"Shirley promised me an insane amount of money for two days because she can trust me to keep my mouth closed," Jamie continued. "If he's still here when I get back, I'll take over if you want me to."

Mav tried to decide if Jamie was saying this because she actually wanted to branch out, or she had just found a way to get Mav off his butt. But he owed her. "Tell me again what you want me to do?"

"I need you to get shaved, showered, and dressed for starters," Jamie said pointedly. "Then I need you to sit behind the desk in the office and reassure him, get details."

Mav took a deep breath and tried to keep the hand holding the coffee from shaking.

"Do you need any help?" Jamie asked gently.

He shook his head and reached for his leg.

His *plastic* one.

Which was the reason he wasn't still in the Air Force being useful, and the reason all he could do to help his sister was sit behind a desk. He couldn't protect anyone anymore.

Not even pretty blue-eyed boys.

CHAPTER TWO

DEACON PULLED his car to a stop and gazed with interest at the two-story house. Quiet neighborhood but close enough to the neighbors to be social, and one of the nicest in Atlanta. A family home, and very different from where he was living. He looked at his GPS to make sure he was at the right address—Vanguard Circle in southwest Marietta—and ran his hand over the buttery-soft leather console almost absently. Shirley had called the BMW his grown-up car. He would have been happier with a minivan because some of them had very cool stuff for Molly, but as that wasn't exactly an issue now, he didn't care that the car would be taken off him soon. In fact, it was probably just as well it was going to get repossessed, because it would likely be stolen anyway if not. Deacon smiled wryly. *Gallows humor* his grandad, Pops, would call it and would chuckle in a mock evil way over whatever joke he had just told.

He scrambled out of the car and couldn't help the automatic glance at the empty back seat. Molly would have been giggling excitedly now. She loved taking any sort of trip with him.

Deacon brushed his sweaty palms down his jeans and tried to slow his breathing. Shirley had said Jamie would be perfect. A mom herself, an ex-cop, and old enough to have the right amount of common sense. Deacon knew the criticism had been aimed at him. Shirley thought he had lost his mind and was about to push away the first decent chance in over a year. But her reaction wasn't as embarrassing as the desk sergeant. Hell, that had been an exercise in humility. This was his last chance to convince someone to listen to him, and as he glanced at the time on his phone, he knew he'd better move. Being late wasn't likely to get Shirley's friend to be sympathetic.

He walked up the path, wishing he was wearing shorts and not caring what he looked like for once. He couldn't help the nervous glances he threw around, but the reporters had all slithered underground again. It was unlikely they were still following him. He pressed the bell, hearing the echo and then the measured steps on what was probably a tiled floor.

The door opened, and his own step back was automatic, even if he had tried to unsuccessfully cover up his shocked reaction. Deacon knew by the way the man's lips tightened and thinned that he hadn't been fooled.

"I'm Maverick Delgardo. The office is directly in front of you."

They shook hands as Deacon muttered his name. Then ducking his head away from the knowing stare, he stepped into blessedly cool air and walked forward across the entranceway and into the office opposite him. He sank gratefully into the large leather chair in front of the desk and looked behind him, wondering where Mr. Delgardo had gone. Deacon heard the main door close and then watched the man walk excruciatingly slowly toward where he was. He turned back before Delgardo could see him watching and was embarrassed again. His reaction to the man's face had been bad enough; the last thing he wanted was to be caught staring. Delgardo was limping, but his steps were so forced it looked like he was hurt in both legs. Awkward silence settled in the room, and Deacon looked up as Delgardo came into the office.

"Mr. Daniels—"

"Deacon, please," he interjected.

"Then call me Maverick or Mav, if you like."

"M-Mav?" Deacon clamped his lips together. For God's sake, he sounded like a little kid.

"My sister sends her apologies. She had papers to serve, and the two appointments clashed. However, if you tell me exactly what the problem seems to be, we will see what we can do to help."

Deacon opened his mouth to launch into the same explanation he had tried to tell the cops. That he'd gotten the note on the windshield of his car. That he had finally been given the chance to start his life again, and it wasn't about to slip through his fingers—it was likely being wrenched from his grasp. But all that came out was "I think I'm losing my mind." And he pushed away from the desk and stood. He couldn't do this. It was pointless and humiliating.

There was a beat of silence while he waited for Mav to agree with him, but Mav just said, "It seems a waste of gas, you driving here and leaving without seeing if we can do something." He sounded so reasonable. Maybe Maverick was good at calming hysterical clients.

"Sorry," he offered and sat down again.

Mav shook his head. "There's no reason to apologize. Do you want to start at the beginning?"

Deacon met Maverick's calm brown eyes and seemed to breathe a little easier. His gaze roamed over the large man, and he felt his heartbeat slow. In any other situation, Deacon would be really attracted to him. And it wasn't just his size. It was the aura of competence surrounding Maverick that pushed all Deacon's buttons.

"I found a note on my car eight days ago."

"You have the note?"

Deacon shook his head. "I threw it away, but the cops kept the second."

"The second?" Mav asked immediately, his focus laser-sharp.

"It was on my car three days ago. It just said, 'I'm watching you, Joker.'"

Mav looked up. "Joker?"

"Only a Joker," Deacon said flatly, wondering if the guy was deliberately being dense. "The number one hit off our first album." When everything had been good.

· "Where was your car both times?"

"Outside my apartment."

"So the cops are thinking this is a joke—*sorry*—just in bad taste?"

Deacon nodded. "I know it probably is…." He'd tried very hard to convince himself it was. "I didn't like whoever knowing what I drive or where I live."

"But you're not sure?"

Maybe Deacon wasn't fooling anyone. "Do you know what happened before?" He kept looking at Maverick until he saw the knowledge in the steady gaze. He didn't know whether to be relieved or ashamed.

"I know about the car fatality last year, if that's what you mean."

"And my niece?"

Maverick's eyes narrowed. "Your niece? There was a threat to your niece?"

"No. My older brother died less than a year ago and named me Molly's guardian, much to the disgust of my mother."

"Your brother who died of an overdose," Mav clarified.

Deacon tried not to wince. "Yes. Molly is two and has lived with me since Mikey died. Mikey didn't know about her for a few months until her mother died."

"Did you know?"

"No," Deacon whispered. "We sent texts, emailed, that sort of thing, but I was too busy being a rock star, and I think Mikey wanted to meet me as an equal this time." He rubbed a hand over his face. "I paid for rehab just over three years ago, and it killed him that I had to. Mikey always saw himself as my protector, not the other way around, so when he lost his job, instead of calling me, he tried to cope." For a second Deacon closed his eyes. He'd been playing the "if only" game for far too long. "Anyway, long story short, Sony and Nickelodeon dropped the band, and my fool agent made up the stalker story, and that poor woman died. My mom got the agent to swear the idea was mine and won custody of Molly last month. Manny completely trashed me in court, saying I made everything up and it was likely my influence that sent Mikey off the rails in the first place. That's why no one believes me."

Mav searched his face for a few seconds. "Well, I'm not a lawyer, so I can't comment on the custody case, but the rest makes no sense. You have your first real chance at a new career. You would have to be a masochist to instigate this."

Deacon blew out a breath and relaxed a little. Did that mean *he* believed him? "Don't get me wrong. I'm hoping to death this is a bad joke by some bitter fan."

"A fan?"

"Yeah, I got a ton of hate mail when we lost both deals and the band split up." Deacon swallowed. "Actual death threats. That's when my agent decided it would be a good idea to invent the story someone was out to get me. He thought it might swing public opinion back the other way. A disaster waiting to happen. I didn't know." He wanted this guy to believe him. He *needed* Mav to believe him… which made no sense whatsoever.

Mav seemed content to let silence settle over the room. Deacon tried not to squirm.

"There's something else," Maverick said.

Deacon looked up in surprise. It hadn't been a question. "Yes, but I didn't tell the cops."

Mav tilted his head silently, waiting for the answer.

"My phone keeps ringing, and no one talks when I answer. It's a blocked number." It had been annoying at first, but after the note, it took on another meaning.

"Have you changed your number?"

Deacon nodded. "And it's unlisted, but it barely took a few days before it started again." And when he got the disbelieving reaction about the note, he hadn't bothered mentioning the phone.

"And?" Mav watched him steadily.

"You're gonna think I'm crazy." *He* thought he was crazy.

"I really need you to tell me everything."

But still he hesitated. Not that it mattered if everyone thought he was insane now. He'd lost Molly. He'd lost her for good. And if this was some crazy fan, much as he hated the idea, Molly was better off with his mother.

"I've seen the same car following me a few times." He laughed shortly. It sounded like a bad cop show.

"Did you get a license? Description?" Mav dragged a notepad toward him.

"It's probably my imagination." He wasn't sure whether to feel worried or vindicated when Mav shook his head. "It's a Dodge Charger. I used to be crazy about them as a teenager, so I tend to take notice of them even now when they're quite common. I've never seen it close enough for any details. It's just all black"—he lifted his hand to forestall any comment—"and I know that's a popular color, but it was exactly what I wanted back then. So when I see one, I notice. Now it's like I see it all the time."

"Do you ever see who's driving?"

Deacon shook his head, but then the cell phone sitting on the desk started dancing across it, and Mav glanced at the screen, then swiped it up. Deacon stepped outside the office, thinking Maverick might need some privacy. No, now he was lying to himself. He needed a minute away from those astute brown eyes that seemed to ask a ton of questions he wasn't sure he had the answers to. He gazed at the pretty teenager whose photos were all over the walls and wondered if she was Mav's daughter. He would have been young, though. Maybe it was his niece?

"Sorry, I'm going to have to cut this short."

Deacon looked up as Mav appeared at the doorway to the office. It seemed to sum up their interaction so far, all the apologies, but then he noted the stiffness in Mav's face. "What's wrong?"

"Jamie just got sideswiped by an idiot who ran a stoplight. Her ankle is the biggest casualty, though." He blew out a breath. "It could have been so much worse."

"You obviously need to go," Deacon said immediately. "Where is she being taken?"

Mav shook himself. "WellStar on Parkway. About a thirty minute cab ride."

"Plus however long they take to show up. You'll have to navigate." Deacon turned for the door, but a large hand stopped him.

"I wasn't asking—"

"I know," Deacon assured him. Not waiting for any other objection, he hurried to the car while Mav was hopefully locking the door.

As Mav got into the BMW, Deacon, even though he tried not to watch, immediately understood what was buried beneath the baggy sweats Mav wore. Mav had to grab his right leg and swing it into the floorboard. Deacon's mind was going a million miles a minute, but he could hardly ask. Was whatever happened to his leg the same as what had damaged his face?

As soon as Mav was in, Deacon set off. "You need to go right at the end and head for seventy-five" was all Mav said. The quiet seemed oppressive, but Deacon didn't know how to break it. Mav was obviously worried about his sister, so small talk would just be insensitive.

He was almost relieved when they pulled up outside the ER. "I'm sorry we had to cut the meeting short." Deacon desperately wanted to go around and help Mav out of the car, but he wasn't suicidal. Mav managed to get out, and then he turned, white-knuckling the hand on the edge of the car door.

"Let me know how she is?" he urged before Mav could say anything else.

Mav looked taken aback that Deacon would care, but he nodded. "Give me your phone."

Deacon handed it over in surprise. "The password is MOL2015."

Mav took the phone, and Deacon tried not to watch his hand tremble as Mav entered the password and typed a quick text. "I've sent myself your number." He passed it back, then hesitated. "Thanks," he said, then shut the door.

The phone rang almost right away, and Deacon recognized the number as Augusta's, Mrs. Sanchez's daughter, who also had an apartment in their complex. He answered it immediately.

"Deacon?"

A chill walked down his spine. "What is it?"

"Deacon, I'm so sorry, but the AC people were late, and when I went to let them in, your door was damaged. It looks like someone broke in. I called the cops." Her voice hitched. "I think you'd better come see."

Deacon sat completely frozen for what seemed like forever, and he automatically looked over to the entrance where Mav had gone inside. "Has anything been stolen?"

"It's hard to tell," Augusta whispered.

The chill in his back turned icy. "What do you mean?"

He heard the breath she took. "It's trashed, Deacon. I'm sorry."

Deacon was moving before he realized it. Another twenty minutes and he was pulling into his apartment complex. He saw the two black-and-whites with blue lights flashing as he pulled up, but he didn't even need to get out of the car to see what was upsetting Augusta. In huge red letters spray-painted over his door were the words "The joke's on you."

It was starting all over again. And this time he was worried it was never going to stop.

CHAPTER THREE

"IT'S BROKEN." Jamie's eyes filled for the second time in so many hours, and Mav hushed her as he wrapped his arms around her. He heard a discreet cough from the corner and looked over to see an older man dressed in a white coat, who he remembered from the man's visits to his sister's. "*Richards*?"

The man nodded in relief, and they shook hands. Mav glanced back at his sister, waiting to find out why Harvey Richards was here, when Richards spoke up.

"Mav, I know we haven't seen each other many times, but I'm David's father. I work in the ER and saw the notification of Jamie's admission." He paused and looked fondly at Mav's sister. "Jamie's gonna be off her feet for a few days and then crutches for at least six weeks. In three days, Melanie and David leave on their school trip to Spain, so Melanie won't be any help to her mom." He coughed. "My elderly mother lives with me, and I employ a nurse to help her with personal care."

Mav had no idea what any of this—*oh*, no, he did. Jamie would need personal care, and he wasn't even capable of taking care of himself most days. He looked back at Jamie, who was smiling even though she was obviously in pain.

"The thing is, I would be delighted to have Jamie come and stay with me while she recovers. Miss Abernathy is more than able to help Jamie at the same time, and I have another spare room for Melanie until they leave for Spain." He paused. "You are more than welcome to the couch in the meantime. I—"

"That is very generous but completely unnecessary," Mav assured the man. He felt Jamie's fingers tighten on his.

"Are you sure?" she asked worriedly.

"Positive." Mav smiled and shot Richards an assessing look. He had a feeling Richards would be more than happy for Jamie to move in there full-time, and that was totally their business, but Mav didn't think Jamie had even halfway recovered from what her bastard of an ex-husband had done.

"They want to keep me in tonight, but I can be discharged tomorrow," she added, and at that moment, a frantic Melanie burst into the room and nearly flung herself at Jamie.

"Mom!"

Mav assumed the young man who followed and greeted Richards was David, his son.

Jamie gave Melanie a big hug, then immediately transitioned into Mom mode, giving Melanie instructions for packing clothes and toiletries. David was going to drive her back now for them. Faced with a task,

Melanie immediately calmed down and seemed to realize Mav was in the room.

"Uncle Mav, do you want a ride home?" she offered immediately.

Mav hesitated and looked down at his sister.

"Oh, I forgot. How did the meeting go?"

"We kind of got interrupted," he said, smiling for
the first time since the hospital had called him, but not
having the first clue what to make of the tinge of regret
that accompanied that statement. Which was a shame.
Deacon Daniels was intriguing. "But I think it was just
someone's idea of a practical joke. Likely to be a dis-
gruntled fan." He shrugged like it was no big deal. "I'm
going to meet with him tomorrow." Not that he'd made
any arrangements, but it wouldn't hurt to talk some
more. He tried to ease his weight without making it obvious. The pain in his back was something fierce.

"Can you manage?" Jamie asked, noticing.

"Absolutely," Mav assured her, with way more
confidence than he actually felt. She didn't look convinced but just nodded. He squeezed her hand and followed his niece, probably walking much faster than he
should.

It was his own fault. He'd gone through the fitting
and the weeks-long process of healing, but after four
months, when he hadn't been able to seamlessly transition into handling and balancing on the leg that was
supposed to make him whole, he'd simply run away—
or *crawled* might be more apt. He'd missed three fitting
appointments, and he knew his residual had shrunk.
He *knew* it. But rational thought had taken a back seat
to disappearing into a Jack and Coke. These days he
didn't even bother with the Coke.

Supposed to make him whole? He was more broken every day.

He was glad Melanie and David didn't notice how long it took him to get into the house. She had run in practically before he'd swung his leg out. Not that he blamed her. And she was a good kid. Just mostly oblivious, as teenagers often were, and she'd had a shock. When one parent proved unreliable, kids tended to hold on to the other with gritted teeth.

He had.

And Jamie had been absent at the time. She'd already been at college when Dad lost his job. Not that any of them had realized for quite a while. The first Mav had known was when he'd heard his mom sobbing in the kitchen. He'd rushed straight in there, thinking she was alone, but his dad was there, and Mav hadn't known what to do. He'd gone upstairs and listened when the footsteps and the slam of the door told him his dad had left. And much to his shame, he had stayed where he was instead of rushing down to talk to his mom. Dad had come home after a few hours, and it was only when he didn't leave for work the next day that Mav found out his dad had gotten fired two whole months earlier but had been too ashamed to admit it. Mav hadn't understood. At only twelve, he'd thought everything would be okay. Even when his dad spent most days slumped in front of the TV and his mom got a job and went out to work.

Even when she had looked more tired. Even when she'd gotten sick, and especially when she'd died.

And through it all, his dad had sat there, drinking and watching TV. Of course, he'd died himself three years later, but to Mav, his dad had stopped living the day he became unemployed.

Mav's phone was ringing as soon as he made it inside. It seemed to be the day for it, and he answered, already heading for the back room and a drink. "Yep?"

"Mr. Delgardo?"

Mav stilled at the official-sounding voice. But Jamie was okay. He'd only just left her. "Yes, what—"

"Mr. Deacon Daniels has asked us to call you. I'm Officer—" Mav sucked in oxygen and missed the next few words. "Mr. Delgardo? Would you be able to collect him? Are you—"

Mav heard muffled voices in the background, and then the phone was taken over. "Mav?"

Mav sat heavily.

Deacon's voice came over the line. "You don't have to collect me at all." But before Mav had the chance to ask what was wrong or what had happened, Deacon started talking again. "I'm sorry. Of course I can go to a motel. It was only that they were asking if I had protection." He sounded shaken.

"What happened?" Mav asked, glad his voice sounded reasonable, and really, that was what the cop should have started with.

"My apartment." Deacon swallowed audibly. "It's been trashed. Although the plus is you are my alibi, so there is that." His voice sounded so brittle.

"Trashed?"

"Graffiti spray-painted. Furniture broken." Deacon laughed bitterly. "You get the idea."

"I'll come for you," Mav immediately said, wondering how fast he could get a cab.

"No, it's completely not necessary. I'm sorry, but I told them you were my protection, or Jamie is." His voice rose as if it was a question.

"Yes, confirm it with the cops. Tell them you will be staying here while we find out what is going on," Mav said, immediately wishing he felt as calm as he sounded. He heard another voice in the background, and then Deacon spoke again. "Officer Fitzpatrick says he can drop me off, and the other officer knows where the house is."

Good, thought Mav, *it's probably an old colleague of Jamie's.* He knew she'd kept in touch, especially with Keith, her old partner, and his wife, Felicia.

Deacon hung up after saying he would be there soon, and Mav sank down onto his couch, feeling every protest in his useless fucking leg… and reached for the bottle of Jack.

His hand hovered for a second. In his mind, he was unscrewing the cap, splashing a little of the deep amber whiskey into his tumbler, and licking his lips after the burning liquid seemed oddly to slide so smoothly down his throat and calm the fire in his gut. He needed it. He needed to take the edge off his shakes and look far more competent than he felt.

He *needed* it.

And for no other reason than that guilty admission—one more among so fucking many—he fisted his empty hand and pressed it down on the shell of what used to be his right knee.

Mav winced as he stood. He'd already walked farther on his leg today than he had all month. The most he had done since he arrived at his sister's was go to the bathroom and the kitchen. He'd even slept on the couch because he said he couldn't manage the stairs. Which was a lie but meant he got left alone. At least this way, there was a room for Deacon.

Mav determinedly picked up the bottle and shoved it on a high shelf above the TV. Out of sight, out of mind? He would be so lucky.

His response to the cops and to Deacon started ringing in his ears like a damn bell. He had said he was Deacon's protection, which was laughable. Jamie was originally going to take on the role, but she couldn't now, obviously, and if tonight was anything to go by, it looked like someone might be taking this to another level. Deacon might need protection for real, and it seriously complicated things.

Of course, Deacon could still be making all this up, but he doubted it. From what he could tell, Deacon seemed genuine. He must have been pretty freaked-out to agree to come here. The offer of a motel seemed half-hearted at best, but didn't these show-business types have loads of money? The car he'd driven was a top-of-the-line BMW, and it wouldn't have come cheap.

"Uncle Mav?" Melanie appeared, David hovering behind her.

He plastered on a smile. "You all set?"

She nodded. "Mom said to tell you the fridge is full and so is the freezer."

"I won't starve." He chuckled, touched she was worried. "Go on. Your mom will be expecting her things." He would talk to Jamie tomorrow when she wasn't in pain and ask her advice about Deacon.

He ought to admit she had a new houseguest as well.

Mel smiled, obviously relieved, and left quickly.

Now what should he do? He glanced at his phone. Nearly ten. He walked into the large kitchen and opened the fridge. It was as packed as Melanie had assured him it would be.

At the last second, he went to the cupboard above the fridge where the pills were. He really needed the ones the hospital had given him, but he would cope with some ibuprofen.

He quickly swallowed three and took another look around the room—no idea why, but it gave him something to do. Then, for the same reason, he made a plate of sandwiches. He was relieved when the doorbell rang sometime later. Schooling his face to try to walk without it looking like he was stepping on nails, he managed to make it to the front door.

He blinked in stunned recognition at the cop.

"Mav?" Hunter "Charlie" Chaplin stood as speechless as Mav. "I didn't…." He trailed off, glancing at Mav's leg.

Mav shook his head. "*A cop?*"

Charlie nodded vigorously. "Long story. We'll have to get a beer."

Shit he hadn't known. He'd been so wrapped up in his own pity party he'd never actually checked whether Charlie had married or even knew he'd moved from Toledo. Charlie had always intended to reenlist, but his girlfriend had been sick or something, so when his term ended a year ago, he'd had no choice but to go home. At least it had kept him alive. If he'd been there when they'd gone to evacuate the aid workers and the bomb had detonated, Mav would have lost another friend. Charlie had texted Mav a few times after Cass died, but not being able to cope with the reminder of how tight the three of them had once been, Mav had ignored him. Which was shit. *He* was a shit.

"No." He couldn't just let Charlie go.

Charlie put out a hand to Mav's arm. "I can't believe Cass…." Mav shared the loss, the regret in

Charlie's eyes for a second before Charlie's radio crackled and he stepped back to answer it.

"We'll be in touch tomorrow, sir," the other officer said and nodded pleasantly at Deacon.

"Let's get that beer sometime soon," Charlie said to Mav before he and his partner hurried off.

"How's Jamie?" Deacon asked immediately.

"Going to stay at her friend's tomorrow and be pampered," Mav replied. "Tell me what happened." Deacon glanced at him, and Mav saw the dark shadows under his eyes. "Never mind. Let's go in the kitchen. I have food, coffee, or something stronger?"

The tiny stab of disappointment when Deacon asked for coffee burned inside Mav. It would have been an excuse for him to have something stronger if Deacon had asked for it. The coffee was brewed, so he simply poured two mugs and dumped the little basket Jamie had full of creamers and stuff onto the table next to a spoon. He got the sandwiches from the fridge and put them on the table, quite pleased when he remembered plates and napkins. He would have probably torn off a piece of kitchen towel and just used that if it had been only him.

No, if it had been only him, he doubted the sandwiches would have ever happened. He only ate when Jamie put food in front of him.

Deacon helped himself to a couple of vanilla-flavored creamers and seemed to take his time stirring them in. Mav knew he was probably still processing, and he looked considerably paler than earlier, if that was even possible. It couldn't be makeup anyway.

Deacon's phone rang, and he lifted it out of his pocket, glanced at the screen, frowned, and then answered it. Mav could hear a voice and saw Deacon half close his eyes, almost in defeat. He ended the call without saying a word.

"Another crank call?" Mav clipped, straightening from where he was leaning against the counter.

"No. I almost wish it was. I recognized her."

"Her?"

"Sara Jeffries. Reporter. She did a fabricated exposé about me holding wild parties and taking drugs. It was supposedly how Mikey got hooked." The wry tilt of his lips told Mav more than any denial. "Then she was like a dog with a bone. Covered the stalker story, the accident, and the investigation."

"What did she want?"

"Wanted to know if I was upset about the break-in."

"Already? That's fast. How did she know?"

Deacon shrugged. "Maybe I should have taken the money she offered for an exclusive."

"Why would the press assume you got Mikey hooked on drugs?" It seemed a stretch to Mav.

"Because I was an idiot when I first went to college. There was an incident with weed and a couple of guys that were in the band with me. Someone dragged that up, and because Mikey was ex-military, it's easier to assume a bad-boy band singer is partying too hard than a hero might need narcotics to get him through the day because Uncle Sam turned his back."

Maverick inclined his head in agreement. He knew the horrific stats. Knew guys himself who had ended up on the streets because the transition to home life had been impossible for them and there wasn't the help they deserved. Then something else occurred to him. "What car does Sara Jeffries drive?" It would be interesting if it was a Charger.

"I have no idea. Do you think it's her that's following me?" Deacon had obviously caught on.

"But why?" Maverick mused. "I can't see her getting any mileage out of a possible break-in."

"*Possible?*"

Mav lifted his hand. "I don't mean it didn't happen, before you bite my head off. I meant I wasn't sure what they class the crime as. Was anything stolen?"

"Hard to tell, but no, I don't think so." Deacon's phone dinged with an alert.

Mav watched the expression of disbelief as Deacon read the text, then held it up so Mav could. Mav frowned while he read the message.

A little sympathy wouldn't hurt your cause, unless this is another made-up instance. I can run the story just as easily without you.

Mav searched Deacon's face as he reread the message. Deacon pressed his lips together tightly, as if to stop words from slipping out. It could be anger, frustration even—totally understandable—but there seemed an underlying sadness to the droop of his shoulders. Maybe he missed his niece? "How did she get the number?"

"It's not listed, so I don't know."

Mav didn't think it was that hard to get unlisted numbers, but he would have to ask Jamie. "Who has it?"

"Shirley. Mrs. Sanchez. Her daughter, Augusta. The clinic. The cops." He hesitated. "My mother. But none of them would give it out."

"Is there any reason anyone apart from a disappointed fan would have it in for you?"

Deacon thought about it for a second, and then his lips tilted in an approximation of a smile. "If you had asked me that last year, I would have said the line is infinite, but it's been months, so I have no idea why it should start up again." His mouth flattened. "Shirley thinks it might be because I just lost Molly."

Mav took a breath, wishing he had something else to give him a shot of courage. He gazed at Deacon to try and decide if he was upset. Either he was a cold bastard and Molly would be better off with the grandparents, or he was good at hiding his feelings.

"I told the cops I was your bodyguard, but we both know that's not going to work." Mav bent down and hitched his pants up in case Deacon still didn't get it and showed him the edge of the metal ankle joint.

Deacon didn't seem surprised. "Up to today, I was going to employ you for a couple of weeks and see if things settled down now I'm out of the media. Shirley said people get bored easily and to give it a few days."

Up to today? Before he saw me. Mav tried not to let the disappointment show.

"No," Deacon said as understanding flashed across his face. "This has nothing to do with your ability to do the job. To be honest, I would think all you have to do is look at people and they would run screaming—" Deacon snapped his mouth closed midsentence, and the dawning horror on his face told Mav he hadn't meant it how it sounded. "Oh my God," he moaned behind the hands he was trying to hide behind. "I swear I didn't mean that. Or I did, but not in any way—"

And suddenly, humor bubbled up in Mav. Deacon stopped when he heard the low chuckle and lowered his hands cautiously. "You're very direct," Mav remarked, realizing he wasn't offended in the least.

"*I meant*," Deacon stressed, "that you look like one of those Ranger-type SWAT Special Forces guys that can kill me with your little finger."

Mav's smile widened. "I was a helicopter pilot."

"Exactly," Deacon said as if that proved his point and nodded determinedly. "The real reason is a little more embarrassing than saying all that, though." He took a breath. "I'm broke. I had a chance at another job yesterday, but they've given it to an established voice actor."

Mav stared at Deacon. "Broke as in you can't afford to engage us for two weeks or not at all?"

Deacon pressed his lips together. Mav imagined the truth was hard to spit out. He should know.

"Look, how about this? You can't afford personal protection, and other than looking like the guy from *A Nightmare on Elm Street*, I can't do shit—" Mav stopped suddenly when Deacon's hand clasped his arm.

"I said I didn't mean that how it sounded." His eyes glittered with sudden moisture. "Please believe me."

Mav nodded. "It's okay." And it was. Unless the guy was as talented an actor as he was a singer, Mav was pretty sure he meant every word. Mav's gaze dropped to the slim fingers wrapped around his arm. Deacon was pale, but he looked like he was a few pints of the red stuff short when his hand was wrapped around Mav's own much darker arm. Deacon followed his gaze and then yanked his fingers back when he saw what he was doing.

Not that Maverick especially minded—but he clamped down on that idea real fast. This was work.

CHAPTER FOUR

DEACON DANIELS would die. *Painfully*, and he would make sure of it. He never knew hate had a taste before he was forced to swallow it down every day like a bitter, stagnant ache that churned in his gut.

The man glanced across to where Jones lay lifeless and felt a little cheated, almost. He'd expected him to last longer. Not that it wasn't a good thing. Getting into Jones's computer had been so easy it had almost been insulting, and he had laid enough crumbs to make messing with time of death interesting.

Then the reporter, but he couldn't hurry that one. She was essential to making Daniels suffer. He wanted him panicked. He wanted him to feel the net closing even if he didn't know who tightened the strings. It would be delicious to throw suspicion Daniels's way for this one, and they could never prove otherwise. He really needed another victim, but Daniels didn't seem to have anyone close. There was always the possibility of the child, though… but that reminded him too much of other things. Maybe someone close to the child? That was worth considering.

He knew enough to be careful and to keep the scene clean, or clean from him anyway. He knew how much blood a human body could hold—of course he did—but he had never seen it on so many surfaces. Some of the cuts he had made had spurted before he had closed them. Leaving them would have ended it far too quickly. Although the pathetic specimen had given up after the last few and never attempted to struggle. Just cried and pissed his pants. He hadn't even begged in the end and seemed confused as to where he was.

Not that Jones didn't deserve to suffer every second for what they had taken from him, but he had intended to keep him alive when the fire started.

He had a second of regret as he squirted the gasoline he had brought. The reporter—she would be next—would be awake to see this part. He would make sure of it. He might not even cut her first. He peeled the Tyvek suit from his body along with the nitrile gloves and mask. They would burn along with any evidence. At the last second, he took out the hoodie he had brought to cover himself with on the off chance he was seen, and then took a quick scan around the room to check he had left nothing. He couldn't help the satisfied smile as he closed the door behind him.

HE ISN'T joking, Maverick thought as they pulled into Deacon's neighborhood the next morning. Or not about his lack of cash anyway.

I'm broke. Deacon's car had been repossessed as soon as he had gone home last night, which was why Charlie and the other cop had to drop him off, and no one had been more surprised than Mav when his old truck, which had been sitting in the garage for weeks because Melanie didn't really like driving it, started right away. They seemed to have reached a tentative if temporary agreement. Basically, Deacon wouldn't pay him for protection he couldn't provide.

He supposed there had to be a joke in there somewhere.

But for now, Maverick would hang around with him unofficially and try to look menacing. *Not difficult for me.* He'd managed a quick call to Jamie this morning as soon as he had woken up. She felt a ton better and told him in no uncertain terms that she expected him to visit before the end of the week. She hadn't mentioned Deacon—she didn't know Mav had seen him since they last spoke—but what surprised Maverick was he didn't mention Deacon to her.

It wasn't like it was some secret.

Mav eyed the small, empty playground and the church advertising "Jesus Saves" before Deacon drove past a strip mall with a 7-Eleven, a barber, three boarded-up stores, and a psychic offering discount tarot readings, which was fitting because after another space there was a funeral parlor. *Every option covered.*

Deacon pulled around the corner, and Mav looked with interest. The first few houses were single dwellings, all lived in and well looked after. Then the larger blocks started. Four apartments in one square building.

"How far away is your apartment?"

"Just over there." Mav followed Deacon's nod to the end of the street, where a two-story apartment row sat, looking like a motel. "Mine's the penthouse on the end."

Mav shared Deacon's smile. "You rock stars are all for show."

"Yep," Deacon agreed. "This is really to throw the reporters off. My other place is in Kingswood."

Mav chuckled, thinking of the million-dollar-plus houses in that neighborhood, and glanced down at Deacon's fingers resting on the steering wheel. Mav missed driving. He'd been ready to retire his old truck after Melanie was done with it, promising himself when he was home on leave he would get a new one, but he'd never given it much thought since he got home. *Liar.* Jamie had shoved some flyers at him about adaptations so he could drive easily, and he had dumped them in the trash because he had been sulking. Or drunk. Or *both*.

"What are you thinking about?"

Mav looked across at Deacon in surprise.

Deacon banged his hand on the dash. "I swear I know how to be a grown-up. I just have this annoying habit of speaking without any filter."

Mav grinned. He'd worked that one out last night. "I was thinking of all the times I acted like a spoiled brat since this happened." He touched his knee in case Deacon didn't get what "this" referred to.

"Did they make you leave? I went to school with a friend whose whole family was in the military. It was something he knew he wanted to do since he was old enough to know what being a soldier was. He had a below-knee amputation, but a year later, I saw on Facebook he'd taken part in this Army race that ended at the Pentagon."

Mav's voice stayed level. "The Army Ten-Miler."

Deacon nodded. "He couldn't run, but he still walked with fifty pounds. I believe he returned to active duty about six months later."

"I heard about that," Mav said casually. "He's a paratrooper. There're more and more amputees returning to active duty. It's a little easier if you have more of a residual limb."

Deacon opened his mouth. "Oh God, no. Please don't think I was trying to say—"

"It's fine," Mav interrupted. "I was leaving anyway. Believe it or not, I was going to go in with Jamie and expand the business to personal protection. This just brought things forward a few months. Plus, I'm thirty-four. Bit of an old dog and all that."

Deacon scoffed, then froze. After another few seconds, he glanced at Mav. "I'd probably better not attempt a reply to that. You know, no filter."

Mav smiled to himself, and he felt the familiar pull of the skin across his jaw. After another few seconds, Deacon drew up outside the apartments and glanced at him. "I'm upstairs." He said it casually, but Mav knew what he was really asking.

"Let's go, then," Mav said. There was a rail. He could do this.

Deacon didn't seem to deliberately keep his strides short, but he didn't run on ahead. Mav couldn't decide whether he was grateful or resentful. "How long have you been here?"

"Just over two months. I was going to get something with a yard eventually." His smile fell, and Mav wondered if he was thinking about his niece. "And there's the money I need. A lot of places want hefty security deposits. At least this was only a thousand."

Mav ran a critical eye over the trash-strewn stairs and the peeling paint as they walked past the doors. Personally, he thought a thousand bucks was too high, but it sounded like Deacon was backed into a corner. They carried on, and Mav managed to get up the stairs without too much problem. The pain in his back would be worse by this afternoon, but he was coping now.

"At the risk of saying something else insensitive, can I ask a question?"

Mav nodded, suddenly wary.

"Did you hurt your back as well? I mean," he rushed out, "it never seems to be your leg that hurts, more your back."

Mav stopped in surprise. How had Deacon known? Most people wouldn't be able to differentiate between pain in his back and his leg. "My fault. I missed half a dozen appointments after I got my permanent leg."

"Well, believe it or not, I started training as a masseuse at college before we got the record deal. I do a really good back massage."

It was a good thing Deacon turned away immediately after he said it so he couldn't witness Mav's entire body tightening at the innocent words. Mav remembered those slim fingers clutching his arm.

"Mr. Daniels?"

Mav looked over to where a man stepped out of the first door on the left and hailed them. Mav would put the guy at about sixty, bald head, squinty eyes. The dislike was immediate.

"Mr. Atkins," Deacon greeted him.

Atkins looked Deacon up and down dispassionately. "Saves me tracking you down." He slapped a piece of paper into Deacon's hand and then bent down and hefted two garbage bags out of the apartment and set them out on the walkway.

Deacon glanced at the paper. "But—"

"The apartment's trashed. You cost me furniture, a new door, and a paint job."

The landlord.

"I only paid you the rent yesterday, two weeks in *advance*," Deacon protested. "You can't keep—"

"I can do anything I like," he interrupted. He nodded to the bags. "That's what I could save. Everything else was garbage."

Mav took a step forward, and Atkins suddenly seemed to notice him, his eyes widening as he took a very gratifying step backward. "I'm within my rights because of the damage to my property," he added, his voice not sounding as sure anymore.

"I paid some of the AC repairs," Deacon added in a bewildered voice. Mav wanted to punch Atkins.

"I checked with my lawyer this morning, and apparently you're bad news. I don't need any reporters around here."

Mav didn't like the defeat on Deacon's face.

Atkins pulled the door shut and pocketed the key. "You don't need to give me your key because I had to change the locks," he said pointedly and looked at the trash bags. "I want them out of the way, or I'll be calling the nice cops who came by this morning." And with that, he stepped past Deacon and Mav and walked to the stairs.

Mav opened his mouth, but Deacon snagged his arm. "It doesn't matter," he mumbled.

"I know half a dozen guys who could make him change his mind real quick." Or did he? He'd avoided the other vets like a plague. Ignored every tentative reach out for a beer or more. Hell, he knew at least half a dozen old buddies based at Dobbins ARB. *If they'd come.* To say nothing of Charlie. Cass might have been the brother he never had, but in a lot of ways so was Charlie. After seven years, when he and Cass had luckily been posted together, their duo had simply added a third.

He caught the small shake of Deacon's head and felt the tug on his arm. "I hated the place anyway." Mav glanced down ready to make another argument or simply offer to make the landlord change his mind, but Deacon was looking at him with an expression he hadn't seen for fuck knew how long, and it made him stand a little taller.

"You can stay with me for the time being," Mav said firmly, knowing his generous-hearted sister wouldn't mind in the least.

Deacon looked like he was going to protest, but Mav guessed his new reality kept his mouth closed.

"I think we need to go talk to the cops," Mav said. "I know one of the ones who brought you to my house last night."

Deacon's eyebrows rose. "You think you can get them to believe me? It sounds like they were here."

Mav nodded. "This is a game changer. There's no way cops aren't going to take this seriously."

Deacon picked up both bags. "At least they didn't get Mikey's stuff."

"Your brother?"

"Yeah. Most of his cash went into savings for Molly, which is good, but he prepaid a year's rent on a small storage unit. I put all his furniture in it until I got somewhere nicer. I guess I should be glad that place was furnished." Deacon swallowed heavily, and Mav gave him a second to get himself under control. So the brother had left some money, but Deacon couldn't touch it? His sister always said babies were expensive.

"Close to here?"

"Not too far. A little farther north of Marietta." Deacon looked like he was going to say something else, but he didn't.

And even though it wasn't his business, Mav raised the subject anyway. "I can't imagine what it must have been like suddenly being responsible for a toddler." And just like that, Deacon lit up. Mav simply paused and basked in the warmth radiating from his smile.

"I was so lucky. Do you have any idea what it's like to be trusted with something so precious? Of course you do," Deacon added before Mav could answer. "You flew million-dollar helicopters."

It was hardly the same, though. "Yeah, but the Huey wouldn't cry if you left it alone." Although Charlie babied them all the time. It was a standing joke among the three of them that faced with a choice in a life-and-death situation, Charlie would save the Huey first.

"You hungry?"

"I guess." Deacon huffed out a surprised breath as if it had just occurred to him. He looked down at his phone as it started ringing, but Mav's rang a second after. They both glanced ruefully at each other and took a step apart to answer.

"Mav?"

Mav recognized Charlie's voice immediately, and he grunted. He'd missed his friend.

"Are you with Deacon Daniels?"

Mav stiffened. Charlie didn't sound like he was shooting the breeze. That was specific. "Yes." His eyes met Deacon's.

"There's going to be a Detective Phan calling him to arrange a meet—"

"I think he's calling him now," Mav interrupted, watching Deacon's worried face.

"Where are you?"

"Outside Deacon's apartment. We're going back to mine." He heard Charlie say something to someone and saw Deacon shove his phone back into his pocket.

"Okay," Charlie confirmed. "We'll see you there."

Mav put his phone into his own pocket and eyed Deacon, who looked a little shell-shocked. "Detective Phan?"

Deacon's eyes widened.

"That was the cop I know from last night. He's actually an old Air Force buddy and was giving me a heads-up."

"They wanted me to go to the precinct, but he spoke to someone else, and they're meeting me at your house."

"This is good, though," Mav encouraged. "I didn't think the cops would be able to get anyone to take notice of this." He nodded toward the apartment.

"No." Deacon shook his head. "These detectives are from over in Athens."

"Why—"

"They wanted to know when I last spoke to Emmanuel Jones."

Mav shook his head. He was no wiser.

"Emmanuel Jones was my old agent. The one who made up the stalker story that got that lady and her son killed." Deacon met Mav's eyes. "They wouldn't tell me why they needed to know."

THE COPS were already at Maverick's when they pulled up. There were two cars waiting for them, and Deacon recognized the friend of Mav's and Officer

Fitzpatrick. The two men who got out of the Buick must have been the detectives, and he eyed them quickly, watching as Maverick's eyes narrowed on the older detective. Sizing him up. The other guy looked like he was some sort of trainee. Deacon's grandad would have said "not old enough to shave." He missed his grandad so damn much. He would never have been in this situation if Pops had still been alive.

Deacon pushed that thought away and climbed out of the car. He noticed the wince from Mav as he straightened up and the way his face slid into a polite mask as he attempted to hide it. Although, it was probably only visible to Deacon. He'd learned very quickly as a child how to read body language, and the familiar hurt curled around his heart.

The cops walked over to Mav, and the detectives came over to him.

Detective Phan extended his hand. "Mr. Daniels?" Phan was the older of the two. Late forties, at a guess. Straight black hair. Pale skin contrasted with the dark gray pupils staring back at Deacon. Smart suit. Looked fit and capable. Deacon pushed that thought away and nodded as he was introduced to Detective Wright, but it was clear Phan was in charge.

Mav walked around the truck and shook hands. Then Mav led them into the house. Deacon glanced at Mav to see if he minded his home being invaded, but it didn't seem so. Mav directed them into a dining room Deacon hadn't seen, and they all took seats around the large oak table.

"I'm assuming this is about the break-in," Mav said as he walked in after having gone into the kitchen to get bottles of water for everyone. He then sat deliberately next to Deacon, and Deacon felt able to take a breath for the first time since they had gone to his apartment.

Phan looked at him, and something in the detective's gray eyes sent a shiver tripping down Deacon's arms. "The break-in is being handled by the local police. As I said on the phone, we wondered if you could tell us the last time you saw Mr. Emmanuel Jones."

Deacon didn't think he was likely to forget. "Outside court four weeks ago after he confirmed what a crap parent I would make."

He didn't dare meet Maverick's eyes as the big man had immediately focused on his words. Manny had done his best to paint Deacon as an unfit guardian, blaming him for the events of the previous year, and it had worked even though he had spent days pretending it wasn't true. That Molly was still there to give him the tight hugs with sticky fingers that clutched him tight and buried in his heart. He would return every one of those big fierce kisses and count himself so damn lucky. Until he wasn't anymore.

It had been chaos outside the courthouse. There had been reporters. A big crowd. People shouting. Manny had done his best to insist he had just been following Deacon's orders on the fake stalker story. And the judge had believed him.

"Are his current whereabouts unknown?" Mav asked mildly.

Phan ignored the question. "And you haven't received any telephone calls, emails, anything of that nature from him?"

Deacon shook his head, puzzled. "I wanted nothing to do with him. Why are you asking me?"

"According to Mr. Jones's email records, he emailed you Thursday and referenced a meeting you had the day before."

"With Manny?" Deacon shuddered. "That man helped to ruin my life, and he destroyed Shelley Young's and her son's. I want nothing to do with him." Deacon frowned. "And if you mean the Deacon Daniels Gmail, I stopped using that when the band split up. And he's lying if he says otherwise."

"It might be a bit difficult to ask, because we found a body yesterday, and we have reason to believe it is him."

Deacon shivered. "But he's married. I mean, can't Helena confirm—" He felt Maverick squeeze his arm at the same time as a hundred appalling thoughts rushed through him. "Oh God," he whispered.

"He separated from his wife last month. There was a fire at his house in the early hours of yesterday morning, and his body was discovered then."

"He died in a fire?" That was awful.

"No," Phan answered shortly. "He was already dead. We need to know your confirmed whereabouts between last Thursday and yesterday morning."

"Why?" Deacon didn't understand, and Phan suddenly looked a little sympathetic.

"We need to establish the whereabouts of anyone who might have a grudge against Jones."

"Oh," Deacon said, feeling very small. He was a suspect? He glanced at Mav, who sat so close their legs brushed. It was nice. Gave him the confidence to keep talking. "Can I look at my phone?"

Phan nodded.

Deacon drew it out of his pocket and looked at the calendar. "I went for an audition on Thursday, then had lunch with my agent. Shirley Maplin," he added. "Friday, I had two more interviews."

"Auditions?" the other detective asked.

"No," Deacon said. "One was in Lenox Square Mall as a retail assistant, and the other was as a massage therapist."

The pause was just long enough to make Deacon feel judged.

"We will need contact details," Phan said. "And the rest?"

Deacon shook his head. "Nowhere I can think of, and I live on my own."

"I understand you recently lost custody of your niece?"

Deacon frowned. "What has that got to do with anything?"

"You said it yourself," Phan pointed out. "Jones didn't do you any favors."

"I guess," Deacon admitted. God, it sounded bad now he thought about it.

"Your brother named you as his daughter's guardian in his will?"

"Yes." Deacon smiled a little. He had been stunned when he found out. Full of regret for the missing years with Mikey, then so touched when he had been trusted with her. And he'd let them both down.

"No mom on the scene?" Officer Fitzpatrick asked suddenly.

Deacon shook his head. "She died. I had very little contact with my brother in the past twelve years, and it was only when she died my brother even found out he had a daughter. She was barely eight weeks old then."

Phan looked curious. "Which seems odd that your brother would name you in his will to be her guardian instead of her grandparents."

Deacon felt Mav's fingers tighten briefly.

"To be honest, until Shelley Young died and I was in the papers, they didn't even know about Molly. My brother left home at seventeen and never reconciled with my mom."

Deacon would never forget the shouts, the confusion, and the total bewilderment that Mikey wasn't there anymore. Twelve years on and the memory was still raw.

"Mikey!" he screamed at the top of his lungs. He nearly made it to the door, but his dad grabbed his arm as he tried to duck past. Mom was crying. It seemed like she always cried or drank. Most times she did both.

"Get out of my house, you bastard," Dad shouted.

But Mikey just scoffed. "I'd rather be a bastard all day long than any son of yours."

That even silenced him, and for a second, he stopped struggling, suddenly understanding that one of his dad's favorite swear words might have a literal meaning. That was it? Was that what had caused the fight this time?

"And don't bother thinking you can take my name either," his dad had railed, not missing a beat and giving him confirmation. Not that he cared. Michael was everything he ever wanted to be. Strong. Brave. Mikey'd taken more than one beating aimed for him, and a few for his mom.

"Mikey?" He started struggling again. He wasn't going to be left anywhere his brother wasn't. He wasn't staying here.

"Shut up." His father backhanded him, and the pain made his head reel. His legs didn't work too well for a few seconds, and that was all it had taken for Mikey to step outside the door without him.

And he never knew why. How his strong, brave brother could suddenly leave him. It had taken a lot of years before Deacon had forgiven him, before he had understood that at seventeen, Michael had still been a child himself. And by the time Deacon was at college and Mikey made contact, six years had passed. Mikey had done what he had to, faked his age and enlisted, and he hadn't known they'd moved shortly afterward when Dad changed jobs. It had been a catalogue of missing things, missing addresses, and missing opportunities. Deacon had never expected Michael to go anywhere without him, and feeling like Mikey had turned his back on him, he'd done the same.

And when he'd finally realized his mistake, it had been nearly too late.

"Deacon?"

Maverick saying his name brought him into the present with a start. He squirmed a little to see all eyes on him and wondered how long he had been lost in his regrets.

He looked at the detective even though it had been Maverick who had spoken. "I would have to think about an alibi for the other days, but to be honest, I know I don't have a complete one."

"We are hoping to get the time of death narrowed down when our ME gets his results," Detective Wright said. "At the moment, we don't have any confirmed sightings for at least three days, but we have Amazon rental activity seventy-two hours prior. If we use that, then the time of death would be the eleventh to the fourteenth or the weekend through Tuesday when the fire started. The email makes it a little closer if true because that was sent on the twelfth."

"Except I didn't receive it and I didn't meet with him," Deacon reiterated and glanced at Mav, but Mav was looking at Detective Phan. Neither of the local cops had said a word, and Deacon wondered what they were doing here. "My landlord said you had visited." He glanced at Mav's friend. "Officer…?"

"Chaplin," he supplied. "Yes, we followed up with the landlord, but he had already cleared your apartment when we got there."

It figured Atkins had lied. Slimy money-grubber. So there was nothing they could do. He wasn't sure what he was expecting, to be honest.

"So that's it?" Mav asked, the disbelief apparent in his voice.

Detective Phan stood up, and Detective Wright passed Deacon a card. "We may need to speak to you some more, so we would appreciate it if you inform us of any travel plans."

What travel plans?

"Can we contact you here?" Detective Phan glanced at Maverick, then Deacon.

"Yes," Maverick confirmed before Deacon even had a chance to think about his reply. Deacon was still musing on it as the detectives left, and when Mav came back in, Deacon hadn't moved. He didn't know what to say. What to think. He watched Mav's hands tremble slightly as he picked up the water bottle he hadn't touched yet.

"Why did he leave?" Maverick asked.

Deacon knew Mav meant his brother. Was he ready to tell him? "They were yelling at each other on the stairs when I came in from my grandad's. Dad said I had to go to my room, and when I tried to go after Mikey, he backhanded me. My dad basically said Mikey wasn't his. It was the first I'd heard about it, but there were five years between us, so I was only twelve. It was another six years—nearly seven—before we finally spoke to each other, and he didn't want to talk about anything to do with my dad."

"Didn't your mom say something, or your grandad? Wait," he said before Deacon could answer. "Your dad hit you?"

Deacon nodded. "Mom all the time. Michael when he could get in between them. Me not so much, but I was good at keeping out of the way."

"Then why on earth did you let him take Molly? She's not safe. Surely to God you could get witnesses. What about your grandad?"

"I—"

"I mean, I guess looking after a small child is difficult, but any home is better than that one."

"Difficult," Deacon parroted. "No—"

Mav shook his head, and Deacon stilled, realization dawning on him. "My dad's dead," Deacon said flatly. "You really thought I would have let that happen if she was going to that *bastard*?" Deacon didn't know whether to be horrified or angry. He'd thought Mav believed him, but really he was just the same as everyone else.

CHAPTER FIVE

MAV'S LIPS parted, but he couldn't form any words. Fuck, he had thought exactly that.

It was Deacon's turn to shake his head. "Pops was in a nursing home by the time Mikey left. My dad had a stroke the year before I graduated high school and died just as I left for college. Mom married her attorney, of all things. Not that I blamed her for it."

But you blame her for other things. "I'm sorry," Mav offered, knowing that was completely inadequate.

Deacon shrugged. "Of course, you wouldn't know, but yeah, Percy Fellhouse the Third is rich. Mom decided she wanted Molly, and Percy paid for it to happen."

"What, you mean *bribes*?"

"I don't know. Honestly, I don't think she needed to. They're rich." He started counting off on his fingers. "She'll go to the best schools. I'm *not* rich. In fact, at the moment, I don't even have somewhere to live." He was silent a beat. "Or a car. I may or may not have a job tomorrow."

"That's why you didn't fight it." The explanation dawned on Maverick. "You think she would actually be better off there." It made a ton of sense even if some things still weren't adding up. "But you said she drank. Why didn't that come out in court?"

"She was sober every time I saw her. I guess she doesn't need it anymore."

Which was bull. Alcoholics always needed it. It was simply that the need to stay sober was greater. When Mav got a chance, he was going to see if Jamie knew anyone who knew this judge, because something seemed off to him.

"I just miss her." Deacon chewed his lip.

"How long was she with you?"

"Ten months."

Mav didn't know whether talking about her made it better or worse, so he kept on. "How old is she?"

Deacon's eyes suddenly became a little brighter, and he dipped his head quickly but not before Maverick saw them. "Two. She was two a couple of days ago."

The words were whispered so quietly Maverick barely heard them. *Deacon missed her birthday?* "Can't you see her?"

Deacon nodded. "Yes, I was granted visitation every Thursday for two hours."

Fuck. That was harsh. "Wait. It was Thursday two days ago. On her birthday."

Deacon looked miserable. "I called there at three as usual, but she had left for her party in some hotel, so I couldn't see her. I left her gift with the housekeeper."

"But that means you should get another day, surely," Mav argued.

"I guess. I've been too distracted to sort it out."

Mav reached out and squeezed his arm before he even thought about what he was doing. "Understatement of the year?"

Deacon returned his smile, and Mav removed his hand. That was the second time he had touched Deacon without thinking, and this was *work*. "Do you need to do anything else today?" He looked exhausted. It was on the tip of Mav's tongue to tell him to go catch a nap when he realized he was overstepping. Deacon was an adult. "I'm hungry," Mav said, not giving Deacon a chance to answer his question. "Jamie said the fridge was full."

"I could eat," Deacon replied, and they both stood at the same time, which was awkward, especially when Deacon walked away from him and took the long way around the table so Maverick wouldn't hold him up. Mav blew out a short breath as he put an unsteady foot forward. Maybe he needed to make some calls. He'd spent the last three months burying his head in a bottle, and while life might not be how he envisioned, he might be able to make it a bit better. Deacon, not surprisingly, made it to the kitchen first and pulled open the door on the large fridge.

He brightened. "What do you feel like?"

Mav kept his face carefully straight. "I can make sandwiches."

Deacon smiled. "I can make a Spanish omelet."

"Sold," Mav said and went to fill the coffee maker.

MAVERICK WATCHED Deacon carefully, quite pleased with himself. They'd taken their coffees into the living room after he had discovered Deacon was a damn fine cook, and Deacon had called and made arrangements to see Molly. It had sounded like his request wasn't received favorably at first until he asked if they preferred the request to come from his attorney, and then they promised to call him back.

Maverick had looked at his own phone then so it didn't seem he was listening, and considered texting Charlie. He also searched for the new prosthetics facility out past Johns Creek he had been referred to and shot them a reply to one of the many emails they had sent him. It was a start. He looked up from his phone after he realized Deacon had stopped talking, and couldn't help the smile. Deacon was sprawled on his couch, asleep. Or he had his eyes shut anyway.

His gaze roamed over Deacon's body. His own body was giving off interested signals for the first time since he'd woken up in Somalia, and he had to keep reminding himself propositioning Jamie's clients wasn't a good business decision. He wasn't dumb either. Deacon's model-worthy good looks or the way he dressed so carefully weren't an indication of anything. He knew gay came in all shapes and sizes, and just because Deacon had accepted a casual, comforting touch, then initiated one when he was under so much stress was in no way flashing a green light. Mav tried to stretch out his leg and winced at the pull in his back.

"When are you seeing your therapist?"

Maverick focused on the tired blue eyes that were open and watching him lazily. "I emailed them a few minutes ago, actually."

"That's good." Deacon yawned.

"I thought you were asleep."

"I'm a little wired, to be honest, and I'm waiting to hear from my mom."

"You could be waiting a long time." Personally, Maverick thought they were giving him the runaround in the hope he would simply give up.

Deacon's eyes widened a little. "You think I should just go?"

"What's the worst that can happen?"

Deacon tugged at his lip with his teeth. "They say she's out."

"So you won't be any worse off."

Deacon swung his legs down from the couch and stood up. "Can I borrow the truck?"

Maverick shook his head. "That's not how this works. Wherever you go, I go. Call me your assistant, if you like, and I can always wait in the truck if they won't let me in."

Deacon's smile turned innocent. "But doesn't hired help get to wait in the kitchen?"

"This isn't some PBS rerun," Maverick growled and stood up. "Where do they live?"

"Ansley Park."

Mav tipped his head. "Big house?"

"Huge," Deacon answered forlornly and followed him out.

"Can I ask," Mav started as they got in the truck. "How many times have you seen your mom recently?"

"Apart from the visits with Molly—two—and the court. I haven't seen her since I was eighteen." Mav shot a glance at him, but Deacon was looking at the road as he drove. "I left as soon as I inherited the money Pops left me for college," he explained. "Dad had his first stroke the year before, but if anything, that made him meaner. The only benefit was he couldn't move as fast."

"I'm sorry he hurt you." Maverick could have happily gutted the bastard.

Deacon shrugged. "I wasn't as brave as Mikey."

Which in no way made it Deacon's fault. But Maverick wasn't sure how to convince Deacon of that. "I don't know your brother, and I mean no disrespect, but I think you mean you weren't as confrontational. It takes as much courage sometimes to stay calm as it does to lash out."

Deacon glanced at Maverick as if the compliment surprised him. "You think?" he asked hesitantly.

"What did you do at eighteen?"

"Went to college and had a blast," Deacon replied and chuckled. "It was like being let out of prison. I probably went a little too far at first, until it was forcibly pointed out to me one day I'd wake up broke with no job and no prospect of getting one."

Maverick smiled. He would have liked to have seen a wild Deacon. It would make a nice change from the too quiet one.

"Of course, it still came back to bite me on the butt."

"How so?"

"Court." Deacon sighed. "About four of us got caught smoking weed, and it's still illegal in Alabama. I was lucky because I wasn't in my room, and the guy who bought it had already gotten into trouble once, so I got away with it. It sobered me up very quickly to what I had nearly thrown away, so I got my head down and finished. I'd done pretty well at school, so even though I wasted six months, it only took me two years."

Maybe not an airhead, then.

"Then we won the talent contest at school, then a local radio one, and someone put a clip of us on You-Tube. The rest, as they say, is history."

"Were you studying music?" He was more of a rock fan himself, but he knew Six Sundays had been very popular.

"No, biology, actually." Deacon laughed. "I can't read music one little bit. My roommate, Jazz, was the music aficionado, except he couldn't sing, and I seemed to be able to write catchy lyrics as well. The other guys were musicians Jazz had strong-armed for the contest. We were all pretty stunned when the clip was aired and Sony contacted us."

"And you don't see them anymore? If you weren't prosecuted, how was it mentioned in court?" But he wasn't an attorney. He had no clue.

"Sara Jeffries found all this out. I wouldn't speak to her, so she just basically made everything up. It was in the papers, and that's when my mom found out about Molly and that I had been given custody. And at the custody hearing because Jazz and the others who ended up having their lives tanked all appeared at court blaming me. My lawyer said they had probably been paid 'expenses'"—Deacon finger quoted the word—"to appear. Except, funnily enough, the guy who actually was to blame, no one could find him. He progressed to the harder stuff pretty quickly, and he hasn't been seen in some time. The whole case was whether I was a fit person to care for an infant, so everyone my mom's solicitor could find to say I couldn't was dragged in. Manny was there, as I said. He was still trying to resurrect his career, so he made out in court I was a hysterical, strung-out junkie like my brother and he'd been following orders."

Mav made a disgusted sound. "I don't blame you for not talking to Jeffries."

Deacon glanced at him as they came off the highway at the next junction. "It's not because she was a reporter, but because we have history."

"You were together?" The sharp stab of disappointment jabbed at Mav.

"Oh God no." Deacon shuddered. "I don't do lady parts." Mav concentrated very hard not to react. "It was what she did to Shelley Young."

Maverick recognized the name of the woman who had died in the car crash. "What did she do?"

"Made her life hell for a few weeks. She was ill. She'd been in psychiatric care but skipped town a few times and ended up in Atlanta with a child."

"No father around?"

"All she would say was when he got back, he was going to marry her. No idea if it was true. If he was away somewhere, or even if she really knew who he was. He could have been a one-night stand."

"A john?"

"I don't think so," Deacon said. "She had money for concert tickets anyway. The first time I met her was after a concert. She'd been one of the fans who had lined up in the rain for five hours beforehand, and Manny invited a few of them in as a publicity thing to meet us." He shook his head. "She was soaked, and I gave her my jacket. Then we went on tour—our first and only one—and she kept turning up. I didn't notice until one of the doormen came in saying a lady was outside insisting she was my girlfriend. He thought it was nonsense, but he promised to ask me because she had the baby with her, and he was worried. I followed him behind the ticketing area, which was restricted. I recognized her right away, and Manny said I mustn't talk to her, so I gave the doorman some cash to get her a cab. The only other time I saw her before the accident was during a concert when she tried to get on the stage, but security stopped her."

"Then the story came out about your brother," Maverick said, understanding how everything had escalated.

"Yes, and it was Sara Jeffries who did that."

Maverick winced.

"Then Manny made up that ridiculous story about the stalker, and Shelley handed herself in to the cops. Sara was on her right away. According to the police, she was in one of the cars that pursued Shelley before the accident."

"She wants locking up," Mav decreed. "But Shelley got the blame because she was high?"

"Yes, but Sara—not being content with ruining just Shelley's life—convinced Manny somehow she had proof he had made the whole story up, and he panicked and blamed me, which was a much better story for her. She ran the piece, which played right into my mom's hands, and I got sued for custody of Molly."

Maverick didn't know what to say. It had been one disaster after another, so he went with the first thing that occurred to him. "I'm sorry about your brother."

"Not half as sorry as I am," Deacon said bitterly, then flushed. "That was unfair."

"And your mom didn't try and help?" She would have had the money.

Deacon scoffed like the idea was ridiculous. "The first time I met Mikey after he left, we'd arranged to meet in a coffee bar near campus. I was still under twenty-one," he added. "It was hard looking at him through an adult's eyes, as the last time I had seen him I was twelve, and he always seemed larger than life then."

Maverick understood unrealistic expectations. "Was he on drugs then?"

"I don't think so," Deacon said, "but if he was, he hid it well. He'd just left the Army, and he was struggling, but I didn't know. I know he did two tours in Iraq and that it was hell, but when you don't know what someone's normal is, it's hard to tell any difference."

"Army?"

Deacon nodded. "I don't even know what he did because he didn't seem to want to talk about it. He'd already left." Deacon paused. "He was driving to San Francisco the next day to start a new job. He'd gotten a post with a security company similar to what you were trying to set up with Jamie. Ex-military personnel."

"When did you hear from him next?"

"He visited one more time when I needed him." Deacon smiled but didn't elaborate. "We texted, but I was doing exams." Deacon slowed for a light. "It was so hard. It was like the elephant in the corner, and he didn't talk about leaving or what had happened. He told me he reached out to Mom after Dad died, but the letter was unanswered. I told him we weren't talking either, and he said as soon as I finished school, if I wanted to move to San Francisco, I would always be welcome. Anyway, the contest happened literally the week of finals, and before I knew it, we were in New York. Five crazy months went by with the texts getting less and less, and eventually I got a call from a rehab center in Daly City. Mikey had been admitted, but his insurance was for shit, so I immediately flew out. He was a mess. Whatever he had started on had progressed to heroin. I got him admitted to the best place I could find, but we had an interview scheduled the next morning and production for the show started the next week. It was ten days before I got back, and he seemed a lot better."

Seemed? Rehab took a lot longer than that, but Deacon wouldn't have known.

"He begged me to take him home with me, but I couldn't. I didn't even have my own place at that point. All the band was living in a huge apartment Sony was paying for, and we were writing as many songs as we could." Deacon fell silent, and Mav tried to process everything. He couldn't imagine what Deacon had gone through.

"The next I heard was a letter telling me he had sorted his life out and was working. It was the time he got Molly, but he never told me." The regret. The bewilderment was in Deacon's voice.

"Do you know why?"

Deacon was silent for a few moments. "It killed him to ask me for help, and it nearly destroyed me that I couldn't bring him back with me. I want to say I wasn't in a position to help, and that's true to a big extent, but…."

"You hadn't forgiven him?"

"What sort of a brother does that make me?" Deacon whispered.

"A young one?" Mav offered. Deacon didn't reply. "We all have regrets." Mav had. "And hindsight is a wonderful thing, as they say. For what it's worth, I think your brother didn't say anything because he wanted to go back to being the protector. The man you could look up to. He wanted to succeed before he came back to you."

"You mean he felt he had to pretend?" Deacon looked aghast.

Mav shook his head. "When my mom died, it nearly destroyed our family with guilt."

"She was sick?"

"Yes, but that's not exactly what I mean. My sister felt guilty because she was away at college when my mom first got sick, and I felt guilty because she and my dad were having problems and I spent a long time pretending it wasn't happening."

"How old were you?"

"Twelve when Dad lost his job and Jamie went to college." Mav looked at Deacon. "The same age you were when Michael left."

"But I was older when Michael had problems."

"And you did your best to help." Maverick clasped Deacon's hand. "When you found out about Molly, did it ever occur to you not to take her? A single guy? And you had enough issues of your own."

Deacon smiled. "No. Molly was like having a part of Mikey back."

"There you go, then," Mav said. Deacon had tried, and then he had let her go because he thought she'd be better off somewhere else.

"Did you ever find out what happened after he got Molly?"

"I called a few times after I didn't hear anything for a while, and in the end I got hold of a friend Mikey used to work with. Apparently, Molly's mom had cheated on him, and it had sent him over the edge. She left him, and he went back on drugs. Then she died, and Mikey got Molly. He straightened up and was good for a few months, but then the company went under and Mikey lost his job. He left Molly with a babysitter, and when he didn't come back to collect her, she called the cops. He'd been going to a job interview, and they called him to say it had been filled. Instead of going home, he shot up and OD'd." Deacon shot him a worried look. "What do you think happened to Manny?"

The complete change of subject took Mav a little by surprise, but then Mav didn't blame Deacon one little bit for needing to talk about something else. "Jones?" Mav had no idea. "I guess they're looking at who else he pissed off. If his treatment of you was anything to go by, I can't see it being a short list. I was going to let Jamie settle in at Richards's, then call her. She has a lot of friends still on the force even though she left years ago. She's always been heavily into fundraising for them and the like."

Deacon turned down a pretty street with large trees on either side. All the houses were set back. All the *mansions*.

"Wow," Mav murmured.

"Uh-huh," Deacon agreed, and of course, he pulled to a stop outside the one that had the biggest set of black gates, then lowered the window. Deacon pressed the call button on the bottom of the panel. Mav took in the security cameras.

"Can I help you?" the tinny-sounding voice echoed from the microphone.

"It's Deacon Daniels to see Molly." There was a silence, and even though Mav was expecting a refusal or another question, the gates started sliding open. Deacon looked as surprised as Mav was.

Deacon put the truck in Drive, and they passed through the gates up to the house. It was nice, if you liked that sort of thing. Very colonial. Big white wraparound porch and shutters at every window. A three-car garage sat to the side, and by the time Deacon pulled up on the gravel drive, the door opened and a woman in full nurse's uniform stepped out. She just missed grabbing the hand of a redheaded hurricane who slipped past her. "Danny!"

Danny? Not Deacon? Maverick gaped as the whirlwind launched herself, and Deacon literally had a second to jump down and open his arms before they were full of what had to be Molly.

Maverick got out of the truck just as Molly realized there was someone else.

"Molly, come here."

Mav and Deacon both turned at the order. Another woman stood at the door in expensive-looking tailored pants and a matching beaded shirt. She certainly didn't look like she was about to play with a toddler, especially one as fast as the one now clinging to Deacon. Maverick looked at the woman for a few seconds. He had the strangest feeling he had seen her before, but it could have been the news about the court case.

Molly immediately shrank closer to Deacon, making it clear what she thought of the order. Deacon transferred Molly to his hip, and she clung on like a limpet and buried her face in the crook of Deacon's neck. Deacon faced the woman but didn't take a step any farther forward. "Hello, Mom."

Okay, so that had been kind of obvious, and Mav really hadn't needed the confirmation. He stayed completely still and waited for an introduction or a request. He wasn't completely certain he would get either.

"Daniel," his mom acknowledged, which answered the question over his name. "Your visits are supposed to be on a Thursday."

"Which I—"

"But seeing as how it was Molly's party," she interrupted, "I am allowing this one." Then she looked at

Maverick like the conversation was over. He ignored her and waited for Deacon to finish it. She really should have gotten her current backbone twenty years ago. Too little too late.

Deacon was silent for a beat, and then he looked at Maverick. "Maverick, this is my mother, Anne Fellhouse. Mom, this is Maverick Delgardo, my protection detail."

Mav nearly snorted. That sounded like a line out of some film, not that bodyguard was any better. Jamie would have to come up with a name.

"Mrs. Fellhouse," Mav said very smoothly in his deepest voice and stepped forward, extending his hand. Her couple of blinks showed he still had some charisma despite the scar. He didn't dare look at Deacon.

She allowed him to take her hand, then looked at Deacon. "You might as well bring her in," she said dismissively and turned.

Then Mav looked at Deacon, and the hurt that flashed in those blue eyes made him want to hit someone. She hadn't protected him when he was a child, and now she still wanted a pound of flesh, and Mav didn't understand why. Kids needed as many adults who loved them as they could get. Why did it need to be fought over?

Deacon nuzzled the top of Molly's head. "How about we go inside?"

Mav caught the nod of her head, but she still didn't look up. It didn't look like she was going to let go of Deacon anytime soon either.

Anne Fellhouse wasn't as confident as she was making out, Maverick decided fifteen minutes later. She hadn't suggested Maverick should be anywhere other than with them, but then she seemed to have decided to ignore him. Or not *exactly*. Deacon seemed to be her main focus, which surprised Mav. He had expected it to be Molly. He couldn't quite decide whether to be pleased or not.

The nurse/nanny/whatever tried to pry Molly from Deacon's arms a couple of times, but that proved pointless, so Anne had suggested she go to the kitchen.

They even had a maid or housekeeper-type person serve coffee, and milk for Molly. Deacon and his mom were still looking at each other like one was carrying explosives.

Maverick eyed the immaculate room and turned to Molly. He picked up the discarded doll off the floor and turned the toy around. Molly watched him but made no move to take it. He picked up the alphabet picture book from the side table, and that immediately garnered interest. Then he spotted her teddy bear and picked it up, and Molly held out her arms for it. "Are you learning all your letters yet?"

"Hardly," Anne said dryly.

Deacon hugged her. "You wanna sing the ABC song for Maverick?"

"You know the ABC song?" Mav teased, pretending to be doubtful.

"She doesn't—"Anne started, but Molly launched into the rhyme and sang it perfectly. Anne watched in astonishment.

Mav leaned over and high-fived Molly. Or nearly—he had to raise Molly's hand and show her when she didn't know what to do.

"Goodness," murmured Anne.

Deacon smiled at Molly. "I bet Grandma sings with you all the time. She can teach you—"

"No," Anne Fellhouse interrupted.

"But, Mom—"

"Absolutely not," Anne said flatly. There was another silence while they stared at each other, and Mav was confused. There seemed to be real resentment, anger, and he had no idea why.

"Good job, kiddo," Deacon said after a few seconds, but he clearly wasn't surprised. After all, up to nearly four weeks ago, Molly was learning all her letters with him.

"Drink your milk," Anne murmured, but the cutie-pie wrinkled her nose.

"She likes it with a small spoonful of Nesquik chocolate," Deacon said with the air of someone who had said that before.

Anne frowned. "I'm not sure how healthy all that sugar is."

Deacon nodded. "It does have a high fructose content, but it also delivers 40 percent of her calcium needs. It's definitely better than the syrup and even better than her not getting any milk at all."

Maverick tried really, really hard not to smile, to the point of lowering his head.

"I need to go pee-pee," Molly whispered very loudly to Deacon and tugged on his arm.

Anne frowned again. "Rachel will take her." She looked expectantly at the door for Rachel—Mav assumed the nurse slash nanny—to immediately appear.

"Danny," Molly wailed immediately.

Deacon chuckled. "You got it, sweet pea." And he stood up.

"I really don't think that's appropriate," Anne interrupted, but she didn't make any attempt to stand up.

"Just tell me where it is, Mom," Deacon said with infinite patience when Mav would have lost his cool at the assumption. He wanted to ask if she was that worried why didn't she take Molly herself, but he kept silent. Scoring points might make him feel better, but it wouldn't help Deacon or Molly.

Anne looked uncomfortable but just waved her hand. "On the right," she clipped out, and Molly giggled as Deacon swung her up. Mav heard Molly launch into the rhyme once more as they disappeared, and he wondered if Molly had inherited her uncle's singing talent. He'd bet that wouldn't go down well with the old cow sitting in front of him.

Silence settled over the room, and Anne eyed him carefully. "Protection detail?"

Maverick nodded. "Ma'am. Your son thought it was wise with the recent court case and all."

"But Shelley Young's dead," Anne returned bluntly.

And Deacon, not having any relationship with his mother where he could confide in her or ask advice, clearly hadn't said he had a current problem. "You have a beautiful home, Mrs. Fellhouse," Maverick said, completely changing the subject. With the half smile gracing her lips, he wasn't sure whether she knew what he was doing or was completely oblivious.

"Why does my son need protection?"

Maybe not completely oblivious, then. "I'm sorry, but you would have to ask him," Maverick replied honestly. Anne looked like she was going to ask another question, but Deacon came back into the room, holding Molly's hand. Molly took one look at her grandma and turned into Deacon again with her arms up, obviously asking to be picked up.

Maverick watched Anne's face as Deacon chuckled and swung her up. Anne seemed confused. Maybe

she genuinely didn't understand the connection between Deacon and his niece. Maybe she believed all
the stories about him? Who knew?

Molly chattered on to Deacon a mile a minute, and
Anne just sat and sipped her coffee. Rachel appeared at
the door like she'd been summoned. "It's time for your
nap, Molly," Anne said, and Deacon looked at her, his
reluctance that the visit was brief obvious on his face.
Molly glanced at her grandmother and then turned and
buried herself against Deacon. Molly's opinion on the
matter was evident.

Maverick caught the hint of sympathy on Rachel's
face and the confused expression on Anne's. He stood
up. "You got a castle up there, Your Highness?" There
was no way he wanted another uncomfortable five minutes with Deacon's mom.

Molly's eyes widened. "No."

"You got a blanket?"

Molly nodded, eyes alight with possibilities.

"Then you got a castle, sweetie." And he held his
hand out, which Molly took immediately, then stretched
out her other arm to Deacon as he set her down.

It was a funny procession. Trying to get through
doors without letting go became a game. Then the
stairs, and of course Molly noticed he had difficulty
climbing them.

He followed Rachel into what was definitely a bedroom fit for royalty, with the Disney Princess bed and
decorations. Seeing her looking at his leg, he lifted his
pants until she could see the metal joint on his ankle.
He rapped it with his knuckles, and she giggled. "See?
Brand-new."

"Because you got an owie?" she asked.

Maverick, impressed with her reasoning, bent down nearer to her height and nodded, keeping it simple. "Yes, honey."

Molly stared at his cheek and put her hand against the scarred flesh. "Did you get an owie there?"

He heard the gasp from Rachel. "M—"

"It's okay." He stopped Rachel and forced himself to stay still while Molly's little fingers traced his cheek. Then his breath caught as she leaned forward and pressed her lips on the torn and ugly skin.

"There." Molly gently patted his face. "All better." Mav couldn't have spoken if his life had depended on it.

"I used to have awful trouble getting her to sleep," Deacon told Rachel, who seemed to have difficulty wrenching her eyes from Mav and Molly. Mav knew Deacon was trying to distract her, and shot him a grateful glance.

Molly yawned but then shook her head. "No nap."

Deacon grinned, obviously used to this. "But I'm tired." And he made a big show of yawning.

Molly clasped his hand and dragged him wordlessly to the bed. Mav watched in amusement as Deacon lay down and Molly snuggled in close.

"I'll come back in five," Rachel whispered and took a step to the door. Mav snagged her arm carefully. "Thank you."

She nodded. "Maybe Mr. Daniels could meet Molly somewhere else?" she whispered, and glanced back at them both. "There's a small café close by. I couldn't… that is if Mrs. Fellhouse—"

"We understand," Mav assured her. It was a sweet offer, and maybe Deacon's mom would be persuaded in a few weeks. It would certainly be less awkward for both of them.

"Sing the bye-bye song," Molly asked.

Maverick sat down quietly and listened in awe as Deacon started singing. He'd heard the song but wasn't sure from where, but what kept him still and determined not to interrupt was the happiness on Molly's face and the pure joy on Deacon's.

Deacon's voice grew to barely a whisper as Molly closed her eyes. After another minute where Deacon just watched her sleep, he kissed her gently on the cheek and climbed carefully out of the bed.

"Daniel."

They both looked around, and Anne stood there with Rachel behind her. "I'd really like you to leave now. It's important that Molly's routine isn't disturbed any further."

It was like a slap in the face.

Anne turned to Maverick. "Mr. Delgardo? If you would please wait in your vehicle? I wish to talk to my son in private."

She swept out, and Deacon gave a sleeping Molly a last kiss before he left the room with Maverick in tow. Mav didn't like leaving Deacon to battle the old cow on his own. Nothing she had said so far gave him any impression Anne was a warm and loving person.

But then, if she had been, Deacon's childhood might have been very different. Mav got to the bottom of the stairs a little after Deacon and Anne and looked at Deacon's face.

"I'll wait in the truck."

Deacon nodded, but he appeared miserable. Every step Maverick took toward the door seemed to hurt more than usual.

CHAPTER SIX

DEACON FOLLOWED his mom when he would far rather have gone with Maverick. She smoothed her pants and sat on the edge of the couch. "I don't want Molly's routine disturbed anymore, so I expect routine visits to be as per the court stipulated."

Wow. "The *court* stipulated that as part of her routine, she is to have a visit with me every Thursday for two hours, but that doesn't mean we can't meet somewhere else. In fact the court never stipulated a place. Perhaps Rachel could bring her if you don't want to, or if you would rather I didn't come here?" He tried to keep his voice even. He tried to keep calm. He tried to not have it really *fucking hurt*.

His mom stared at him for a few seconds. "Don't think that Rachel can be easily manipulated."

Deacon blew out his anger on a long exhale. Losing his temper wasn't going to help anyone. "I'm not sure what I ever did to give you such a bad impression of me. You should have known the things they said in court were untrue."

She arched a manicured brow. "Why should I?"

"Oh, I don't know…." Deacon pretended to consider. "How about the eighteen years I lived with you? How about my immaculate behavior for all of it? How about the perfect school grades?"

Anne leaped to her feet. "Get out."

"Why, Mom? Truth hard to swallow?" Deacon knew he had blown it, but the words just kept tumbling out.

"It was all your fault," she hissed, the veins standing out in her neck.

"What was my fault?" Deacon said. "I spent the years after Mikey left keeping as much out of the way as possible, and the second I could, I left."

"Exactly," she screeched, and Deacon heard a door open from the corridor. "If you hadn't been so bookish, your dad would have been much better. He tried so hard with you, but you'd never so much as kick a football. It was no wonder he got so frustrated."

Comprehension floored Deacon. "Are you really trying to blame Dad's behavior on me?" He couldn't have heard properly. She couldn't possibly—

"Of course it was your fault," she nearly screamed and took a step closer, just as the living room door opened and the housekeeper hovered. "You were the child I promised to make up for him taking in Michael. You were supposed to be a son he could be proud of, not some weak, pathetic thing that wouldn't even look him in the face."

"Mrs. Fellhouse?" the housekeeper tried to intervene.

"Get out," Anne nearly snarled at the poor woman, who backed away quickly.

"Do you know what he used to say to me? Do you?" She was in his face now. He should move, but horror froze him to the spot. "That I might as well have had a girl because you acted like one. At least I could have put you in a dress," she spat, her thin pretense at civility completely gone.

Deacon heard the door open again but couldn't tear his eyes from the disgust on her face that she didn't bother to hide. "You never complained about me being weak the number of times I stood in front of you when Dad raised his hand. You should have been standing in front of *me*. I was a *child*."

Deacon saw her raise her own hand then and had a second to flinch, but instead of pain and the harsh memory of flesh meeting flesh, there was only silence.

He didn't seem able to breathe, but when he opened his eyes, his mom was standing there looking as horrified as Deacon felt, and Maverick had his fingers wrapped around her wrist, preventing her from slapping Deacon.

Deacon found his feet and stepped back out of the way. Maverick let go of her wrist.

"How dare you?" she shrieked. "I will have you arrested for assault. I will—"

"Shut up and listen to me," Maverick interrupted. "I work in security with access to the latest electronics. We always have to protect ourselves from being accused of rough handling a bail jumper or beating on any other lowlife we happen to meet. Do you really think I would be so unprepared I wouldn't be wearing a body camera?"

Deacon gaped at Maverick. *A body camera?* Then before he had the chance to even think of a response to his mom or even if he'd want to make one, Maverick took him gently by the arm and steered him toward the door. Maverick paused just before they exited the room.

"My client will let you know the meeting place of his choosing for next Thursday as per the court terms stipulated. Should you get any ideas about Molly not being there, we will have no choice but to return to the court with the images and recording I now have. You have fueled untrue speculation to your own ends, and that stops now. I am ex-military with a spotless reputation. My sister, who runs the company, was a cop for eighteen years and knows a lot of people both on the force and in the justice system. You made the mistake of steamrolling your son at a vulnerable time in his life." Maverick paused. "He is not on his own any longer, and he is not without friends. Should you wish to be difficult, the first thing his new attorney would do is petition for the release of your medical records."

Deacon watched the barb find its mark, and his mom went white. Maverick turned without another word, and Deacon let himself be led outside and into the truck.

"Are you okay to drive?" Maverick asked, concern threading his words.

Deacon nodded and got in almost on autopilot. He waited until Maverick did the same, then set off. The gates opened automatically as they approached them. Thoughts, words, images were all swirling around his head. His heart squeezed in the vise she had tightened until he struggled to breathe.

"Pull over here," Maverick urged, and through the fog, Deacon saw where he could stop. *I need air.* He couldn't breathe, and he scrambled, hands shaking, to get out.

He tried to take a breath. And another. He whimpered as blackness encroached at the edges of his vision. So cold. He couldn't seem to inflate his lungs… and then, hard strong arms pulled him back into warmth and safety.

"Breathe," Maverick ordered, warm air tickling his ear. "Breathe," he repeated. And Deacon did. He gasped and shuddered in relief as his vision cleared, and he took another breath. "Slowly now, that's it." Maverick's calm voice soothed him, and he sagged back against the hard body that was effortlessly holding him. "C'mere." The slight hint of frustration was obvious in Maverick's voice as he gently turned Deacon around and wrapped him up in the strongest, safest arms Deacon could ever remember being held in.

He closed his eyes and clung on.

In a few seconds, he was breathing normally, but he still didn't move. He should, he supposed, but then Maverick made the decision for him. "Hey," he said unoriginally.

Deacon inhaled the smell of… something wonderful—*Maverick*—to keep him going, because he doubted he would get another chance, and he looked up into warm brown eyes. He opened his mouth to apologize, but Maverick must've been psychic, because he shook his head, then thumbed the wetness from Deacon's cheeks, and Deacon couldn't help leaning against the rough skin of Mav's hand. For a second, Maverick cradled his face. He was crying? He didn't even know. Then the familiar tightness grew in his throat, and he swallowed forcibly.

"I didn't know," he finally got out. "I never knew." He rested his forehead against Mav's chest. Mav was tall. He'd never thought about just how damn big he was.

"What your mom said?"

"Mmm." Another few seconds passed. He raised his head again and took a breath, then stepped back. Maverick let him go, and Deacon immediately missed him.

He swiped at his eyes. "I never cry." And he didn't. All through the court case. When he found out about Mikey's death. When they lost the contracts and the money. "Not once. Only when they took Molly," he added.

"I don't blame you," Mav said.

"I owe him so much," Deacon whispered.

"Do you mean Michael?"

Deacon nodded.

"Do you want an ice cream?"

Deacon blinked stupidly at the completely random question, and then he followed Mav's gaze and saw the small row of stores across the road. There was a liquor store, a barber's, and a small café advertising home-made ice cream. Deacon huffed in surprise but straightened his shirt where it had become rucked up, then nodded cautiously. Mav guided him across the empty road, and they walked in.

A woman looked up and smiled from where she was refilling some pans. "What can I get you?"

Deacon stared unseeing at the menu. What was he even doing in here? He wanted to go home, except he didn't have one anymore, and that thought brought on another round of tears. He turned away in case the lady saw him.

"A slow kiss," Maverick said clearly.

"What?" Deacon lifted his head in surprise, convinced he'd misheard. Maverick pointed to the menu board, and sure enough, a Slow Kiss was chocolate mixed with fudge and a brownie. Deacon stood for a few seconds staring at the board. The words came into focus. That actually sounded pretty good. He paused. *The ice cream.* His gaze ran over the flavors while the lady made Maverick's, and he decided. "I'll have a Threesome," Deacon said, feeling a little silly. Vanilla, butter pecan, and peanut butter. That also sounded amazing. It was like he was having some out-of-body experience. He'd had one of the worst afternoons of his life, and he was standing here making jokes and eating ice cream. He quickly held his hand to his lips because he wasn't sure whether the next sound out of them would be a laugh or a sob. At the moment, it could go either way.

He felt the hot breath on his cheek as Maverick leaned forward. "I would never have that," he said quietly. "I don't share."

Deacon didn't answer because he couldn't think of what to say. Maverick could be shooting the breeze. Teasing to make him feel better. He could mean something entirely different from what it sounded like. Deacon didn't even know if Mav was *gay.* And Deacon could be hearing what he wanted to hear.

All of it. Or none of it.

Maverick paid the lady, and she thanked him, informing them she had to go in the back, but she would hear the bell if the door opened and they were to just holler if they needed anything else. Mav steered him to the table in the far corner. Deacon slid in around the back to give Maverick more room to maneuver.

"Thank you," Maverick acknowledged, and Deacon's icy insides warmed a little.

"Is your mom still drinking?" Maverick asked, and Deacon's head shot up in surprise.

"What?"

"You mentioned her drinking when she was younger, and I simply don't understand where all this resentment of you comes from. I mentioned her medical records on a hunch, and her reaction was very telling. She's definitely got something to hide."

Deacon sighed. "She hates me because of the singing."

Mav frowned. "Hates you? I would have thought she would be proud of you."

Deacon picked up his spoon. "Have you ever heard of The Sammy Gee Band?"

"Weren't they something in the seventies? Jamie was into them I think. She may have even gone to a few concerts." He shrugged.

Deacon chuckled. "They were a four-piece group. Very famous, and Annie Redding was one of their backing singers."

"Oh," Mav said, suddenly understanding. "That's what all that about singing songs to Molly was about? Your mom was a singer? I thought she reminded me of something. I'm sure Jamie has still got their old albums."

Deacon nodded. "And she was getting noticed. There was talk of a record deal, and then she got pregnant with the drummer's baby."

"Your dad."

"No," Deacon chuckled. "The drummer denied everything, and the record label paid her to go away. She met and married Dad when Mikey was a year old."

"Are you saying all this hatred is because your mom is *jealous*?"

"She always said music was a waste of time. I wanted to learn an instrument when I was younger, but Mom said it was pointless and did no one any good.

It was Pops who explained to me why she resented Mikey. I guess I know now why she hated me as well."

"Tell me what he was like."

Deacon tilted his head, his brain still trying to catch up. "Mikey? Oh, you mean when he was younger?"

Maverick nodded.

"The best brother in the world." Deacon's voice caught on the last word, and he took a breath. "He was like a wall."

Maverick squinted at him. "Big?"

"No, not in size. He was only a little taller than me. I mean more like something to protect me, a kind of shield."

Mav took another bite of his ice cream and swallowed. "Did he ever tell you what caused the last row between him and your dad?"

Deacon concentrated on his ice cream because at that moment, he couldn't speak. After another couple of beats while Maverick waited patiently, he said, "He covered for me when I needed some money."

"Go on," Mav encouraged.

"There was a talent contest at school. You know, one of those end-of-term things, and I was singing. Except they'd made it a charity thing, and we had to give donations to enter." He'd been desperate. "Mom said it was a waste of money, but I had to go ask Dad. If I'd left it any longer, I would have been too late, but he was asleep." Deacon swallowed some more ice cream. He couldn't remember the last time he'd had some. "No one ever woke Dad up or interrupted him when he was asleep. No one dared, and I knew there was no way Mom would. Mikey came home as I was pleading with her to ask. He immediately gave me the ten dollars from his pocket."

Mav paused while finishing off his chocolate. "Why would he get into trouble for that?"

"Because Mikey had to pay rent."

"When he was seventeen and at school?" Mav sounded incredulous.

Deacon nodded. "It started when he was fourteen, which was why he missed so many classes."

"If your dad wasn't already dead...."

"I didn't know Mikey had bought himself a cell phone. Only a cheap thing, but with the ten bucks he gave me, he was short for the rent. Mikey knew if he said why, I would be in trouble as well, so he lied and said the phone had cost him more, so he was short."

"But your mom said you could ask."

"It didn't matter. He could change his mind instantly, and she didn't really want me to in the first place. His favorite thing was telling us we could have something, then changing his mind at the last minute." After a while, they had stopped asking. Deacon really had had enough, and pushed his half-empty dish to Maverick.

"I'd called at Pops's after school because it was my night to visit and he would worry if I didn't show, but then I had to run over to my friend's house, who was lending me an outfit. We were walking there together, so I never knew all this. I came back as Dad was throwing him out, but it was nearly seven years before I found out why."

Deacon brushed a hand on his face again, and it came back wet. "It was all my fault. For a stupid singing competition, I got my brother thrown out of the house." He raised his eyes to Maverick. "What if it was *all* my fault? What if had he stayed he would never have done drugs?"

"It was your dad's fault, not yours," Mav said gently. "And from what you told me, there were quite a few years in between. I doubt that had anything to do with it." But Mav was just saying it to make him feel better.

"And—" He swallowed. "—he reached out to me as soon as he found out I was in college, and I *ignored* him. How could I have done that? After all he did." Deacon buried his face in his hands. Michael had always protected him. "I thought he'd left me," he mumbled from behind his hands until he felt Mav's fingers easing them away from his face and passing him a wad of napkins. "I should have known better." He would never forgive himself for that.

"But you saw him before you finished college."

Deacon smiled. "You remember I said I had it pointed out to me if I carried on I would be left with no job and no money?"

"It was Michael?"

"He rode to the rescue one last time. Intervened with the college for me. Talked to the cops. He was amazing, and I saw him two more times, but the year I graduated, he was in rehab. The year the band was successful was when he got Molly, and all I got were emails telling me he was working and doing okay. It was such a crazy year, I never checked." Deacon put his head in his hands and took a breath. He would never forgive himself, never. "I didn't see him again, and then the police contacted me about Molly."

He looked around the small store. They sold coffees as well. It would be nice to bring Molly. He swallowed down the lump in his throat and wiped his nose again. He needed to change the subject. "Do you really have a body camera?"

"Nope." Maverick took another bite and swallowed. "But she doesn't know that."

Deacon nodded. Shame, but it was quick thinking.

Maverick put his spoon down. "I heard her when I came back into the hallway."

"How did you know?"

"The housekeeper came for me. Or at least she opened the door and shot me a look that had me moving as fast as I could. I'm sorry it wasn't faster." He briefly squeezed Deacon's arm.

The lady came back out behind the counter. "Can I get you gentlemen anything else?"

Mav stood up and bought two bottles of water. Deacon picked up both dishes and took them to the counter. "Thank you. They were delicious."

She beamed, then tilted her head slightly as if she was considering what he said. "Has anyone ever told you, you look like that good-looking boy from Six Sundays?"

Deacon reddened and dipped his head, and the lady's hands flew to her mouth. "Oh my goodness, it *is* you?"

He nodded glumly. "We're leaving, though, now, ma'am." It would save her from throwing them out. A shame because he couldn't bring Molly now.

"And I don't want to hold you up, but is there any chance I could get your autograph for my niece? She's word-perfect on every song from *Just Joking*."

Deacon's mouth opened in shock. She wanted his autograph? But….

"Here." The lady grabbed a small pad from next to the register and nearly pounced when she saw a pen.

Deacon took it gingerly, like it was going to explode or something, and then his brain finally kicked into gear. "What's her name?"

"Amelia." The lady flushed. "I so wish she was here. She has a T-shirt, the single, and the album. Three posters in her bedroom."

"How old is she?"

"Thirteen now." The age Nickelodeon wanted to target. It had worked, then.

"I don't mean to be nosy, but are you by any chance writing any more songs? I mean, I know the band split up, but I know all her friends love you."

Deacon smiled. "I don't honestly know, but if I do, I will let Amelia know," he told her, and they left.

Maverick nudged him as they paused to cross the road. "Fan, huh?"

"That was surreal," he replied. "I thought she was going to throw me out."

They headed back to the truck. "Maybe Sara Jeffries wasn't as successful in her witch hunt as she thought she was."

"Meaning?"

"Meaning maybe your ordinary fans—the teenagers—just want to hear your songs and don't care about the other bullshit."

Deacon highly doubted it, but it was a nice thought.

"Would you consider it? If there was any chance of another contract, would you go back to singing?"

Never. "It isn't that lucrative unless you can write your own songs, and I wouldn't know a treble clef if I fell over one." No, it was cool while it was good, but he would never put himself out there like that ever again. "It was gratifying she was so nice, but Deacon Daniels has officially retired from the music industry."

"Yeah, *Uncle Danny.* What's with that?"

"My real name is Daniel Brown. It was too boring for Sony, so I changed it up. Deacon was my grandfather's name. I'm going to change it back as soon as I have a second to breathe."

They both climbed into the truck. "Oh, I don't know. I quite like Deacon."

He does? Deacon shot him a look to see if he was joking, but Maverick's warm brown eyes just regarded him steadily.

"So, if you could do anything you wanted, what would it be?"

Deacon didn't have to think. "A physical therapist." Mav raised his eyebrows in inquiry. "But it's another seven years of college. I was looking into being a PT assistant, which is only eighteen months full-time, but I need to earn money as well."

"Didn't you say you were a masseuse? Maybe you could do that and study part-time?"

Deacon nodded, suddenly shy but pleased Mav had remembered. "But I'm not qualified. I would have to take a test." Something else he'd never finished. He started the truck, and then on an impulse he didn't want to name put his hand on Maverick's where it was resting on his leg. "Thank you." Mav had looked after him. Bought him ice cream with funny names.

"For?"

Deacon chuckled, feeling so much lighter despite his mom. "A *slow kiss*."

Maverick paused, and for a panic-inducing second, Deacon thought he'd gone too far.

"You're welcome."

And Deacon, not wanting to push his luck, started driving home, all the time wishing a slow kiss was for real.

CHAPTER SEVEN

THE MAN looked down and pasted on his best nervous expression just before he got into the stupid bitch's car. She smiled eagerly, but then she would, because she thought he was doing her a huge fucking favor.

She didn't know she was going to die.

"You're sure my name isn't going to be leaked?" he said, pretending to be worried. "I need a promise of complete confidentiality."

Sara Jeffries put her hand on his arm in what he was sure she thought was a comforting gesture. "Absolutely. No names. I can promise you complete confidentiality." She tittered like she'd just said the funniest thing in the history of forever. He wondered if she'd still be giggling like they were sharing some big fucking secret when he was pouring lighter fuel all over her naked body. He licked his lips, and she patted his arm again. The bitch thought it was a nervous gesture, but really he was imagining all the things he could do to have some fun first. This one he was going to take his time with.

"Nice car," he complimented. He would have preferred to meet in his, but that would have been awkward when they went home together.

She smiled again and opened an iPad.

"No," he said. "Nothing electronic. You promised you would show me your notes first when we are done." He couldn't take the risk of her saving something externally. He was content at the moment to let her think he was paranoid. He brought a pad and pen out of his pocket. "You can use this."

"Very traditionalist," she snickered but took them and stowed the iPad away in her purse. "Now," she said. "You were going to give me some information about Deacon Daniels."

"Why are you so interested in him?" She'd been like a dog with a bone.

Her eyes gleamed. "Because he's my ticket out of here. I have an interview next week in New York."

He leaned forward as if he was sharing a confidence and clasped the syringe in his pocket, sliding the cap off the needle. "Did you know he's got a new boyfriend?"

She stilled. "My readers won't care he's gay. He's not exactly kept it a secret." She sighed as if she was disappointed, and he smiled to himself.

"Did you know his old agent is dead?"

Her head whipped up. "Jones? No. Accident? Suspicious?" She started trying to take notes, but the pen wouldn't work as he knew it wouldn't. She tutted and bent forward, reaching in her purse for another. It had been exactly the move he had been hoping for, and before she even had a chance to think about screaming, his hand was covering her mouth, and he plunged the needle into her neck. He held her effortlessly while she struggled.

"Quit fighting," he crooned, even as he felt her struggles getting weaker, "because I'm going to give you an exclusive." Her eyes widened, not because she wanted the story, but because she knew what was coming.

"There's going to be another murder," he whispered in her ear as she gave one last pathetic jerk, and he watched as her eyes closed. He gave her another second to give the ketamine a chance to work properly, and then he let her go. He stuffed everything into her bag, got out of the car, and walked around to the driver's side. He'd insisted because of his job he couldn't be seen, and she had understood, so no one was around here to see him lift her out of the seat and stuff her in the trunk. Then he would take her home. He'd already checked she had a garage he could just drive into when they got back to hers.

The man smiled to himself again. That had really been way too easy.

A SLOW kiss? Maverick thought. *Deacon was half-teasing, I think.* His body was noticing Deacon more and more with every minute they spent together, and it was getting harder to ignore.

But he would. Apart from being incredibly vulnerable, Deacon was a client. Mav couldn't mess this up for Jamie. Which reminded him, he needed to call her. Deacon pulled out of Lafayette Drive and headed for the I-75. It would take them about thirty minutes. Another quarter of a mile and they might hit traffic, though. The ice cream store had been close to the Arts Center, and there would be lots of students coming out soon.

"I have another interview tomorrow."

Maverick glanced at Deacon, but he had his eyes on the road. "While I understand the need, of course I do, I'm just not sure that's such a good idea at the moment."

"I have no car, nowhere to live, and no cash. I also have no choice," Deacon said. His words were harsh, but his voice was soft.

"Okay," Maverick conceded. "I'm going to call Jamie when we get home, and I might give Charlie a call as well. See if he knows how Detective Phan is doing."

Deacon did glance at him then. "Should I be worried?"

Mav scoffed. "You couldn't hurt—"

"A fly?" Deacon interrupted. Mav kept his mouth closed. He was the last person who should be making assumptions. They made a right turn, and Mav glanced in the side mirror.

And froze.

A black Charger pulled out of the street they had just come from and joined them. He might not have noticed if he hadn't seen it turn, because it was tucked behind a Toyota sedan and some sort of large Ford, probably an Explorer. Was it a coincidence? He couldn't see the plate, obviously, as it was behind him. "Take a right here," Maverick instructed.

"What?" Deacon questioned it but turned right onto Spring Street. "What is it?" Deacon looked in the mirror. The Toyota went straight on, but the Explorer followed them. After another few seconds, so did the Charger.

"We might have a Charger following us."

Deacon gripped the wheel a little tighter. Then the Explorer turned left into a museum, which left the Charger. "Take the next right," Maverick said. "I want you to head back to Seventeenth and pick up I-75." The Charger slowed behind them as Deacon signaled, and suddenly Maverick realized what a precarious position he was putting them in. It was pretty deserted around here. Whoever was in the Charger might intend harm to Deacon, and Mav had no gun.

Fuck. Mav nearly swore out loud. He had his Glock 22 at home, but it was locked up as per Jamie's conditions of him living there, along with her own Sig Sauer P328. Although, she would have taken hers with her when she went to serve papers to Aaron Malloy.

Deacon turned again, but this time, the Charger went straight on and disappeared. "I couldn't tell if it was the same one," Deacon said, the distress in his voice clear.

It was no good. Mav had to get his ass back behind the wheel. That was twice today Deacon had to drive when it should have been Maverick's job.

"I doubt it was. To see it this far out is unlikely. We didn't tell anyone we were coming here. I think it's a coincidence. Like you said, it's a common car." He tried to sound nonchalant, except Maverick didn't like coincidences, and they could have easily been followed from Deacon's mom's, or even Maverick's.

Deacon didn't look convinced, and Maverick decided he was definitely going to call Charlie.

Maverick was relieved when they got back. He'd caught Deacon checking his rearview mirror what seemed like a hundred times, but there was nothing he could say because Maverick was just as guilty even if he wasn't as obvious. He eased his leg out of the truck and hid the jab he felt in his back.

He walked around—maybe he *limped* around—the truck but epically failed at keeping it from Deacon.

"A bath would help," Deacon said randomly, looking him up and down. "Do you have one?"

Mav had a sudden urge to smell his armpits, but seeing as how he'd showered that morning, he didn't think that was what Deacon meant. He hoped it wasn't.

Humor lit Deacon's eyes as if Mav had said all that out loud. "I'm going to give you a massage. Warm water helps you relax first."

Maverick wondered if it did anything for your breathing, because at the moment, his lungs seemed to have stopped working. He shook his head. There was one upstairs—two actually—but they were impossible to get in and out of without help.

"That's okay. We'll manage. My oils were all trashed in the apartment, but I spotted some good hand cream in the bathroom, so I can use that. Go up and get comfy on the bed. I'm going to see what Jamie has for supper."

"Pizza. She has pizza." That was all Maverick seemed able to contribute to the conversation.

Deacon screwed up his nose. "If we ever eat pizza together, I'm taking you to Giordano's."

He'd never heard of—

"Chicago." Deacon grinned. "And don't bother ordering what's on the menu. You let Matteo make you what's good."

He'd forgotten. For one second, actually maybe a lot more, he'd forgotten this man in front of him had once had the trappings of wealth. Deacon had probably been to more countries than Mav even when he had served.

He'd called Deacon an airhead to Jamie, but in the space of barely a couple of days, Maverick had realized how wrong he was. Deacon was intelligent. He loved Molly like it didn't matter she was a spoke in his carefully crafted wheel. She needed him, and he had come running. He had survived the bastard of a father and had just been cut down by someone else who should have loved him unconditionally.

Mav hobbled upstairs when they went inside, and Deacon disappeared into the kitchen. He really didn't know what to make of the offer of a back massage and was worried he was setting himself up for awkwardness. He'd managed to keep a lid on his attraction, but the thought of those slim fingers doing anything other than touching his arm was getting him hard already.

And that hadn't happened much lately either. Some headshrink they had sent him had cheerfully told him the rate of sexual dysfunction among amputees could be as high as 33 percent. Something to do with how he saw his body afterward. Which Maverick didn't need a psychiatric degree to work out. The private in the bed next to him at Walter Reed had had some serious fucking issues that freaked him the hell out. He'd wake up at all times screaming in agony to the point that the nurses had to sedate him.

Problem was the pain was in his foot, except he didn't have either anymore. Maverick had wanted to cry with the guy after his girlfriend had also freaked out and never come back. And it wasn't that he hadn't felt for him. He wasn't completely cold, just really fucking scared he was going the same way. So, he'd gotten tunnel vision. Did every exercise they told him... *more* than they told him.

He'd pretended to Deacon he'd casually heard about the paratrooper who returned to full active service after an amputation, but he was lying. He could recite every word of the article he'd dreamed about while he'd lain in that bed. Every time he'd gotten himself up on the parallel bars to learn to walk, he'd been like that guy going on missions with his M4 and carrying fifty pounds of body armor.

Then he'd gotten his new leg, and because it hadn't worked instantly, the depression everyone else had seemed to go through in the hospital had hit him like a ton of bricks, and he'd turned his back on the lot of them. It had been true when he'd told Deacon he didn't want to go back to active service; he just wanted to *walk*. A small very selfish part of him had for a second been glad he'd never had to tell Cass he wanted to leave. After eleven, nearly twelve years, he was done. Ready to come home for good. Then in another bad moment, he convinced himself wanting to avoid the conversation with Cass had tempted fate and she had come and delivered some sick retribution. Maybe—no probably—that was why he'd avoided Charlie as well.

The thought made him pause, and then he heard a knock on the bedroom door.

"Do you like chicken?" Deacon called.

"I like everything," Maverick answered instantly.

"Good." There was a pause.

"You can come in. I'm not sure whether you just want me to lie down or not." He badly wanted to take his leg off, but would that freak Deacon out?

Deacon stepped into the room and glanced at the bed. "Towels?"

Mav nodded to the bathroom, and Deacon went in and came back out with a pile of them. He pulled back the comforter and spread them on the sheet. Then he looked up at Maverick, who was still standing there. "You need to get undressed, and if it won't bother you, why don't you take your leg off for a while."

But it might bother you.

He glanced down at his body, and he could feel his pulse spike. His burns were bad on his face, but the scars really came into their own down his leg.

"I've done this before," Deacon said as if he was trying to encourage him.

He had?

"It gave me the extra cash I needed for college, even if I'm not fully qualified," Deacon explained. "I'd never had money, so when I got Pops's, I pretty much set about blowing it in the first few months." He shook his head. "Really dumb. So after Michael made me see sense, I got a part-time job and stopped partying. It helped that it only took two years."

Mav started with his shirt. If Deacon could cope with the burn scars on his body, he'd progress to the leg. Before he had a chance to talk himself out of it, he pulled off the shirt.

Deacon's gaze roamed approvingly over his chest. "Nice definition," he murmured, and Maverick snorted in disbelief.

"You should have seen me last year."

Deacon arched an eyebrow but just said, "Leg?"

Maverick swallowed. "I'm not a pretty sight." He hated looking at it himself, and the thought of showing it to others made him feel physically ill.

"I don't care about pretty," Deacon said firmly. "I care about you being in pain." Which made Mav reach down and press the button on the side of his socket to release the suction. He eased it off and rolled down the inside liner.

"Does it hurt?" Deacon bent down to look.

"Not there. The limb aches occasionally, but the pain's in my back."

Deacon considered his answer. "I'm pretty sure you know more about this than me, but a lot of it is because of compensatory gait."

Mav had heard the term obviously, but he was surprised Deacon had.

"My roommate for the second year in college had a lower leg amputation because of meningitis as a child. Once he knew how interested I was and that I was thinking of becoming a PT, he shared all his experiences. I even went to a couple of appointments with him."

"Did you keep in touch?"

Deacon looked ashamed. "No. Everything changed when we got the record deal."

"But you could now," Maverick pointed out, feeling quite daring because Deacon had seen his residual and wasn't too disgusted. In fact, it didn't appear to be bothering him at all.

"You have to remember, after the accident, a lot of people didn't want anything to do with me. One lady in an ice cream store isn't a good cross section of the population."

Maverick grinned. Deacon sounded so serious sometimes. For someone who was only twenty-four, he seemed older, but then, most twenty-four-year-old's hadn't gone through what he had.

"Can you lie on your front?"

Maverick nodded and pulled a pillow down to raise him up a little. He had softened as they were talking, but he knew one touch from Deacon would make him hard again.

Deacon went to the window and closed the blinds to dim the light and carried on talking. "I like using jojoba oil because it doesn't stain and it's fragrance-free, but this will have to do." Maverick heard him rubbing the cream onto his hands. "Where's the pain? Lower back?" And then he climbed on the bed, which threw Maverick for a second until he realized Deacon simply had to be closer to reach him.

Maverick opened his mouth to reply, but the first touch of Deacon's fingers silenced him. He'd taken his jeans off and left his boxers on, but for a giddy second, he wished he was naked. He tried to muffle a moan that seemed to come from nowhere as Deacon lightly ran his hands over his skin.

"Take a slow deep breath," Deacon instructed, and Maverick did. Soon Deacon was sliding his hands up Maverick's back in a smooth gliding motion. "This is called effleurage," he said conversationally. "I'm moving my hands in the same direction as blood flowing to your heart and warming up your back muscles."

Maverick might have answered. He wasn't sure.

"Now I'm using petrissage techniques." Deacon moved slowly over his entire back and shoulder area, making small circular movements with his hands that seemed to make Mav's body feel really heavy, and his breaths grew easier and slower. Deacon was talking, murmuring quietly, and Maverick was starting to drift.

Maybe I've died. He must have. Maverick had never especially been religious, but somehow, he must have earned himself a slice of heaven. Deacon started ed lightly tapping on his back and explained they were percussive strokes.

Maverick didn't care. He could call them whatever the hell he liked, so long as he didn't stop. Deacon added more lotion to his hands. "This is called a tapotement technique." And Maverick felt nimble fingers almost walking up his spine. He did groan then, a deep sound of contentment he couldn't have held back if his life depended on it. He heard the smile in Deacon's voice.

"That good? Just relax. Feel free to fall asleep if you want to."

Maverick mumbled something that might have been words, but they had passed through his brain so fleetingly, he wasn't sure what they were. Deacon changed position and started sliding his hands widthways in opposite direction. They met briefly in the middle, then slid away to each side. "I can't use the fanning technique because I can't get above your head, so I'm going to move to your legs. Turn over."

There was a pause. "Mav, turn over."

Maverick groaned. He wasn't sure he might not have fallen asleep there for a few seconds. Zoned out, certainly. He barely opened his eyes as he shuffled onto his back, but the feel of Deacon's hands pushing the material of his shorts up woke him up a little. Woke him up *all* over.

Then Deacon moved back and had his hands on his foot. Maverick jerked slightly. "Are you ticklish?" Deacon chuckled.

"A little," Maverick admitted and shut his eyes again, not daring to look him in the face. He felt exposed. At least on his front, Deacon hadn't had to look at his scars.

"Shh," Deacon murmured soothingly, which made Maverick wonder if he'd said his thought out loud, but he was soon relaxed again as the firm fingers treated his foot with the same care his back had gotten. Maverick felt the bed dip as Deacon climbed on again so he could reach higher up Mav's calf. "Will your residual hurt?"

Mav shook his head, staying mute. It wasn't his residual he was worried about. Deacon used long, gentle strokes up and down the side of his calf, and soon Maverick was relaxed again. "I'm going to make scooping passes up and down your thighs to stimulate your muscles."

Maverick had a second to process what Deacon meant, and the first touch of his hands on the inside of Maverick's thigh made him gasp. He opened his eyes and caught both Deacon's wrists with his hands. The silence settled in the room. Maverick shook his head in apology. He only had so much control.

Deacon's eyes narrowed, but he pulled back, and Maverick let him go. "I don't know what you thought was going to happen, but contrary to popular belief, gays have as much control as the next person." He straightened and wiped his hands on the towel. "Take your time. The food will be ready in around half an hour."

And then without giving Maverick a chance to correct him, Deacon slipped out of the door, and Maverick heard him jogging downstairs. *Shit.* Mav had offended him. But he hadn't meant to. How could he explain he wasn't worried about Deacon's self-control but his own?

By being honest?

Maverick took a breath and reached for his leg. It was probably time. He just wasn't sure what good that would do either of them.

CHAPTER EIGHT

DEACON DIDN'T know whether to be angry or just feel sorry for the guy. He was so sexually inexperienced, he'd still been a virgin before he went to college. He might have made up for it a little then, but when the band had gotten together, it had suddenly been so much more difficult. Because of their contract and their image, Deacon had pretty much stayed alone for the time they had performed together. Not that the other boys being straight had made it any easier. They were all so terrified they were going to screw things up, they lived like monks. And afterward, he had so many greater problems than his love life, or lack of it.

Deacon took a cloth and pulled the casserole dish with the chicken breasts out of the oven to check they were ready, poured the sauce all over them, and then put them back to finish cooking. He grabbed the salad from the refrigerator and put a couple of potatoes in the microwave. He quickly put some silverware and glasses of water on the table, took a steadying breath, and turned around to face Maverick. He'd heard him come downstairs and into the kitchen.

"I didn't stop you because I thought you had a problem. I stopped you because I seem to have very little self-control when it comes to you."

Deacon stilled. Was Maverick saying what he thought he was? "I'm not some experiment." He'd come across that in college.

Mav looked surprised and took a step back. "No, you're not. What you are, though, is a client, and very much off-limits. You're in a bad place at the moment, and I don't want to put you in a worse one." Mav leaned against the counter. "I had to stop you up there before I embarrassed myself," he admitted. "You have very talented hands."

Deacon smiled. Maverick had no idea the effect he had on him. But he was right. He would never admit it, but his own self-control had wobbled some up there. "Hungry?"

"Starving." Maverick inhaled appreciatively.

"The sauce is just out of a jar," Deacon said, hoping for a compliment, which was so not like him.

"Stop fishing," Maverick scolded.

They ate in companionable silence. Deacon was mollified to see Maverick eat everything and have what was left. Maverick stood up, holding his plate, but Deacon stopped him. "I know the rule about cleaning up if you didn't cook, but you were going to call Jamie and Charlie." He looked at the clock. Mav followed his gaze and nodded. Deacon watched him walk out of the room and gave himself a mental pat on the back when Mav seemed to move easier.

It took barely a few minutes to clear up, and he filled the coffeepot. He could hear Maverick from the other room, but wanting to give him some semblance of privacy, he stayed where he was until he heard quiet, and then he poured out the coffee and carried it into the small room Maverick liked.

Maverick looked up from where he sat on the couch. "Jamie's going to make some calls and get back to me." He smiled. "I have to visit, and you have to come with me."

"Me?" Deacon nearly inhaled his coffee instead of swallowing it.

Maverick sobered a little. "I told her I'm going to the car dealer tomorrow, and she wants to meet the person who has kicked my ass into gear."

Deacon sipped his coffee. "I'm a good driver." Didn't he feel safe with Deacon?

Maverick acknowledged him with a tip of his head. "But you needed a break today, and I should have been able to step in." Mav paused as if he was trying to decide if that was a joke or not and smiled ruefully. He glanced down at his knee, and Deacon followed his gaze. Mav was wearing shorts, Deacon realized, and he would bet anything that was significant. He'd never seen Maverick in anything but cargo pants and sweats, and he was thrilled if Maverick had managed to relax a little around him. They both sipped their coffee, so when the question did come out of his mouth, it took him as much by surprise as it did Mav. "How did you get hurt?"

Mav's eyebrows rose, as if the question surprised him. "I was a helicopter pilot, and we were evac'ing US charity workers outside of Mogadishu after rebels were trying to overrun their compound. We weren't supposed to be getting involved, leaving it to the locals, but they overwhelmed us pretty quickly, and we had to move."

He stopped, and Deacon searched his face. Why had he asked? But he knew why.

"It was chaos. The locals were running to the helicopter, but we wouldn't have been able to get everyone in. Even if I dumped some gear, we couldn't have gotten more than twelve in at the most. Cass was trying to sort it, and I turned just as this teenager ran toward us. I remember one of the aid workers screaming, but it was as if I couldn't hear her. I always thought it was before the explosion, but the screaming could have been after." He shrugged. "Seven people died, including five aid workers and the teenager. He was the bomber. I lived because I was in the cockpit."

He said it so matter-of-factly, but Deacon heard the pain in his voice loud and clear. He saw Maverick glance toward a picture above the fireplace. It was obviously Maverick, but he wondered who the other two were and if they were still alive. His eyes narrowed a little as he glanced at the photo. "That's the cop," he said. "Officer Chaplin." They all looked so young and vital. Maverick was stunning. Whoever had taken the picture had captured such a carefree moment as they all shared a joke.

"Yep, that's me, Cass, and Charlie. Cass and I trained together. Charlie joined us for two tours, but he left when his time was up because he had problems at home with his girlfriend."

"And Cass?"

Maverick shook his head. "Killed in the blast."

Deacon glanced back at the picture. Cass and Maverick were in flight suits; he thought they were supposed to be flame-retardant, but he guessed they wouldn't protect his face. "Your friend looked surprised to see you."

"And me him. He lived in Toledo, and as far as I knew, he went back there. I had no idea he'd moved to Atlanta."

"Maybe you can catch up. Did you talk to him?"

"He's working now, but he's going to call me tomorrow."

"My interview is at eleven." And he so needed this job.

"Doing?"

"Audio narration." Deacon met Maverick's eyes. The room seemed hot, or maybe it was just the look he was getting. Deacon stood up. "I noticed some books in the dining room. Mind if I borrow one? It's ridiculously early, but I'm beat, and I thought I'd read."

He tried to tell himself the look he got was regretful as he left even though he knew Maverick had been right. It had been true what he told Maverick about him going a little wild when he got to college, but his three partners had all been the result of alcohol-induced attraction and simple availability. None of them had been looking for any other commitment, and he guessed at eighteen or nineteen, that was about right.

He'd briefly toyed with becoming a counselor for a while, and he'd done enough reading to make the leap between his lack of a loving home and his need for a connection. Deacon grabbed a couple of books and returned to go upstairs. The door to Maverick's living room was closed now.

The biggest regret of his life was he could never return the care Mikey had shown him. So many wasted years because he had been selfish. He'd apologized over and over to Mikey when they had finally met, but when he'd seen him for the first time after so long, he had

chuckled and called him Squirt like he always had done.
It had seemed so much more recent than six years ago.

"You were a kid," Mikey soothed.

*"So were you." They were silent for a while. "What
are you doing now?"*

*"Security." He patted his pocket, and Deacon's
eyes widened. He had a gun? Mikey chuckled again.
"Met any nice boys here, then?"*

*Deacon gaped at him. "How did you know?" He'd
been twelve when Mikey had gone.*

Mikey shrugged. "I'm not wrong, though?"

*Deacon shook his head, suddenly wondering if he
should have denied it.*

*"It's no big deal, so long as you're careful." He
raised a brow. "Do I need to have a safe-sex talk
with you?"*

*Deacon must have turned crimson, and Michael
grinned, but then he seemed to get serious. "I mean it.
It's cool, you're having fun, and you're way too sensible not to get gloved up, but I didn't mean just that."*

Deacon frowned. "What did you mean, then?"

*"I mean, you're a one-woman—sorry, one-man
guy. You've been like that all your life. You had one
friend that you hung on to for all you were worth. Remember Tim?"*

*Deacon nodded. He'd been devastated when his
friend had moved away. They'd been inseparable all
through kindergarten and up to fourth grade. Then
Tim's mom and dad had gotten divorced, and he'd
moved out of state. Mikey had caught Deacon crying so
many times. He'd thought his world was ending.*

*"We may be free of them both, but we still carry
that shit around every day."*

Deacon had understood Mikey meant their parents. He even understood Mikey was probably right. He'd just never applied it to Mikey and tried to understand what demons were following him around. The day he'd found out about Molly, he felt like the world was giving him a second chance to get it right with his brother. To make it up to him.

He was going to get this job tomorrow, and he'd give Shirley a call and see if there was any chance of some voice-over work. Audiobooks were huge at the moment, and everyone had told him to give them a try. He could always use another name, but Shirley had hinted that when enough time had passed, curiosity might make people give him a second chance.

He'd dismissed it at the time because he didn't think he deserved it, but if he was ever to have the chance of giving Molly a home….

Woah. Give Molly a home?

He went over the events of the morning. He'd seen no signs that Molly was deprived or abused. She had everything money could buy. But he hadn't seen love. And what if Maverick was right? What if his mom was still drinking? If he got himself together, maybe he could get the court to increase the visits and be trusted to have her on his own. His lawyer had said Michael's wishes normally would hold sway, and he'd encouraged him to fight, but at the time, he'd genuinely believed Molly deserved better than him.

Now he wasn't sure.

THE NEXT morning, Deacon was awake before dawn, which wasn't surprising as he was pretty sure he'd been asleep before eight. He took his time getting showered and dressed. The door to Maverick's room was still closed as he crept downstairs, and he decided to make some coffee and email Shirley before he thought about breakfast and what he was going to wear for his interview.

He had three changes of clothes he'd managed to save from the apartment, but his black jeans were clean, and he had a cream shirt that would pair well. He was on his second coffee, and he still hadn't heard Maverick stir when he decided to make fresh coffee and take some in to him.

Deacon knocked carefully, and when he was met with silence, he gingerly pushed the door open. One look at the room told Deacon exactly why he hadn't heard from Mav this morning. The room was dark, but the nearly empty bottle of Jack next to the tumbler with some dregs in it told Deacon that Mav wouldn't be stirring anytime soon.

So much for my bodyguard.

Maverick grunted and tried to roll over. It looked awkward as hell, and he flung his arm out just as Deacon was going to close the door. The glass shattered as it hit the wooden floor, and Maverick jerked upright. "The fuck?"

Deacon met Maverick's wide eyes for a second, then went to get the brush and pan he'd seen in the kitchen.

Maverick was sitting up with his head in his hands and glanced over at Deacon ruefully when he came back into the room. His leg was on the floor. "I'll do that," he said immediately, but Deacon pointed to the mug.

"Drink your coffee first."

It took a couple of minutes to sweep everything up. Maverick picked up his phone and squinted at it. "Charlie says he will call around after one."

Deacon picked up the bottle of Jack and started screwing the top on. Maverick's warm hand wrapped around his wrist. "Empty it down the sink."

"What?" It wasn't a cheap brand.

"I didn't realize how much I'd been drinking until the last couple of days without it," Maverick admitted. "I thought I could have one glass last night." He met Deacon's eyes. "I was lying to myself. It needs to go."

"Then you need to do it," Deacon said firmly. It had to be Maverick's decision. Exactly the same way he had reached his own. The night before he had met Michael for the first time in six years had been the last time Deacon had taken a drink, and he didn't miss it at all.

Maverick nodded, then glanced at his phone. "We have plenty of time. I'll get ready, and then we'll go for some breakfast before your interview."

Deacon smiled. "I have a better idea. I'll make us breakfast while you're in the shower, and we can go to the car dealer before my interview instead." Deacon tried and knew he had failed to keep the challenge out of his voice, but Maverick held his gaze in silent agreement.

He understood. Of course he did. But Mav seemed so strong, and maybe Deacon's problems were giving him the focus he needed. There had been a couple of times where Mav had made a decision for him, and it wasn't that Deacon wasn't either capable or a doormat, but maybe somehow, they had found a way to help each other.

Deacon heard the knock at the door twenty minutes later before Maverick had come back into the kitchen, and he dried his hands and walked into the hallway just in time to see Maverick letting in Detective Phan.

Maverick shook hands with him and led him into the kitchen. Deacon wasn't especially surprised to see him, and he hoped they might have some news on what had happened to Manny.

He put a black coffee down in front of the detective and glanced over at Maverick. He looked a million times better than when Deacon saw him less than an hour ago. He waited until Maverick glanced his way, wanting to share the memory, but when he did, all trace of humor vanished. Maverick's eyes glinted, and his normally easy smile had gone. Deacon glanced at Phan, wondering if he had missed him saying something, but the cold in the detective's expression sent a shiver down Deacon's spine.

"What's happened?" Maverick asked.

Phan gave no indication the question surprised him. "At 7:00 a.m. this morning, fire trucks and EMTs responded to a neighbor's call about a fire at 1173 Wickham Avenue."

Deacon shared a confused look with Maverick. He was no wiser.

"The home was ablaze when we got there and completely impossible for the fire crew to enter. After it was successfully extinguished, a body was recovered. We won't have a definite identification until the MEs have looked at her—"

"Her?" Deacon picked up on the word right away.

"It's an assumption based on the car in the driveway and the homeowner."

"What has it got to do with me?" Deacon asked. He wasn't stupid, and this definitely wasn't a social call.

"Because we think the body is Sara Jeffries."

Deacon heard the next words through a fog and felt himself being lowered to a seat, and he grasped the arm wrapped around him. *Maverick.* The room came back into focus along with Phan's worried face. Maverick was at his side, but he pulled out the other chair and sat down, never letting go of Deacon. He concentrated on Phan's gray eyes because if he looked at Maverick he might cry, and he knew Maverick would let him. It was all he could do to concentrate on what the detective had said.

"And you can't be sure?" Deacon managed to get out.

Phan sighed. "It's an educated guess. And I have to ask if you can provide an alibi for yesterday. Ms. Jeffries's last known whereabouts was at her office when she told colleagues she was leaving to follow up on a story at ten yesterday morning."

"He was with me yesterday all day," Maverick confirmed.

"And last night?"

The hesitation was obvious, and Deacon jumped in. "I went to bed at eight. No one can vouch for me after that."

Phan looked over at Maverick for confirmation. "If Mr. Daniels had gone out, would you have heard him?"

Deacon recognized the torturous look Maverick sent him. He doubted if a helicopter landing would have brought Maverick out of his drunken stupor. He knew it, and Maverick knew it. "I didn't hear him go out," Maverick confirmed, which wasn't exactly the answer to Phan's question, and he doubted if the detective would have missed it. Deacon almost shook his head but stopped himself. There was no point borrowing trouble.

"Did the fire kill her?"

"We don't know yet. There doesn't seem to be any obvious injuries, but parts of the body were badly charred, so until the ME takes a proper look, we don't know."

Deacon rubbed his hands. He was suddenly very cold.

"Mr. Daniels, can you tell me the last time you spoke to Ms. Jeffries?"

Deacon put his hand in his pocket for his phone, then nearly dropped it because his hands were shaking. "The text," he croaked, and Maverick took the phone. He entered the code, found the text, and then passed it to Detective Phan, who took a photograph of the text with his own phone. "There's some more, but that was the latest."

Phan scrolled through all the texts. "How did she get your number after you changed it?"

"I don't know," Deacon whispered miserably.

"Are you staying here for the time being?" Phan asked after another few seconds of studying his texts. Deacon didn't care. He could keep the damn phone if he wanted. He had nothing to hide. Or nothing the detective would care about. Deacon glanced at Maverick.

"Absolutely," Maverick confirmed.

Phan nodded. "As soon as I hear anything else, I'll be in touch," he said, and he left them.

Maverick came back into the room carrying the bottle of Jack and walked over to the sink and emptied it out. He threw the bottle into the recycling bin, then reached into one of the top cupboards and brought an unopened one down, which he solemnly unscrewed and emptied. He washed his hands after and squirted some dish soap in the sink to chase away the strong smell. When he was done and had dried his hands, he turned around and leaned back on the side of the sink.

"I'm sorry, Deacon," he said carefully, "but I'm not going to be able to offer you personal protection services any longer."

CHAPTER NINE

"YOU THINK I hurt her?"

Maverick blinked. "What? No."

"Then what the hell do you mean?" Deacon burst out.

"I screwed up last night," Maverick admitted. He had. Anyone could have come in, and Deacon would have had no protection whatsoever. "If you'd have had problems last night, I couldn't have done jack shit."

He could see Deacon's face soften, but the last thing he wanted was Deacon feeling sorry for him. Things could have gone badly wrong last night while he was having his own pity party all because he wanted so desperately to follow Deacon upstairs and join him in bed. He'd had the drink to dampen the urge. He'd had the second because he'd had the first. He couldn't remember how many he drank, but the first one had been one too many.

"And it's not only that." He tapped his leg in case Deacon still didn't get it. "I'll be completely honest, when Shirley offered Jamie this job, she intimated a couple of days babysitting while you calmed down." Deacon stiffened, and Maverick held up a conciliatory hand. "She was obviously wrong and misjudged you and the threat itself." He swallowed. "Deacon, there is the real possibility that there is a killer picking off people you know. What if he or she comes for you?"

"Maverick, I have no money."

"I'll pay."

"You try and I'll leave here and check into a motel," Deacon threatened.

"You've just said you've got no money," Maverick pointed out dryly.

"The papers would pay for it."

"*What*?" Maverick exclaimed.

"I have three that have offered to advance me the cash for my 'exclusive' story." Deacon finger quoted. "I could be out of here in thirty minutes."

"Absolutely not," Maverick thundered, wondering how this was going so wrong.

"Says who?" Deacon challenged.

"Me, for starters." It was ridiculous. "You can't go wandering about on your own." It wasn't safe, and the thought of Deacon getting hurt made him feel distinctly ill.

"If I can't have you, I don't want anyone," Deacon said firmly. "So make up your mind because I will have to go get my things together."

"I'm no good for you," Maverick tried again.

"Can you shoot?"

Maverick scowled. Of course he could, but he knew what Deacon was trying to say. "Okay, I'm your protection, but you have to promise me something." Deacon arched an eyebrow but waited. "You stay here, and I will look after you. If this escalates, I may bring in further help from my contacts who I was going to ask originally when Jamie wanted to start this type of business."

Mav looked at the stubborn set of Deacon's jaw, the pale face, and the very light dusting of freckles across his nose that were so like Molly's. The blue eyes were wide open and flashing fury, and Deacon was standing, hands on his hips, and preparing to do battle.

And how Maverick stayed still and didn't gather him in his arms and kiss him senseless was completely beyond him.

AN HOUR later, they were ready to go. Deacon seemed quite nervous because he kept smoothing down the too-tight shirt he wore. When Maverick had watched him come downstairs, he had nearly swallowed his tongue. He'd managed to stop himself offering to loan him one of his, even though it would have looked like a tent on him. Deacon was small but had well-defined muscles that the soft material clung to.

That Maverick wanted to cling to.

Shit. He had it so bad. Maybe he needed to think about getting laid, finally. Or maybe he ought to admit that the only person holding his interest was the one standing in front of him. "Hungry?" Maverick was suddenly starving.

"I don't think I could eat anything," Deacon nearly wailed.

Maverick kept his face straight. "How about if we go through the drive-through on the way to the dealership? Then we could get a snack and go for lunch after your interview?"

Deacon nodded gratefully, and they both got into the truck. "Where am I going?"

"Marietta Ford on Roswell Street." He'd been looking at an F-150, and he leaned back while Deacon drove the truck competently. Now that he had decided to drive, he couldn't wait.

They pulled into the large dealership nearly an hour later after fortifying themselves with a coffee and a breakfast burrito. At least Maverick had. Deacon had just gotten coffee and a water.

Maverick gazed at row after row of brand-new cars. In his mind, he had already picked either the black or the metallic gray, but it depended on what they had available.

The salesman was there before Deacon had even turned the engine off. Deacon and Maverick got out of the truck at the same time, and the young man, who for a second Maverick doubted was even old enough to drive himself, plastered on an eager smile and approached Deacon. The start he gave when he glanced over at Maverick was as equally embarrassing as it was pathetic. For a second—because the way he looked was never an issue to Deacon—Maverick had nearly forgotten the effect his appearance had when people saw him for the first time. It wasn't going to ruin this for him, though.

"I want to talk to someone about getting an F-150 adapted," he said. The salesman glanced over at him and then looked at Deacon like it was him who had spoken.

"Of course, sir. What exactly do you have in mind?"

Deacon glanced at Maverick, and Mav took a deep breath. "I'm a right-side amputee."

The salesman glanced at Maverick nervously, and Deacon spoke up. "Perhaps you have someone who is responsible for mobility adaptations?"

The young man nodded but still didn't seem to make eye contact with Maverick, which was starting to annoy him. "I'm assuming you are able to have any vehicle adapted?"

"Providing it is less than twelve months old," he confirmed, "and"—he glanced at Maverick like he was going to eat him—"it, of course, depends on if you need room for a wheelchair." He looked at Deacon expectantly.

"I'm over here," Maverick said flatly, and the man shot him another nervous look.

"Of course, sir." But this time he kept his eyes on the ground, and suddenly Maverick couldn't be bothered.

"Come on," he said in resignation and turned back to the truck.

"Are you sure?" Deacon said and glared at the man.

Maverick nodded. He was sure. He wanted to kick himself. He knew what he wanted, but he would try a different dealership. Maybe one that employed *grown-ups*.

He was so fucking angry. For a second, he nearly ordered Deacon to head for the nearest liquor store, but as the angry words were rolling around in his brain, he felt the featherlight touch of Deacon's hand on his left leg. "I think you intimidated him."

Maverick's anger turned to hurt.

"Some people don't know how to react when they see someone else is braver, better, and probably smarter than them," Deacon continued.

"What?" Maverick was confused.

"It's a confidence thing. He knows he can't hope to measure up to all this awesomeness." Deacon's eyes trailed the length of Maverick's body, and Maverick couldn't help how every cell in him reacted to Deacon's gaze.

"He's young," Maverick managed to get out. He dragged his eyes away from Deacon's with difficulty, then saw the young man still standing in the lot, watching them in apparent mortification. He looked like someone had kicked him. What had Mav just said about adults? It was Maverick who was behaving like a spoiled brat, and he should be ashamed of himself.

Maverick nodded to himself and climbed back out of the car and walked back over to the salesman. "What's your name?" He nearly added *son* but managed to stop himself sounding like he was ninety not thirty-four.

"P-Philip Mathewson, sir."

"Well, Philip," Maverick said with a friendly smile. "What I should have done was ask how long it takes to get a vehicle adapted."

The young man was openly staring at Maverick's face now when he'd been trying to avoid looking at him before, and it seemed baffling to Mav.

"I also need to look into what help I can get," he added. "My sister says Ford has a special program for veterans?"

The young man nodded eagerly and fished out a business card. "We have a special deal for veterans for up to a $500 free adaptation. Your gas pedal would have to be moved to the other side, sir, and the state of Georgia doesn't need an evaluation done beforehand. We can even make it easily changeable depending if someone else also needs to drive the car."

"Sounds good." Maverick held out his hand, and Philip shook it. Philip opened his mouth but hesitated, clearly wanting to ask something else. Maverick tilted his head enquiringly.

"Can I ask?" He looked at Maverick's burns again.

"It was the result of a suicide bomber outside of Mogadishu."

Philip went so pale, Maverick became concerned. "Somalia?"

"Yes." Maverick frowned. "Why, did you know someone stationed there?"

"No," he whispered. "My dad was in Baghdad. He died driving over a roadside bomb. The Humvee he was in caught fire." And suddenly Philip's reaction to Maverick's scars made complete sense. It was a stark and painful reminder, and Maverick was so thankful he had swallowed his pride and gotten back out of the truck.

"I'm sorry to hear that," Maverick admitted. "He was an instructor for years, but then his best friend got killed, and he requested a transfer. He did a full tour and called my mom to say he'd gotten it out of his system and he was coming home. She was so happy. The bomb happened the day before he was due to fly home." Philip glanced down. "I'm sorry if I offended you, sir."

Maverick was lost for words. It was all complete shit. He glanced back at Deacon, who had gotten back out of the car and was watching him with what he hoped was an approving smile. Philip probably worked on commission only.

"I'm sure you have got guys to help you and your mom, but if you ever want to talk some more about this, I want you to call me, and we can meet for a coffee. Anytime," he pressed. Philip smiled hopefully. "And now, how about we go discuss colors, and you show me some dotted lines to sign?" Maverick glanced inside the showroom.

"Of course, sir," Philip said as Deacon joined them. "But I can get my manager to help you as he has more experience—"

"No, I don't think so," Maverick decided. "You'll do just fine."

"I THINK you made his day." Deacon smiled. Maverick chuckled as they pulled out of the dealership an hour later. "Why didn't you want to trade in the truck? I doubt if you'll get much privately for it."

"I'm not going to get anything for it," Maverick snorted. "But this way you can borrow it until you get your own, or it dies of old age."

"You didn't have to do that," he protested, but Maverick knew.

"Where's your audition?"

"Shirley's offices off of Park Street where the new construction is. We can cut behind the back of the Baptist church." Maverick sat back as they turned. His world seemed so much brighter this morning. "What sort of book—"

But Maverick didn't get the chance to ask about Deacon's audition because he had a split second to register the loud rev of an engine, and then he was flung forward against his seat belt as something rammed into the back of the truck.

The fuck? He glanced in the side mirror to see a blue pickup reversing. "Deacon, floor it," he roared, but Deacon didn't get the chance to react fast enough to stop the pickup from ramming them a second time. The belt caught again, but the truck was pushed sideways into the wrong lane just as a car came around the bend toward them. Another squeal of tires as by some miracle the driver managed to avoid them. The car's driver slammed on his own brakes, and Maverick saw the pickup swerve to avoid it, then accelerate and disappear around the bend.

Silence. For a second. For a breath. And Maverick looked over at Deacon, who groaned and leaned back in his seat, hand to his head. "Are you okay? Deacon?" His heart beat punishingly in his chest.

Deacon turned his head, but his eyes weren't focused. A trickle of blood ran from his temple.

"Is everyone all right?" The door was wrenched open, and the concerned face of the driver—Maverick assumed—who had missed them coming in the opposite direction peered at him.

Maverick scrambled. "Call 911." As fast as he was able, he was out of the truck and around to the driver's side. The guy from the other car obediently pulled out his phone and did as he was instructed.

"Deacon?" Maverick had to physically stop himself from pulling Deacon into his arms. "You hit your head. Stay still," he cautioned as Deacon would have tried to climb out. He took his hand—still cold and even more fragile—and willed the paramedics to get their butts here.

"My head hurts," Deacon said as if he didn't understand why.

"Shh," Maverick soothed. "They will be here soon."

"I crashed your truck," he said pitifully, like it was the worst thing in the history of forever.

Maverick brushed a blond hair from his forehead. "It's your truck now."

"So thassokay?"

Maverick's heart clenched as Deacon slurred his words. *How long was this fucking ambulance going to be?*

"They're on their way," said the other driver as if Maverick had spoken the question out loud. Maverick glanced at the man. He was around forty, worried. He looked like Maverick felt.

"Stay with me?" Deacon suddenly asked, the question coming out of nowhere.

"I'm not going anywhere," Maverick tried to reassure him. He wasn't. Then he heard the sound of sirens, and he didn't realize how fucking scared he'd been. Everything happened really quickly then. Cops, paramedics.

No one liked the idea that Maverick insisted he went with Deacon. They seemed to think he should stay with the car and talk to them. Maverick soon changed their minds.

An hour later, he was sitting in the most uncomfortable white plastic chair known to man when he looked up and saw Detective Phan walking toward him.

"I wondered when they'd call you," he started, and Phan sat down.

"I understand he's got a concussion."

Maverick nodded. They'd called Deacon's next of kin—Anne—and she'd said she wasn't interested. Maverick didn't understand how any mother could be like that with her son. He'd made it clear then and there that he was Deacon's *interested other*, as they called it. The nurses were so dumbfounded at Anne's reaction, they treated Mav like Deacon's family. Which suited Mav just fine. He even went as far as to hint there was more between them than there actually was.

He didn't care. He was waiting while they gave him permission to go see Deacon.

"We found the pickup truck burned out and abandoned. It was stolen earlier today from a Walmart. I have someone looking at CCTV."

"So you believe him now?"

Phan didn't rise to the defensiveness in Maverick's voice. "The driver of the other car witnessed the pickup try and push you into oncoming traffic, and unless this is an elaborate setup—"

Maverick nearly growled.

"Which is unlikely," Phan continued, "then yes, APD are taking it seriously."

Maverick eyed the detective. "But this isn't your case."

"I don't believe in coincidences." He got out a pad. "Can you tell me everything you know from the beginning? All your dealings with Mr. Daniels?"

Maverick glanced at the nurses' station. He caught the eye of the nurse he had spoken to earlier, and she held up ten fingers to him. "I can give you ten minutes."

Phan started taking notes. "We will need to confirm everything with Mr. Daniels but not while he has a concussion."

"Mr. Delgardo?" It was ten minutes, and then another fifteen after Phan had gone, that someone came to speak to him. It was the doctor who had treated Deacon on admission. "We are in a difficult position."

Maverick might have gasped or done something as equally telling.

The doctor's eyes widened. "No, sorry. He's resting comfortably. My problem is unless Mr. Daniels gives us permission, I can't share any details with you."

Maverick grunted. "Can you tell me he's okay?"

The doctor nodded and breathed a sigh of relief. He must have thought Maverick was going to cause trouble. "Then that's all that matters. The only trouble you will get from me is if I can't sit with him."

The doctor smiled. "I'll let the nurses know, unless Mr. Daniels objects, you are allowed to be there."

Maverick exhaled slowly and stood up at the same time as the doctor. "I fully expect Mr. Daniels to be discharged in the morning." He hesitated. "I wouldn't want him to be alone for at least twenty-four hours."

"Oh, he won't be," Maverick assured him. "He stays with me." He nearly added the words "for a long time." But wishing didn't always make something so. He should know that.

CHAPTER TEN

FOR A second, Deacon was back to being eighteen and really stupid. His head certainly seemed to think so. No, that wasn't right. At the same time as his memory filtered back, he registered the large warm hand holding his own and knew who it was. And suddenly his head didn't throb quite so much. He tried to pry his eyes open and instantly regretted it.

It *hurt*.

He must have made some sort of distressed noise, because the warm hand tightened. "Hey," Maverick said quietly, gently. "The nurses gave you something an hour ago, but they can't give you anything that might increase your chance of bleeding."

Deacon would have nodded, but keeping his head still seemed a better idea. He swallowed. "I feel sick."

"Mr. Daniels?" It was the doctor, and Maverick moved his hand. The doctor asked Deacon some questions, then checked his eyes. Deacon hated it. "I don't think there's any worsening of your symptoms, even the nausea, but we'll keep you in tonight."

"Headaches always make me nauseous," Deacon whispered. "I got them a lot when I was younger."

"Migraines?" the doctor asked.

"I don't know," Deacon admitted. He and Michael would have to be dying before his dad would let their mom take them to the clinic.

"We'll see how you are in another hour. Increased pain or if the nausea gets worse or any indication he is confused, please press the call button." He must have been talking to Maverick.

"What happened about the guy who rammed us?"

"Detective Phan's been in and told me the car was stolen and it was dumped shortly after. The other driver gave a statement, and Phan took a statement from me updating him on everything. They're taking this seriously."

"I guess that's good."

Then Deacon processed the doctor's words. "I haven't got any insurance," he said, despair washing over him. How had he gotten into this mess? Without even being consciously aware, he reached out with his fingers, sighing in relief when Maverick clasped his hand again.

"You have nothing to worry about," Maverick said firmly.

But even an overnight stay could cost thousands of dollars. Taking a deep breath, he tried to open his eyes fully without wincing and pushed up with his elbows. "I need—"

But firm hands stopped him from moving. "You need to lie down, or I'll make that nice doctor sedate you."

Deacon couldn't help the smile. "I don't think you can sedate people who have concussion."

"Then I'll just tie you down to the bed."

"You're into bondage, hmm?"

He heard the soft chuckle from Maverick and rolled over a little toward him. He took another breath and gripped Mav's hand. He was really getting sick of worrying.

THE NEXT morning, Deacon was sick of everything. Sick of being woken up when he wanted to sleep. Sick of being poked and prodded, and especially sick when Maverick wasn't there. In fact, he told the doctor he would have a relapse if they didn't let his visitor in, but the nice nurse finally said they'd found Maverick a cot in their break room because they were worried he seemed in pain from his residual, and he'd refused to go home.

He could have told them it was his back, but it didn't really matter. What did matter was Maverick had spent at least seven hours with him without a word of complaint, and Deacon was acting like a baby. So he shut up and closed his eyes. When he heard the nurses sometime later and opened them with barely any headache, he saw two smiling brown eyes looking at him.

"Hey, you," Maverick murmured. "How are you feeling?"

"I can't believe you stayed," Deacon admitted honestly.

Maverick's smile deepened, and Deacon was struck with just how damn good he looked. The scar was bad, yes, but Deacon had stopped seeing it and started noticing the dark umber skin warmed even more by the full lips that smiled indulgently at him, and the deep brown gentle eyes framed by lashes so thick he knew Sascha—the makeup artist who had always fussed with his makeup before a magazine shoot—would have gone crazy for them.

And bashed up, lying in a hospital bed, maybe wasn't the best place to start noticing this kind of thing. *Who are you trying to fool?* He'd been noticing Maverick like this since the first time he had seen him. Especially how Mav had stood up to his mom.

His breath hitched as he remembered Maverick bending down and staying completely still while a two-year-old kissed his damaged cheek. If it had been him, Deacon didn't think he could have been so gentle. So understanding. There was something so touching about a huge guy being so protective about a little girl.

Okay, so it might have been bone-meltingly hot as well. But it went further than that.

"I'm your bodyguard." Maverick interrupted his thoughts, answering his question. "I have to be here to protect you because I think there's at least one nurse who wields her thermometer like a scalpel."

"Was that the only reason?" Deacon tried not to groan. He didn't bother with the excuse of the no-filter problem and hoped Mav might blame the concussion. But he knew it wasn't that simple. He was falling for this big Ranger-type SWAT Special Forces guy that could kill him with his little finger whether he could fly helicopters or not.

"No," Mav replied softly, and Deacon opened his eyes. He just lay there and smiled and hoped that this might be his new reality.

Well, not the hospital bed, because that would suck.

A few hours later, the doctor discharged Deacon with what seemed every warning possible short of a nuclear apocalypse, and gave strict instructions to Maverick to rush him to an ER if he was at all worried. Detective Phan—apparently—had some questions but would meet them at Maverick's later that morning. The nurse he liked wheeled him solemnly to the main doors, and only then did it occur to Deacon the truck was likely damaged.

"Are we getting a cab?"

"Nope," Maverick said and pointed to the APD car that a smiling Charlie was standing next to.

"I'm pretty sure this is illegal," Deacon mused as he was helped into the back seat.

Charlie shook Maverick's hand and grinned. "We're a full-service police force," he explained dryly and got in. They were back at Maverick's in thirty minutes.

"Do you have time for a coffee?" Maverick asked Charlie as they pulled into Jamie's neighborhood.

"Shit," Charlie swore, obviously not answering Maverick's question, and Deacon leaned sideways to see. Charlie had to slow down as reporters swarmed out of two news vans when they approached. Deacon heard Charlie calling it in as they stopped.

Mav turned to him. "We need to get you inside as quickly as possible." At which Deacon wanted to swear himself and sarcastically say, no, of course he wanted to chat to the nice reporters, but all he did was nod his agreement.

Maverick opened the door and tried to ignore the shouted questions as he helped Deacon from the car that seemed to have child locks on. "Deacon Daniels," the cry went up, and Deacon felt Maverick's hand tighten on his arm as he pulled him up to the house. Deacon clung to Maverick but for as much Maverick's benefit as his own. He knew Maverick would suffer later for the clip he was walking at. Then another cop car rolled up, and Maverick unlocked the door as two more cops took charge and stopped the cameramen from walking up Maverick's pathway.

He shot Mav a desperate look as his phone started ringing, and seeing it was Shirley, he answered it immediately.

"Deacon, are you okay? Have you spoken to the police?"

"We're with them now. What's the matter?" He listened in disbelief and promised he was staying there and if anything changed, he would let her know. Shirley wasn't bad. Not like Manny. But her motives were businesslike just the same, even if her methods weren't as questionable. What Shirley might think was good for him might differ from what he himself thought.

He looked at Maverick. "Someone's told the papers about both murders."

"I'd say," Maverick agreed somewhat flippantly. The telephone in the hall started ringing, and so did Deacon's cell. He eyed the screen and pushed the mute button. Maverick strode to the telephone, answered it, listened for five seconds as the reporter started to introduce himself, then hung up. He set it to silent and glanced at Deacon. His phone started buzzing, and he answered it cautiously.

"Mr. Daniels?"

He breathed a sigh of relief. "Detective, we're being mobbed by the press. How did they find out about this?"

"Unfortunately, there are a hundred ways, not least the fact that Ms. Jeffries was a reporter herself. I wanted to check you were at Mr. Delgardo's so we can come and interview you?"

Interview me? It sounded so serious. But he confirmed he was fine.

"That was Detective Phan. They are on their way." There was a knock on the door, and Maverick quickly let Charlie in.

"My sergeant's authorized us to stay. We'll make sure the reporters stay off your property." Deacon breathed a sigh of relief. He liked Charlie. "I'm going to walk around and shut all your blinds," he said calmly and did so.

Deacon shivered, and Maverick noticed immediately. "Come and sit down. You're supposed to be resting."

"I don't know what's happening," he admitted and knew Maverick understood what he meant. His whole life had just spiraled out of control *again*. He sat down on the couch, suddenly so cold. Maverick frowned and took his hands.

"Jesus, you're freezing."

Deacon closed his eyes. He was exhausted between the stress of yesterday and being constantly woken up by the nurses to make sure he was okay. Maverick was warm, and he leaned closer trying to soak up the heat.

"I can make coffee?" Charlie said from the doorway, but Maverick shook his head.

"Jamie's got some teas in there. Stick a chamomile one in some boiling water, will you?" Charlie must have gone because the room became quiet again, and Deacon kept his eyes closed but inched a little nearer. It was nice, and he yawned.

"Sorry."

He felt Maverick's chest rumble, and with a start realized not only had he actually nodded off for a few seconds, he was now leaning on Mav fully. He ought to move. But he didn't. Then he heard Charlie open the front door and knew when he heard Detective Phan that he must have nodded off for longer than a few seconds. He sat up blearily, and Mav solemnly handed him the cooling tea.

Phan walked into the living room, shook Maverick's hand, acknowledged Deacon because he had both his hands wrapped around his mug, and took a seat. Charlie left them to it, but Deacon didn't expect him to go far. Phan fixed his gray eyes on Deacon, and Deacon sipped his tea for warmth, missing Maverick's body.

"We have definitely identified Sara Jeffries."

"And was she dead before the fire started?" Maverick asked.

Phan hesitated, then shook his head. "Not according to the ME."

Oh God. Deacon clamped a hand over his mouth in complete horror.

Maverick glanced at him in sympathy before turning back to Phan. "And so, you're what? Thinking it's the same person?"

"The only evidence linking the two fires is the lack of it. The accelerant wasn't a special preparation and could be commonly bought at a retail store. The main differences were that Emmanuel Jones was dead before the fire started, and Sara Jeffries wasn't. The only connection the two of them ever had to each other was you." Phan looked right at Deacon. "Coupled with the threats and the accident yesterday, we are worried that this may have something to do with your joint history."

"You mean connected to the poor lady that died?" Deacon asked. "She had no family that came forward.

Or none that we knew about. My attorney was worried about a lawsuit, but they couldn't even find the little boy's father. No mention of him at all, and he's not recorded on the birth certificate."

"And why now?" Maverick asked.

"There could be any number of reasons. The loss of custody could be a trigger—"

"But surely if someone has it out for me, that would make them happy?" Deacon interrupted. That made no sense.

Phan inclined his head as if agreeing with Deacon's point. "It also might be down to opportunity and planning. The custody issue might not have anything to do with this."

"So...." Maverick tilted his head as if concentrating. "Are you thinking someone is punishing those they think had anything to do with Shelley Young's death?" He glanced at Deacon, and Deacon recognized the worry cooling the usual warm brown eyes.

"It's one theory," Phan agreed.

"Which means what? Protective custody?"

But Phan was shaking his head. "We will ensure the house is regularly patrolled, but apart from that, unless there is a definite attempt on Mr. Daniels' life, my hands are pretty much tied."

"You are joking," Maverick burst out. "What do you call the car wreck?"

"The reason the APD will put a car outside your house," Phan said dryly. "And there is nothing that makes this case a federal one to access their funding." He glanced at Deacon. "I'm assuming Mr. Daniels will stay here until this is sorted out?"

Maverick huffed a breath out, and Deacon's heart thudded. Mav didn't want him? "I can go to a motel," he started, but Maverick interrupted him with an incredulous look.

"Absolutely not. You're not going anywhere."

Deacon might have objected to the order if he wasn't completely freaked-out by what the detective had said. "But what if this goes on for weeks?"

"That's unlikely," Phan said and stood.

Unlikely? Which meant what? That they were expecting the crazy with the pickup to try something else. Deacon's head started throbbing again.

Maverick came back in after showing the detective out. "Charlie's shift has ended, but we've got a patrol car outside."

Deacon nodded miserably.

"Why don't you try and get some sleep?"

He would never sleep. The noise of the squealing tires ran around in his head on a constant repeat. And he was cold. Maverick made some kind of noise in the back of his throat and sat back down, then gathered Deacon close. Deacon didn't object. He soaked up the comfort.

"I think it's time I thought about making some calls," Maverick said quietly.

"I can't pay for them," Deacon whispered.

"I'm owed some favors," Maverick said, and then he smiled. "You may have to cook."

"I can cook."

He stayed curled against Maverick, sitting quietly. The oddest thing was that it didn't feel odd. He felt... *safe*. Maverick didn't seem to object. It wasn't weird. It wasn't even sexual. Not right at that moment.

When was the last time he had felt like this?

Was there a time?

And then going to sleep felt like something he could very easily do.

CHAPTER ELEVEN

MAVERICK DIALED Jamie, all the while keeping an eye on a sleeping Deacon.

"Well, shit, that's my landscaping job ruined." He had to smile at his sister. "Did you turn on your TV?" she asked dryly.

He did but kept it low so as not to wake Deacon. The front of Jamie's house was shown in full color, including where the vans had parked over the grass and flattened a few bushes. He saw the camera focus on him as Maverick steered Deacon into the house. A petite brunette in heels she was struggling to balance on spoke into the camera.

"And News Fifteen has been told that Deacon Daniels's agent, Emmanuel Jones, died in similar but equally tragic circumstances three days ago. No one from the APD was available to comment on whether Mr. Daniels, lead singer for the band Six Sundays, was a suspect or in danger himself."

The screen immediately changed to Deacon leading the band up to the stage where he received an award, and then to a performance of "Only a Joker." It then changed back to the reporter, who continued by stating that News Fifteen was devastated by the loss of one of their own.

"We've had Detective Phan here. Did he call you?" But Jamie wasn't a cop anymore unless professional courtesy extended to a warning about her house.

"No, I got a heads-up from Keith." Which made sense. Keith had been her old partner for years before she left the force and he took the sergeant's exam. Mav hoped Keith was working this case. Jamie was godmother to his twin boys. "And apparently, your Detective Phan is furious. They were keeping a lid on everything until they'd done the PM, and they have no idea how the press made the jump with Jones, unless Jeffries herself told someone."

"Phan told us she was going to meet someone yesterday morning. I'm assuming they will try and track her GPS." He hadn't bothered to say that to Phan because it was so basic, and he didn't think the detective was stupid.

"Mav, can you talk?" Jamie was suddenly hesitant, and he took a step away, but Deacon was fast asleep. He needed to sleep.

"What is it?"

"Are you completely confident Deacon didn't have anything to do with this?" Jamie was blunt as ever.

"Yes, absolutely." And he was.

She let out a slow breath. "Then much as I have every faith in you, bro, I think you might need a bit of backup."

He told Jamie about the conversation he'd had with Deacon and the calls he could make, and he could tell she approved. Before he hung up, he promised to speak to her later. Deacon moved restlessly, and Maverick turned the TV off. *Enough.*

The silence was kind of nice. Charlie had walked around and closed all the blinds, warning them of zoom lenses, which made sense. Maverick wandered into the kitchen. He put the coffee maker on and stood rubbing his lower back. Now he'd decided on the car, he wanted to go the whole hog and think about an apartment. It didn't need to be huge. He'd seen a lot of shower adaptations that would make his life so much easier. The key was getting a seat like Jamie had installed, but he hated the fact that the shower always took a minute to heat up while he was getting freezing water jetted at him. He knew there was some instant-heat power showers, and he wanted one of those.

Money wasn't exactly an issue, even with the dent refunding Melanie's college money had made. His truck had been his only expense for years, and while he had, at different stages, always had his own place, he never rented anything big or fancy because he was never there.

He'd given up his last place shortly after the accident, and Jamie had cleared it out for him and put all his big furniture in storage while he decided what to do. He really ought to go take a look.

Then he laughed shortly. In less than a week, he'd gone from verging on being an alcoholic to a new job, a new car, and possibly a new life. In twenty years, family had never been a major issue in his life. He loved his sister, but his mom was long gone, and Cass had been the brother he had never had. Starting his own family had never been on his radar. He'd always known he was gay, but it wasn't why he was on his own. Circumstances, the job. There were a lot of people who got married, but the job got them divorced just as quickly. Some people weren't cut out for managing a relationship long distance, and it was even harder on the ones who managed to, then came home.

He'd lost count of the number of friends who had split with their wife or husband once they had retired because living full-time with the person they thought they loved was too much of an adjustment.

Look at Charlie. They needed to grab a beer and talk, or maybe only a coffee now, when this shit was all over.

There was a knock on the door, and Maverick rolled his eyes. Then he realized the reporters seemed to have been pretty silent for a few minutes, and he walked into the hall to see. He immediately spotted the cop's uniform through the colored glass panel and opened it. Charlie hurried through, shaking his head. "We've got them off your property and made them take the vans away, but we can't stop them coming in on foot."

Charlie put out his hand, and Maverick grinned and pulled him forward for a hug. "Thank you for coming this morning. It's been too long, and I know your shift officially ended."

"Shame it's like this, but the good news is my sergeant says to stick close while they decide what's happening." Charlie looked around. "Where's Daniels?"

"Asleep."

Charlie nodded, then suddenly the silence was a little awkward. "I'm sorry about Cass," Charlie said regretfully.

"I can't believe it's been nearly eight months." Maverick pulled out a chair and glanced at Charlie. "Grab a tea." They'd always teased Charlie because he hated coffee. Although Mav didn't blame him with the swill that passed for coffee on some of the bases.

Charlie smiled and fished around for a teabag, then dunked it in his mug carelessly. He took a sip. "That's a hundred percent better than the last stuff I drank with you."

Maverick smiled, remembering. It had been the day before Charlie had left for home. "I was stunned to see you here," Maverick continued, not actually coming out and asking what he really wanted to ask.

Charlie shrugged. "Bad breakup."

"Aww, man," Maverick sympathized. Charlie had left the Air Force for her. He'd worked his ass off and was nearly at RL 111. His promotion to crew chief was just about nailed on, but then who was to say it didn't keep him alive.

"My cousin offered me a place to crash when I told him I wanted to get out of Dodge, and I applied and got a transfer down here. They like ex-military." He nodded to Maverick's face. "I guess you can still pull the pretty ones, huh?"

Maverick huffed because he knew Charlie meant Deacon. "My sister is friends with his agent. The new one," Maverick added in case there was any confusion.

Charlie grimaced. "I see. So, what's it like living with a rock star?"

"I'm not a rock star," Deacon said, and they both turned to see him walk into the kitchen. Maverick frowned because he needed way more than a thirty-minute nap.

"Maybe not," Charlie allowed, "but my ex used to love your music."

"Thank you." Deacon smiled politely.

"Stay inside," Charlie said. "I'm off soon, and I have to check in, but then I have two days. I can help to watch your back while Phan works things out."

"What…." Deacon swallowed. "What if they contact my mom?" His eyes widened. "Molly?"

"Molly?" Charlie looked puzzled.

"My niece. She's with her grandparents out in Ansley Park."

Charlie nodded, pulled out his radio, and stepped out of the kitchen.

Maverick thought hard. It was certainly a consideration, and he was surprised Phan hadn't mentioned it. "We should call your mom, but it might make any progress we made yesterday null and void."

Deacon shook his head. "I don't care. I just want her safe. If I never see her again, I want her safe." His breath hitched, and he lowered his head quickly as if he had something to be ashamed for, and Maverick couldn't stand it. He gathered Deacon close, and Deacon didn't protest. For a few blissful seconds, Deacon gave Maverick all his weight.

"I need to call my mom," Deacon reiterated.

"How about we get Jamie to call her?" Mav said. "Mother to mother and she's an ex-cop?" Deacon looked hopeful, and the more Mav thought about the idea, the more he liked it. He sent Jamie a text immediately, and she confirmed nearly as quickly.

Deacon sat back. "We should eat," Mav said and was met with a doubtful expression. "Then I think you ought to get some rest. Concussions don't magically heal themselves," he pointed out.

Deacon glanced down at himself but didn't seem able to think of an answer.

"At least try and rest on the couch?"

Mav could reheat a ton of stuff when Deacon was ready. Charlie walked back into the living room and nodded to the TV. "You might want to see this."

Deacon turned it on quickly, and Mav recognized the reporter who had been outside earlier.

"And furthermore, we understand from the driver who was nearly an unwitting fatality himself, his quick reflexes might just have saved more than one life today."

The screen immediately showed the older guy from the other car who had called 911 for them. Mav groaned. The guy had a microphone pointed at him. "Butler Cross, you were telling me you think it was only your previous experience as a Hollywood stunt double that saved everyone's lives this morning?"

To his credit, the man looked embarrassed. "I'm not sure I'd go that far, but yes, I guess swerving out of the way was an old habit."

"We understand the pickup was intent on pushing Mr. Daniels and his passenger deliberately into oncoming traffic?"

Butler Cross nodded. "That's sure what it looked like to me, and I understand it was the second time. He'd already reversed back once."

The camera panned back to the reporter in the studio. "The police aren't saying whether they have any description of the driver." The news anchor pressed a finger to her ear. "And in further startling developments, we understand all Mr. Daniels's friends and family have been warned to keep their distance."

"What?" Maverick shook his head. "They make this up as they go along."

"The cops have contacted your mom," Charlie answered, then checked his watch. "I'm off shift now, but there will be patrols on all night. Anything I can do to help, call me." He shook hands with Mav and Deacon and left.

"I'm hungry," Mav said, and Deacon shot him a guilty look, which was exactly what Maverick was hoping for. He was perfectly capable of foraging for himself, but Deacon needed something else to think about, and apart from three cups of coffee, he hadn't eaten all day, and it was after three o'clock. Deacon's phone rang, and he pulled it out of his pocket and frowned. "I don't recognize the number."

Maverick held his hand out and merely said, "Hello," as he answered.

"Deacon, this is Percy Fellhouse." Maverick immediately pressed the speaker and mouthed *Percy* to him.

"What's the matter?" Deacon answered.

"Nothing," he reassured in what sounded like a kind tone. "I was calling to see if you had a passport for Molly?"

Deacon looked bewildered. "A passport, no, why?"

"Because Anne has gotten in a state about the cops calling around, and then we've had three reporters trying to call us for an interview. I have a villa on the Amalfi coast, and I think it's better if we all go there until this dies down."

Deacon opened his mouth but then closed it seemingly at a loss for a reply.

"Mr. Fellhouse?" Maverick took the phone off speaker. "This is Maverick Delgardo, Mr. Daniels's assistant. How is my client supposed to see his niece if you take her out of the country?" He felt a hand on his arm, and Deacon shook his head. It killed Mav to see the complete defeat on Deacon's face.

"It's okay."

"Mr. Delgardo, with the recent instances and the obvious threats, my lawyers will have no problem getting a judge to remove any visitation rights," Percy threatened.

Deacon held his hand out for the phone, and reluctantly Maverick passed it over. "Percy? It's okay, I understand. Just keep Molly safe." Percy must have said something Maverick couldn't hear because Deacon paled before he nodded and ended the call. He raised desperate eyes to Maverick. "They're going for a month but may stay longer. He said he has cousins out there with young children and Molly would be very happy."

Maverick took the phone from his slack fingers.

"What if they decide to stay?" Deacon whispered. "What if I can never see her again?" Tears filled Deacon's eyes, and he brushed his hand across them angrily. "I am so sick of this," he burst out. "Why? Why does my life have to be ruined? I was kind to her. I never knew Manny would be so stupid, so irresponsible." He clamped his hand against his mouth and raised horrified eyes to Maverick and swallowed, lowering his hand cautiously. "I can't believe I said that." He licked his lips and brushed another hand over his cheek. "Manny is *dead*." His voice broke again on the last word. "And I'm behaving like a baby who should be grateful he's still alive and not complaining—"

His last words were muffled as Maverick couldn't stand to watch this anymore and not do something, so he clasped Deacon's arms and pulled him into him, tucking his head against his chest and sliding his arms protectively around his back.

Deacon cried, big ugly sobs that seemed to wrench something so vital out of Maverick and nearly turn him inside out. But he didn't move, and he didn't let go.

He hooked his finger under Deacon's chin and raised his face gently. He was going to tell him everything was going to be okay. Not to worry. That whatever it took, Maverick would do. But as Deacon raised storm-tossed but beautiful blue eyes to his own, a completely different emotion took over. Slowly but very deliberately, so Deacon knew exactly what he was going to do, Maverick lowered his face until their lips brushed.

The noise that was dragged out of Maverick was loud and needy, so much more so because Deacon had gone perfectly still. What was he doing? He couldn't believe he—

But the light fingers that threaded through the hair on his nape silenced the demons, and the sigh from Deacon as their lips met settled the beating of his heart. Lazily, leisurely, Maverick sucked and licked and tasted. Like he had all the time in the world. Like *they* had all the time in the world. With a slight contented sigh, Deacon parted his lips some more, and Maverick willingly answered the invitation. He ran his hands firmly over Deacon's back, tugging the material until he could feel skin, soft silky skin that enticed his wandering fingers as if they had lives and made decisions of their own. He certainly didn't consciously remember the decision to tuck them in Deacon's waistband and slide them to the front.

Deacon shivered, but his fingers tightened some more, encouraging, pleading. He broke off. "We shouldn't be in the kitchen," he pointed out, the breathless catch in his voice making Maverick's body throb.

He smiled against Deacon's throat. His lips brushed the soft stubble, and he felt the vibration of each hurried breath Deacon took. "I don't think we are in any danger of offending the coffeepot."

Deacon's teasing slap on his arm took him by surprise, but the chuckle warmed him. "You know what I mean." Deacon stepped back, and Maverick immediately reached for him, but Deacon took his hand. "Let's be comfortable. This isn't a quick hookup behind some club."

But what was it? They'd known each other... *three days*? "No." And it wasn't. Maverick wasn't ready to hang a name on exactly what it was.

Deacon paused. "What are you afraid of?"

Maverick's eyebrow lifted to be rewarded by another smile. "What makes you think I'm afraid of anything?"

Deacon tilted his head, considering the answer, but he tugged on Maverick's hand to get him to walk. "I think you doubt yourself." He stilled. "Or maybe you doubt me?"

"No," Maverick said. "I don't think for one minute you had... *have* anything to do with this. I'm just worried this isn't crossing a line, it's annihilating it."

"Depends who drew it, I guess," Deacon said as he steered Maverick through the kitchen. "I was never very good at geometry."

Maverick's lips twitched again, but he let himself be led. Deacon, at least, seemed able to navigate a straight line upstairs.

CHAPTER TWELVE

WHAT WAS it about this man that gave him so much confidence? Deacon should be a basket case. He had, in fact, gone from nearly crying all over Mav to basically ordering him upstairs in the blink of an eye.

It was the kiss. Deacon was a goner for a good kiss. Not that he had much experience of really good kissing, but having Maverick's strong hands roam over his back and smooth out what seemed to be every jagged edge inside him made him instantly want more. And he wasn't stupid. He knew the kisses were only promises of a good time, but at the moment, the thought of a good time—a great one—without hurting anyone else was exactly what he needed. Maverick definitely walked easier and the strain around his eyes was less, but he needed another massage, and that in itself wasn't a cure-all.

It was his fault Maverick hadn't—

No, no it wasn't. Maverick's PT or lack of it wasn't his fault, and he had to stop assuming blame for everything. Just because other people had blamed him for so long didn't mean they were right all the time.

They got in the bedroom, and Maverick gently turned him around. "One thing." Deacon moved in closer, but Maverick stopped him and dropped a kiss on Deacon's head. "I can hear the gears in that head of yours turning. If they're in a different direction to what they were downstairs, or you want—"

Deacon lunged, and Maverick caught him. He fastened needy lips on warm ones and simply took what he wanted. What he *craved*. Maverick stilled in shock for a second, and then Deacon heard the groan of surrender, and Maverick took the kiss and made it his own. He might be unsteady with his leg, but Maverick's arms and lips worked just fine, and Deacon melted into them.

Before Deacon knew what was even happening, Maverick had taken his own shirt off, and eager to comply, Deacon simply lifted his arms up. Deacon ran his hands over the burned skin on his neck and collarbone. "Does it hurt?" He bent and kissed it gently.

"Not really," Mav admitted. "My face got the worst, and I have to slather moisturizer on that. I don't grow hair on the scars either."

Deacon—feeling brave—continued his gentle exploration of Maverick's scars. "I thought flight suits were supposed to protect you."

"It did," Maverick admitted. "Not that it would have protected my face, but it was so damn hot, I risked an Article 15."

"Which is?"

"A reprimand. Anything from a slap on the knuckles to a reduction in rank. I guess they thought the injury was punishment enough," he said.

"What did you do?"

"I lowered my zipper."

Deacon's lips parted, and Maverick smirked. "Not that sort of zipper. The one on my flight suit. It's supposed to be closed to three inches below the neckline. It was more like seven or eight, so it was my own fault." Deacon cupped the side of Maverick's face, and Maverick's brown eyes deepened. "Does it not bother you?"

Deacon let his eyes roam obviously up and down. "All this awesomeness in one package?" He snickered. "Actually…." He leaned in and hooked Maverick's waistband with one hand, and with the other, traced the line of Maverick's lips until Maverick caught his finger in between them and sucked. The involuntary shudder that ran down his body was delicious. "There is something wrong with these."

Maverick smiled and let his finger go. "What?"

"Too much talking and not enough kissing."

Maverick bent his head, and all thoughts of protest disappeared. Deacon carefully unzipped Maverick's pants, and they broke free from each other for a minute while Deacon stepped out of his own, but then he realized Maverick had to sit down to get out of his. Deacon tugged him to the bed, and he sat, then leaned down to pull off his pants.

"Let me," Deacon begged, and obediently Maverick lifted his hand away. Meeting Mav's eyes, he carefully tugged at Maverick's waistband and saw the flash of uncertainty as Maverick allowed Deacon to undress him. "*Oh my.*"

Maverick shrugged.

"You're not wearing anything," Deacon said unnecessarily as Maverick's cock lay thickening against his leg. Maverick arched a brow, but his hesitation seemed to have subsided.

Deacon took in the mouthwatering sight. He trailed his fingers over Maverick's inner thigh, remembering the reaction from last time, and Maverick moaned and widened his legs. How had he gotten this lucky? Or was he? The thought that Maverick might be paying him attention because he thought his current choices were limited was a sobering one. He would just have to make himself be memorable, and with his goal in mind, Deacon bent and followed his fingers with his lips.

Maverick's cock jumped as Deacon closed his eyes, and Deacon felt the reaction in his own. He kissed and nibbled the skin at the side of Deacon's knee and up the softer skin of Deacon's thigh until he got as high as his groin but deliberately skated over that part and gave his other leg his attention. He walked his fingers down to where he felt the first scar, and Maverick suddenly clamped his wrist. Deacon opened his eyes and looked up. "Did I hurt you?"

Maverick shook his head and swallowed, and Deacon understood. Very gently he wiggled his wrist out of Maverick's hold and bent his head all the while keeping eye contact. Deacon had paid attention and pressed the button releasing the suction. The leg and liner came next, and Deacon pushed Maverick until he scooted back. He breathed the gentlest kiss he could on the end of Maverick's residual and smiled. Not speaking, simply peppering small kisses all over the scar tissue until he noticed Maverick's eyes had become very bright, and he had to swallow again. Satisfied he'd banished that particular ghost, he closed his eyes and kissed higher until he got to Maverick's groin.

The breathy moans from Maverick were getting louder, and Deacon closed his fingers around Maverick's very erect cock. "You're so hot," he murmured and continued to mouth the delicate skin. His fingers brushed the tip and came back wet, so he used the precum to help the slide of his hand.

And then it wasn't enough, and he had to taste him. He shuffled higher, and at the first touch of his tongue, Maverick groaned loudly. "Jesus fucking Christ," Maverick whimpered, and Deacon hummed in pleasure, snaking his other hand down the front of his shorts to wrap his fingers around his own.

"You are way too good at this," Maverick gasped out as Deacon hollowed his cheeks and drew back, swallowing around the thick length. "Deacon, you have to stop," Maverick begged.

He drew off and opened his eyes. "Why?"

Mav took a hurried breath. "Because I don't want it to be over with that soon."

And faster than Deacon ever thought he could move, he was on his back and Maverick was looking down on him. "Top, bottom, or neither?" Deacon asked lightly, but he knew he wasn't fooling Maverick for one second.

"Any way I can have you," Maverick replied, pulling at Deacon's shorts. He paused and glanced up. "Seriously, I've done both." He winced. "Though not for a while."

Deacon huffed. "It's not been anytime recently for me either."

"I find that hard to believe," Maverick murmured and bent to suck on Deacon's nipple, and Deacon arched as the frisson of pleasure ran straight to his cock.

Maverick made an approving noise and felt for Deacon's length and wrapped his large fingers around it. Deacon squirmed helplessly. "Not fair," he gasped and felt the rumble of laughter in Maverick's chest. By the time Maverick had finished with his other nipple, Deacon was barely holding on to any shred of control.

He wanted to finish the blow job he had started, but when Maverick closed his lips around his cock, he was done. He lost himself in a maelstrom of heat and pleasure unlike he had ever felt before, and when his orgasm slammed into him, he was helpless to do anything other than cry out and hold on.

Deacon concentrated on breathing while he floated, not especially in a hurry to surface until he became aware that Maverick had moved and had tucked him in close, murmuring sweet nonsense words and kissing him lightly. But as awareness returned, so did the thought that Maverick was still hard. Deacon bit his lip. He knew what he desperately wanted to happen, but Maverick might not like that. He'd seen it a million times online….

"What is it?"

Deacon opened his eyes, startled.

"Your breathing changed. One minute, you were floating on all those endorphins, and the next second, reality checked in." Maverick sighed and sat up. "This doesn't have to be weird."

"No," Deacon nearly shouted and grabbed Maverick's wrist. *Now or never.* "I wanted to do something— well, you to do something—but it's totally okay—"

Maverick silenced him with a finger across his lips. His eyes were shining in anticipation. "What?"

Deacon opened his mouth, but nothing came out, and he pressed his lips together.

"Hey." Maverick cupped his face. "You saw my scars. I don't think you have anything that's going to frighten me."

"I wanna watch," Deacon blurted out. Maverick looked confused, and then a slow smile spread over his face.

"You want to watch me jerk off?"

Deacon swallowed but nodded. He was dying inside, but his cock was interested in the idea. "So, let me get this straight, *or not*," Maverick added with a smirk. "You want me to take my hand and rub myself until I shoot?" Deacon forgot to breathe. Maverick watched him intently. "Or even better, shoot all over you?"

Deacon might have made a noise, he wasn't honestly sure. Maverick traced his jawline with his finger. "Your pupils dilated. That's exactly what you want, huh? What you need?"

Deacon whined. Speech, actual coherent words, was beyond him, and his cock gave a valiant jerk. "And do you like the way I talk to you? Or are you a strong and very silent type?"

"Talk," Deacon managed to get out before he died from a lack of oxygen because he didn't seem able to inflate his lungs.

Maverick hummed to himself and rolled onto his side. Deacon shuffled lower down in breathless anticipation. He had seen this online, but nothing had prepared him for the real thing. Maverick rolled on his back and opened the top drawer in his nightstand. He smiled and brought out the lube. "Believe it or not, my sister bought this for me on one of her shopping trips. She told me she'd stashed it hoping that would make me climb the stairs."

Maverick rolled back and flipped the top. "I like a smooth ride." And Deacon nearly swallowed his tongue. Mav trickled a little on his hand and leaned over and smoothed it over Deacon's rapidly hardening length. "Damn, good recovery time," he murmured and glanced at Deacon. "I want you to touch yourself while you watch." Maverick watched the effect his words were obviously having on Deacon. "Why have I never realized before how much of a turn-on this would be?"

A shard of something kind of like jealousy pierced Deacon. He didn't like the thought of Maverick realizing anything with someone else. Maverick smiled again but didn't comment, and he closed his eyes, his slick hands around his cock. Deacon's moan was as loud as Maverick's, and he rolled his balls in his fingers, not taking his eyes away from the glorious sight in front of him for one minute.

"I have things I like," Mav murmured, his voice deep and low and doing all sorts of funny things to Deacon's insides. "I love when I smooth my palm over the tip and scratch the side of my nail under the head." He opened his eyes and stared at Deacon. "Sometimes a little pain brings a whole lot of pleasure."

Deacon licked suddenly dry lips.

"Roll your balls in your fingers, feel the weight," he directed, and Deacon obeyed. The instruction, the *order*, making things so much more intense.

"Oh yeah," Maverick said and pulled the skin down until it was taut. "I like to squeeze a little and twist my hand when I get to the bottom."

Deacon could feel the ache start in his groin.

"Then I like to speed up. Sometimes push my nail right in the slit. Oh fuck," Mav growled, and Deacon's cock throbbed. "But what really makes it amazing is when I lie on my back and use one hand on my cock and the other in my ass. Just a finger, but it's incredible." He looked at Deacon. "I think you should." And he reached out for the lube and drizzled some more first on Deacon's hand and then on his own.

"I'm not going on my back because when I shoot, it's gonna be all over you."

Deacon gasped and moaned. What he was *seeing*, what he was *hearing*, rendered him incapable of any thought other than doing exactly as he was told.

"I'm close," Mav groaned. "I can feel the heat starting in my balls and the base of my spine. It's starting. Getting pressure. I have to jerk faster, squeeze harder. Can't stop. I'm coming. Fuck, it's coming."

And it was. Deacon was. He gasped in shock and bone-deep pleasure as cum erupted from Maverick and coated Deacon's chest and throat. He even had some of his own spurt in his hand, which he would have said impossible so soon after coming once already.

"Fuck," Maverick repeated eloquently and collapsed onto his back, continuing to rub himself for a few more seconds to finish. Maverick rolled his head to look at Deacon, satisfaction etched on his face.

Deacon sighed happily. That was him, and he hadn't realized how satisfying contentment could be until he knew he was responsible for it in another person.

CHAPTER THIRTEEN

THE MAN knocked once on the kitchen door, confident of his welcome. Preparation and planning. That was what it amounted to, and really, she was pathetic. In love with what he was as much as the attention. The air of desperation sat on her as unattractive as the shapeless dress she wore. He'd originally intended on three and done, but the urge to make more of a statement had been too hard to resist. He mused, you could always class it as a public service. People this brainless shouldn't ever be responsible for children.

He'd followed Daniels yesterday more out of curiosity than anything else, but when he'd seen what the pathetic runt was doing, he'd gone and taken the first car he'd come across, like candy. He was getting bored, which would never do. Bored people made mistakes. He'd let his temper rule his actions yesterday and that could have cost him.

Now, what to do with her? The possibilities were endless. "You sure we are alone?"

She nodded. Indecision and longing written all over her face. "They're catching a flight out of Harts-field tonight direct. They've gone with Molly to get a passport and left me to pack for her. Mrs. Taylor has the day off." She bit her lip, possibly thinking it was some-how alluring. "I don't have to go." The words were so hopeful.

"You won't be going," he said and stepped closer, inhaling the distasteful scent of whatever cheap perfume she had bathed in obviously for him.

"I-I won't?" Her smile grew.

He shook his head and uncapped the syringe in his pocket. "How long do you think we have before they get back?"

"Oh at least a couple of hours," she answered quickly, eagerly. "Should I call them so they don't get me a ticket?"

He moved quickly to kiss her neck, and she sagged against him. Plunging the needle in was easier than it should have been.

He let her drop to the floor where she lay unable to move, and carefully, slowly, undid his belt buckle where she could watch. Her dazed green eyes changed to wide and terrified ones.

DEACON STRETCHED every blissful bone in his body, which was challenging because the larger body he was nearly wrapped up in didn't like him moving.

Maverick grunted. "You're like a cat."

Which was quite accurate because Deacon could happily start purring anytime soon.

They both heard the sound of the front door opening at the same time. "Mav?" a woman shouted.

Maverick swore, and Deacon sat bolt upright. "It's
Jamie," he groaned. "I'm just going in the shower," he
shouted back. "Put the coffee on."

"I thought she'd broken her ankle," Deacon whispered, and Maverick sat up.

"That's not gonna stop her." They both heard a
man's voice and the door closing, then footsteps going
to the kitchen. "I guess Richards brought her."

"Was that the friend you mentioned?"

Mav nodded. "Yeah, but I think he wants more.
My brother-in-law had a midlife crisis quite spectacu-
larly three months ago and ran off with another woman.
Jamie's strong, but they'd been married twenty years.
You can't get over something like that so quickly."

"And you're the expert?" Deacon grinned suddenly, not as shy as he thought he would be. "I need a
shower," he confided. They'd cleaned up hurriedly last
night and changed the sheets, but then they'd lazed in
bed, and Deacon had brought snacks upstairs. He had
passed out pretty quickly after that, which was good
because he had no idea what to say to someone after
the best sex of his life. He chuckled, and Mav looked
amused at him as he reached for his leg.

"I'll go down and see what's up. You take your
time." And then to Deacon's delight, Maverick leaned
forward to grab a kiss, which thrilled him. He had been
worried it would either be awkward or back to business
this morning, and Deacon was so pleased it obviously
wasn't going to be.

Deacon made a show of reluctantly letting go, to
which Maverick answered by nipping Deacon's bottom lip with his teeth. Which didn't have the effect

Maverick intended; Deacon still wasn't out of bed when Maverick left the room.

MAVERICK WALKED into the kitchen just in time to see Richards carefully balance Jamie's foot on a cushion covering one of the chairs. She beamed up at him. "Where's Deacon?"

"Just getting in the shower," Maverick answered and waited to be grilled. Richards switched on the coffee maker.

"I'll be going, then," he said hesitantly.

Jamie's smile was wide, and her eyes softened. "I'll talk to you when you finish work." He brightened a little, shook hands with Maverick, and left.

"You're home?"

Jamie nodded. "I was giving him the impression it would be permanent, and while he's a sweet guy, I'm not ready for that. Why? Am I in the way?" Jamie asked innocently.

Mav sighed, suddenly feeling about ten years old. "No," he replied honestly. He'd never had any secrets around his big sister. "To be honest, I could do with some advice."

Her eyes softened. "With the case or with your love life?"

He shot her an exasperated look.

"Well, you didn't sleep downstairs last night because I checked." She eyed him. "If Deacon is responsible for your current look, I like him already."

"You're gonna love him." And she would. He relaxed a little.

"Why don't you tell me what you've got so far, and we'll put our heads together?"

Maverick got up and got his own coffee. He heard the shower turn off and knew Deacon would be down soon, so he poured a second one and grabbed the vanilla creamers.

He glanced up to see Jamie watching him with interest. "It's not… I'm not—"

"It's new, I get it," she interrupted, and Maverick launched into an explanation of what had happened so far. He just got to them getting home to find the reporters when Deacon walked in and smiled shyly at Jamie and put out his hand.

She grinned and shook it. "Glad to see you're keeping my brother out of trouble." Deacon shot a surprised look at Maverick, but Mav simply pulled out the chair next to him.

"I've been bringing Jamie up to speed," he told him, and he finished describing the calls he had gotten and his decision to try and track down some colleagues. He'd left a few messages last night, but Gazza and Pip were both deployed. He'd left a message with Troy—who, coincidentally, had been Charlie's first lieutenant at one point—and he was waiting to hear back.

"I left messages with my friends, but Charlie offered if we need him."

Jamie looked taken aback. "There's no way Charlie's sergeant will give the green light on that. Way too much a conflict of interest."

Maverick shrugged. "Then maybe Troy will call back soon. He probably knows another couple of guys."

"So do I," Jamie said thoughtfully. "I spoke to Keith this morning, and while I would never put him in a difficult position by asking him to reveal anything that would cause him problems, he said the trouble was there was no evidence and no leads. There's nothing forensically to link anyone. The accelerant was basic, but the fire pretty much destroyed everything."

"Detective Phan did say that one of the similarities was the lack of a connection," Deacon agreed.

"And he has a point. A crazy way to link the murders, but yes."

"And me," Deacon said in a small voice, and Mav reached out and clasped his hand. Deacon's hands were on his knee, but Jamie still wouldn't have missed it.

"Jones was also dead when the fire started, but Jeffries wasn't." Jamie shot Deacon an apologetic look.

"How is that significant?" Maverick asked.

Jamie put down her coffee. "A number of reasons. It's quite possible this was the guy's first murder. Panic, inexperience, any of that could have made him either rush accidently or rush on purpose. By victim number two, he has a little more confidence."

"He's not making any attempt to hide the victims, though," Maverick pointed out. "Both in their homes, and Sara Jeffries would have been missed quickly even if he didn't torch the place."

"So it's someone who either has such a good disguise—" Deacon said.

"Or someone that's invisible," Jamie finished.

Maverick frowned. "What, small you mean?"

Jamie chuckled. "No. I mean, for example, witnesses often notice the job not the person. If someone walked past a man or a woman in a white coat, their mind would think *doctor* but not be able to describe features."

"Or construction workers in yellow vests," Deacon added.

"Yes. There are dozens of jobs where the uniform is so recognizable, but witnesses never see what's underneath it."

Maverick thought of Army fatigues and knew she was right.

Jamie glanced at them both. "So which one of you is going to make breakfast? I'm starving."

Deacon jumped up. "I will." Jamie beamed at them both.

"Eggs? Bacon? Harvey's mother insisted on muesli and rabbit food. I'm sure my body's going into shock from lack of fat and carbs."

Maverick snorted. "So that's really why you wanted to come home, huh?"

Jamie fixed him with her best innocent expression.

"How about pancakes with syrup and bacon on the side?" Deacon asked.

Jamie put a hand on her heart. "My arteries are dancing as we speak."

AN HOUR later, Jamie groaned and pushed her plate away. "You're going to have to keep him, you know." She waved her finger at Maverick, and Mav was thankful Deacon had gone to put some laundry to wash while he cleared up but felt his heart jump at her *possibly* innocent words.

"I doubt he's going to want to stay when he gets his life back. I think I might make him feel safe, and he was out of options." He doubted it very much.

"That's not what Shirley told me."

"The reporters, you mean?"

"Not just. Did you know about the custody ruling?"

"I know he got granted Thursday visitation, and I know his mother is a frigid cow who doesn't deserve Molly. I also don't know how he turned out to be such a decent human being with his examples."

Jamie smiled. "Yes, but did you know the mom's new husband tried to buy Molly first?"

"*What*?"

She nodded. "Straight after the court case when the band got sued and Deacon lost everything. He was offered half a million dollars to voluntarily give up parental rights." Jamie watched him, letting the words sink in. "And he said no, so they took him to court, which was why things were dragged out."

And Maverick had thought Deacon wasn't that upset at first. He'd been so wrong.

Deacon came back into the kitchen and smiled at Jamie. "I hope this was okay, but I stripped your bed as well. I thought you'd like fresh sheets, and it was easy to wash them together."

"Thank you, Deacon."

There was a knock at the door, and Maverick held up his hand when Deacon took a step. "No answering doors. Leave it to me."

Maverick walked into the hallway and immediately saw the flashing police lights through the glass, and his heart sank. "Now what?" he muttered, opening the door and stopping in surprise. He didn't recognize the cop standing on the step, but he definitely recognized the tear-streaked face of the little girl clutching the hand of the woman standing next to them both. "Deacon," he shouted over his shoulder and stepped back to let them through. There didn't seem to be any reporters there at the moment, thank fuck, and he breathed a sigh out when the lights on the cop car stopped.

"Sorry," the cop said, glancing back. "It was the only way I could get her in the car."

"Molly?" Deacon's astonished cry was loud behind him, and Molly looked up and promptly burst into tears. He held out his arms, and the woman let her go, and Molly ran and jumped. Deacon caught her. Jamie hobbled out of the kitchen, balancing on her crutches.

"Loretta?" Jamie said in surprise, and the lady smiled.

"I was hoping you were going to be here."

"Come in." Jamie pointed to the living room, and the cop looked at the woman and followed them all in. "My sergeant has also asked me to check the reporters are leaving Mr. Daniels alone."

Deacon carried Molly into the living room and took a seat on the couch, where she buried her face in his chest and clung on. Jamie took an armchair, and the woman took another. Maverick sat down next to Deacon. Deacon talked quietly to Molly while she cried herself out for another minute, then yawned. The woman pulled out a teddy from her bag and passed it to Deacon. Molly's eyes were drooping then, and she sighed, putting her thumb in her mouth. In what seemed no more than another few seconds, she was asleep.

"Melanie was like that," Jamie said conversationally. "She always fell sleep after she'd cried."

Deacon dropped a kiss on Molly's head and glanced at the woman expectantly. Maverick had to give him props. He would have been demanding answers the second they appeared, but Deacon had made sure Molly was okay first.

"Mr. Daniels?" The woman drew some ID out of her purse. "My name is Loretta Marsh, and I'm with the Division of Children and Family Services." She hesitated and glanced at the cop.

"Officer O'Roarke, sirs, ma'am," the cop replied politely.

"There's been an incident at the home of Mrs. Fellhouse this morning," she carried on. "Detective Phan will come and explain things to you as soon as he can, but it was necessary to remove Molly from her grandmother's house this morning—"

Deacon gasped. "Are they all right?"

"Yes," she said. "The detective will be here soon, and I'm sorry I can't say any more. I know Jamie," Loretta continued. "And as I understand you are living here, I thought it would be less stressful for Molly to be here." She grimaced slightly. "I'm probably going to have to jump through some red tape on Monday, but following the guidelines in the strictest sense, I am encouraged to grant kinship to an adult family member in these circumstances."

Deacon looked dumbfounded but tightened his hold on Molly reflexively.

"If I had been in any doubt, her reaction when she saw you would have been very telling." She glanced at a sleeping Molly and then at Jamie. "Unless of course you tell me that she can't stay."

"No," Jamie and Maverick both said together.

The cop smiled. "She was all packed for a trip, but we weren't allowed to bring anything from the house. She wouldn't leave without the bear."

Deacon swallowed. "I bought it for her birthday."

Loretta brought two cards out of her purse and handed them over to Maverick. "You should also know that Detective Phan was also of the opinion she was to be brought here."

Mav watched as Deacon hugged the little girl close. He didn't seem able to speak.

"This is temporary," Loretta cautioned. "We will need to see what your long-term plans are regarding living arrangements. Check everything out, but there is no immediate rush while you are here." Loretta stood up. Maverick rose to show them out and walked to the door with the cop.

"Is it bad?"

Her eyes told him it was. "Two patrol cars are going to wait outside. Please wait here until Detective Phan gets here."

Maverick followed them and locked the door as soon as they left.

"Mav?" Jamie said as soon as he walked back. "I have friends that can easily drop some clothes off for her, and she can have Melanie's room."

Mav picked up the small blanket Loretta had left and draped it over the sofa. "Why don't we lay her here?" he asked gently. "And we can go in the kitchen when he gets here. We don't want Phan having to explain anything where there's a chance she can hear."

Deacon let Maverick carefully take her out of his arms and lay her on the blanket. It was large enough to drape back over her as well. She was soon cocooned warmly and safely.

"And I will stay in here," Jamie volunteered just as there was a knock on the door.

Deacon bent down to brush a kiss on Molly's cheek and stood to follow Maverick out. Maverick had a really bad feeling about this, and Deacon had barely said two words since Molly arrived.

The detective nodded to them as Maverick opened the door. "Your niece is here I understand?"

"She's asleep," Deacon confirmed and gestured to the living room.

"My sister is staying with her while we talk," Maverick added.

Phan breathed out a sigh and followed them to the kitchen. Maverick closed the door behind them.

"Mr. Daniels, when was the last time you spoke to Mr. or Mrs. Fellhouse?"

"Yesterday morning."

"I was with Deacon when he took the phone call," Mav confirmed.

"Can you tell me what was said?"

Deacon took a breath. "The reporters had been bugging them after Sara Jeffries had been found. Percy called me asking if Molly had a passport. They informed me that they were taking Molly to their house in Italy for a month, maybe longer."

"And you said what?"

"Mr. Fellhouse informed us both that if we objected in any way, their lawyers would have no problem in altering the custody agreement to exclude Deacon completely," Maverick said.

Phan grimaced. "Look, I'm no lawyer, but I'm not sure that's right."

"What's happened?" Deacon burst out.

Phan held his hand up. "Just another couple of questions." He glanced at Maverick. "Can you provide an alibi for Mr. Daniels between 9:00 a.m. and 10:45 this morning?"

"Absolutely. I can provide an alibi since the last time you were here." A small smile graced Phan's lips as the implication sank in. "And my sister was here at nine if not before."

"Did you know a Miss Rachel Mackenzie?"

Deacon frowned. "That's Molly's nanny. We last saw her on Saturday when we went to visit Molly."

Phan sighed. "Sometime this morning, while Mr. and Mrs. Fellhouse were out getting Molly's passport, someone murdered Ms. Mackenzie. They found her dead when they returned."

Deacon's hand flew to his mouth in horror. Maverick shook his head. "A fire?"

"No," Phan said, "but there is a chance he or she was disturbed by the housekeeper returning. It was her day off, but the housekeeper said Mr. Fellhouse had called her from the car, asking if she could go to the house and pack for them. It was a hurried decision."

"Okay." Maverick was confused. "So the housekeeper found her?"

"Yes," Phan confirmed. "She arrived home moments before the Fellhouses."

"And they are all okay?"

Phan hesitated. "They aren't physically hurt. The killer was gone."

"Then much as I know Molly and Deacon are thrilled, why is she here?"

"Because Mrs. Fellhouse became hysterical, and her husband had to physically restrain her. She was admitted into temporary psychiatric care, and Mr. Fellhouse made it clear he doesn't consider Molly his responsibility. Apparently he did everything for his wife, but when she wasn't in a condition to care for her, he called Children and Family Services, and the duty social worker knows Jamie, and apparently her old partner was also the sergeant on duty."

"I'm so sorry Rachel was killed. I know Molly seemed to like her." Deacon paused.

"But you're wondering how this has got anything to do with you?"

Deacon nodded.

"Does the phrase 'Only a Joker' mean anything to you?"

Maverick watched as every bit of color drained from Deacon's face. "It's the name of their single," Maverick answered for Deacon.

"Those exact words were written near the body."

"Written?" Maverick queried, and then he saw the answer in Phan's gray eyes and wished he hadn't asked.

Phan looked at Deacon. "We will have officers here outside the house. Please stay here for the time being. If you need to go out for any reason, I want to know about it first, and the APD officers will accompany you. This puts everything in a different light. I will be in touch later if I have anything else."

Maverick stood up, and Deacon shook hands with Phan and let himself back in the living room. Mav walked Phan toward the door. "Are you any further forward in finding this lunatic?"

Phan rested his steady gaze on Mav. "We are concentrating on Deacon and why someone would have it in for him, even if the nanny was a very tenuous connection."

"And you think it still might be connected to the death of Shelley Young?"

Phan nodded. "The first two certainly."

"And Rachel?"

Phan hesitated. "What if someone wants to turn the knife? There were no signs of a break-in. The housekeeper thinks Rachel had a boyfriend, but we can't find anyone who has seen them together, although it's very early days. The thing is, if this was a boyfriend, that means there is a chance he has had access to Molly, and I need someone with better skills than I to ask her. If that's the case, though, what better way to torture Deacon? The thought that someone would have had access to his niece and could have killed her at any time?"

Maverick swallowed. He hoped it hadn't occurred to Deacon yet, because it would kill him when it did.

CHAPTER FOURTEEN

JAMIE JOINED Maverick in the kitchen while he pulled out snacks. "They're okay?"

She nodded. "I texted Keith." The change in his sister's voice made Maverick look up from the fridge.

"What is it?"

"You can't tell Deacon."

Maverick shook his head.

"The nanny was ripped to shreds. She had a needle mark, but they haven't done the PM yet. 'Only a Joker'?"

"The song title?"

Jamie swallowed. "It was carved in her skin, and with the way she bled, while she was still alive, and if you tell anyone that, Keith will get fired."

Maverick sat down heavily. "There's no way I want Deacon to find this out." It would be something else to make him feel guilty about.

"I made those phone calls you asked me to yesterday." Jamie changed the subject.

Maverick frowned, and then he understood. "The custody?"

"Apparently the grandparents had Thompkins and Russell."

Maverick drew a blank.

"They're one of the most expensive legal firms in the country, and Deacon wouldn't even have gotten a court-appointed one for a custody case."

"Meaning?" But he thought he knew.

"Meaning they had plenty of dollars to drag this through court as long as they like, and they took their time hoping it would never even get to court before Deacon caved. I've been told—completely off the record—that Deacon was threatened with losing all contact and that the judge is heavily involved with the same charity Percy Fellhouse supports financially."

"So he had no chance."

Jamie shook her head. "I've also been told there are a number of complaints from ex-employees of the Fellhouses who were paid off, including one alleged sexual assault of a secretary."

Maverick gaped. "Wow."

"I also understand now that Loretta is involved, should the grandmother suddenly decide she wants Molly back, no amount of money will cut it after Percy called the office. Technically there is even a case for child abandonment, but Loretta has a lot of sway and is on our side. The department knows they screwed up last time, and I think they will want this to just go away."

"So she's safe?"

They both turned at Deacon's voice from the doorway. He looked completely shell-shocked.

Jamie smiled. "You have a lot of people in your corner this time."

Deacon pressed his lips together, and Jamie held out her arms. "You're gonna have to come to me, but I want a hug."

And Deacon flew straight into her arms. Maverick nodded approvingly. If anyone needed a big sister, it was Deacon.

"I was just going to wake Molly up. I want her to be able to sleep tonight, but I also think I need to talk to someone about her."

Maverick looked at first Deacon, then Jamie. Jamie seemed to know what Deacon meant. "About custody? Loretta said—"

"No," Deacon interrupted. "She's moved house—*homes* at least four times in the last two years. She's gone through three different sets of parents or guardians, four counting her mom, and it was obvious my mom wouldn't know love or affection if it hit her in the face."

"Plus trauma can cause regression," Jamie agreed. "Unless you already have someone, I know an excellent pediatrician, but I would say she's going to be very clingy for the time being. It may involve bed-wetting etcetera."

"She's been dry during the day for over three months," Deacon said proudly. Then he glanced at Maverick. "I'm sorry. Guarding me was one thing. I don't think you expected *actual* babysitting duty."

Mav smiled at his own words being used back at him. "She's no problem."

Jamie grinned. "And it's been a while since I had to read stories."

Deacon looked at both of them. "You're sure?"

"What does she like to eat?" Jamie asked, the subject clearly done.

"Pancakes," Deacon said ruefully. "But she also likes fruit and toast triangles with peanut butter."

"Well, how about you go get her, and we'll make my brother cook?" Mav chuckled, knowing what Jamie was going to say. "He was always in charge of the PB and J sandwiches." He had been, and he had forgotten that until Jamie reminded him. It was nice to get a good reminder.

"Then I need a plan," Deacon said.

"Plan?" Maverick bit out.

"How about you just concentrate on not giving Maverick heart failure, huh?"

Deacon glanced at Jamie in confusion and then to Maverick.

"I mean," Jamie said, "you say the word *plan*, and that indicates movement to him. Like it or not, you're stuck here and with us for the time being."

Deacon pulled at his lip. "But—"

"And if you give me any of that money crap again, I'm definitely tying you to the bed." Everyone was silent for at least three heartbeats while Maverick wished the ground would open and swallow him up. Deacon went bright red, and so did Jamie, but that was only because she was struggling not to choke with laughter. Maverick brushed a hand over his face and raised his eyes to the ceiling.

"I'm sure your sister doesn't need to know our bedroom habits," Deacon said slowly. Maverick stared openmouthed as Deacon smiled impishly, and Jamie laughed so hard she nearly fell off the chair.

"Danny?" They all heard the panic in Molly's cry and rushed into the living room. She was sitting up, rubbing her eyes, but opened her arms for Deacon as he got there first. Mav was a few seconds later, and Jamie was slower. Molly snuggled against his chest, watching Maverick and then Jamie with big eyes as they both sat down.

"Are you thirsty, Molly-Moo?" Deacon pulled her into his lap.

Maverick stood up. "Water, orange juice, milk?"

"Water, I think, for now," Deacon murmured. "Are you hungry?"

Molly didn't answer, just turned into Deacon and clung on.

"Coming right up," Maverick said and walked into the kitchen for the water. He popped a couple of slices in the toaster, got the peanut butter from the fridge, and thought about what Phan had told him. He was right in a way about whoever was doing this having found a way to turn the knife. Threatening anyone close to Molly was so petrifying, Maverick didn't know how Deacon was holding it together, unless the responsibility of caring for Molly was exactly what he needed to do so.

While he waited for the toast, he left the kitchen, hearing Jamie asking Molly if she wanted to watch a show on TV, and he headed for the stairs, trying to ignore the constant ache in his back. He walked into Jamie's room and toward her closet. After moving the rack of clothes to one side, he punched the numbers into the safe. Glancing at Jamie's Sig, he reached for his Glock. He also unhooked his holster that was stored with Jamie's and clipped it on his belt. He wanted the gun safe and fastened to his side, but now there was a child in the house, he also didn't want it visible and covered it under his T-shirt.

Satisfied, Mav closed everything up and headed for the stairs, ignoring the twinge and wondering if he should use his crutches a little more in the house.

Stubbornness had stopped him. As soon as he had gotten his first leg, he had been determined to get rid of them, and the consequent blisters had been a painful reminder. He was walking easier. His residual itself was giving him little problems, but he really needed to go and get it checked or let the PT guys get their hands on him.

Then he brightened. He was getting his new truck today. But what did that mean? He was pretty sure they needed to go get some basic groceries, like milk, if they were going to be holed up in the house for the time being. And were they? What if they hadn't caught this guy in a day, a week, a month? Did their lives stop?

And shit, Melanie would be home from Europe in a week. There was no way he could put her life in danger. He didn't like risking Jamie, but she was an ex-cop and a grown-up. His seventeen-year-old niece was entirely another matter. He could easily rent an apartment for him and Deacon, but Deacon not living with Rachel hadn't helped her, and at least them all being together kept the patrol cars outside.

He strode into the kitchen and quickly spread the peanut butter on the toast and cut it up in little triangles. He grabbed a glass from the cupboard and got some ice water and carried everything into the living room. Molly was smiling at some cartoons Jamie had managed to find on the TV. "Here, munchkin," Mav said and put the glass and the plate on the small table next to Deacon.

She looked at him out of Deacon's eyes, the blue just as startling. "What's a munchkin?"

"Magical people," Maverick replied. "Only very short ones."

Molly seemed to think about that. Her eyes ran the full length of his body to his face, making Maverick feel the size of a house.

"Sometimes big people can be magical," Maverick tagged on.

"Who?" Molly wanted to know.

Maverick desperately tried to think of someone.

"The fairy godmother in *Cinderella*," Jamie supplied.

"Or the giant in *The BFG*," Deacon suggested helpfully.

"Yes," Maverick agreed, searching for a change of subject, not sure he liked being compared to a giant, even a friendly one. He glanced at Jamie. "My new truck will be ready today. And we ought to get some supplies." He nodded at Molly. He glanced at his phone. It was after one already, and it only seemed like he'd just gotten out of bed. The phone lit up as he was going to put it in his pocket, and seeing it was a restricted number, he answered it cautiously.

"Mav?"

He recognized the voice of Barry "Troy" Helenar immediately and walked into the kitchen.

"How's my favorite ugly bastard?"

Mav chuckled. Troy was a US citizen, but being born and brought up in London's East End until he was fifteen and his father had gotten posted to Patrick AFB in Florida, he'd never lost his Cockney accent. Mav had been posted twice alongside Troy earlier on in his career, and they had remained friends. Troy said exactly what he thought most of the time, and commenting on Maverick's scars wouldn't be off-limits either. Troy had visited him twice in Eglin, but he'd taken a new posting as a TACP along with the incredible responsibility of calling in an air strike in exactly the right place at exactly the right time. It had taken a few messages to track him down.

"I'd say congratulations, but I think Uncle Sam must be getting fucking desperate."

He heard the answering laugh. "What do you need? I'm nowhere near Atlanta, or I'd be up for a beer. They give discounts to cripples, don't they?"

"Well, I'd get one, but you have to be a grown-up to drink in this country, so you'd have a problem." He heard a breath and quieted. "Need some help," Mav admitted, and he gave Troy a quick rundown.

"Shit," Troy said eloquently. "What are the cops saying?"

"Actually, that's why I called. You're never going to believe who's here."

"Father fucking Christmas?"

Mav shook his head even though Troy couldn't see him. "Hunter Chaplin."

"No shit," Troy said in surprise. "I thought he was in some place like Tampa."

"Toledo," Mav corrected dryly. "Anyway he broke up with his girlfriend and became a cop. He got transferred. Thing is I know he wants to help, but it makes things awkward because he's working the case. But it gave me the idea of asking around for some other help." Maverick paused. "The guy that's in danger has a kid. They're both with me, but you know the cops. I don't know how long this is going to go on, and a few patrol cars driving past the house isn't gonna do shit."

There was a pause. "Sounds personal," Troy said mildly, but Mav knew what he was asking. Troy knew

Mav was gay and didn't give a shit about something that didn't affect his competence.

"Yeah," Maverick confirmed. "But I tried who I can think of, and every fucker seems to be deployed."

The amusement was back in Troy's voice. "War is just so bloody inconvenient. I can ask around, though. Keep your lights on." And without another word he hung up.

He felt the arms go around his middle before he turned around. "I'm sorry we're causing you so much trouble."

Maverick turned and wrapped his own arms around Deacon. "You listen to me," he said. "Some psycho do-ing whatever is *not your fault*. You didn't instigate this. You certainly aren't responsible for it. The only thing you have to worry about is keeping Molly safe." Dea-con nodded and laid his head on Maverick's chest. Mav pressed a kiss to the top. "Leave everything else to me."

"That doesn't sound very fair."

Maverick grunted and pushed him back a bit so he could see his face. "It is what it is." Maverick tried to be casual, but he seemed to fail spectacularly when Deacon moved back in closer.

"When we're both safe and this is over, will I see you again?"

Maverick raked his eyes over Deacon's face. The pale skin with the few freckles that were so like Mol-ly's. The slight pink on his cheeks and throat. The way he moistened his lips with his tongue that Maverick had sucked and tasted. Groaning, he closed his eyes and bent his head. He just had to. Deacon was enthusiastic for a few seconds until he heard the giggle from the living room and Jamie laughing, and drew back.

Maverick's phone rang for the second time, and he answered it. It was Detective Phan. "Delgardo? Is Deacon there? Can you put him on speaker? I need to talk to you both." Mav pressed the button.

"Deacon, have you ever met a Jared Upchurch?"

Deacon frowned. "Jared? No."

"He's the Fellhouses' handyman—"

"Oh, you mean Jimmy?" Deacon interrupted. "Yes. Once I think. Why?"

"Did he know who you are? Were?"

"Actually—" Deacon smiled. "—the first time I visited Molly after the court case, he asked me for my autograph. My mother nearly had a fit." Deacon paused. "A little unusual for an adult, but Jimmy has a few mental health challenges, so I understand. He seemed nice, and my mom told me he practically works for nothing." The last was delivered with a certain amount of disgust.

"Have you had any other dealings with him? Given him any memorabilia for example?"

"You mean from the band? No, why?"

"Because his name came up in connection with Rachel when we were asking about the possibility of a boyfriend. The housekeeper said he had a crush on her and she was kind to him, so we went to his house, thankfully with a warrant. He has an upstairs room completely dedicated to Six Sundays. And when I say completely, I mean floor-to-ceiling posters, clippings from magazines, album covers, and something more significant."

Phan paused. "We have other evidence I'm not able to share—"

Deacon gasped. "You think it's him?"

"Honestly?" Phan sighed. "I don't know what to think. I don't for one second think he has the capability to murder the other two victims, but this is different. There was no fire or any indication there was going to be. The other two victims may have been the crazed revenge we assume, and someone completely different could be responsible for Rachel. It looks bad for Jared, but at the moment, he's not talking, and our doctors are looking at him. We need him fit for interview, and until that's signed off on, we can't ask anything."

Deacon didn't seem able to speak.

"I was actually going to call you," Maverick said, feeling selfish for introducing another topic. "We need to go get my truck and go for supplies for Molly."

"I'd really rather you didn't," Phan said. "At least until tomorrow." Which was reasonable.

In the end, Jamie called her friends, and soon the fridge was full again. Clothes were even dropped off. They spent the evening watching films with Molly. Molly had taken to Jamie almost instantly but seemed to still be unwilling to be more than six feet away from Deacon at all times. Not that he blamed her. Jamie went upstairs early, and Deacon just let Molly fall asleep on the couch after her bath.

"I'm gonna sleep down here," Maverick said as *The Lion King* finished, and Molly never stirred. Deacon looked up at him. "She must be completely confused, and I know you'd rather have her in with you, not in Melanie's room."

Deacon's gaze mapped his face, but Maverick knew it was the right thing to do. Molly had had enough upset in her short life. He saw the understanding settle on Deacon's face along with the gratitude. He hoped he saw a little longing, but it could be wishful thinking. He brushed a kiss on Deacon's lips to say he understood and groaned as the brush caught fire and the kiss was enthusiastically returned.

"Go to bed before I change my mind."

SOMETIME LATER—Maverick couldn't sleep—he was coming back from the bathroom when he heard a noise from upstairs and instantly knew it was Molly, and he heard Deacon trying to hush her. He grabbed the rail and pulled himself up the stairs, then quietly pushed the door open to Deacon's room. Deacon smiled. "I'm sorry if we woke you. She won't settle."

Maverick glanced at the clock on the nightstand and was surprised to see it read 2:00 a.m. Deacon looked exhausted. "Has she slept at all?"

Molly peered at him from where she sat cuddled on Deacon's lap. "Hey, munchkin," he said softly.

Deacon bent down to her. "Will you wait with Uncle Mav for a few seconds while I run and get you some milk?" Deacon glanced at him. "I was going to warm it."

Mav smiled. He could go do it if the little imp wouldn't stay with him. He sat in the old recliner in the corner of the room, his tracksuit bottoms hitching up and showing his prosthesis. Molly's eyes became as round as the O shape her lips made. He rapped his knuckles against it like he had done the last time. "Wanna see?"

Molly immediately glanced at Deacon to see what he thought of the offer, and Deacon nodded.

"It's really cool, and I can take it off," Mav confided.

Her surprise was funny, and Deacon stood and sat her next to Maverick in the huge chair that had belonged to Mav's dad many years ago. When his dad had died and they had sold everything, Jamie had wanted to keep it, and Mav was glad she did. Mav suddenly had a memory of his dad sitting in it and them reading something together.

He forgot sometimes he'd had a lot of years of good before the last few bad ones, and he felt guilty he didn't think about them enough. "I have a button to push to take it off." And that was it. He wasn't sure Molly even noticed Deacon running downstairs.

"Did it get broken?" Molly said when his prosthetic was off and she had examined his residual.

"Uh-huh," Maverick replied as Deacon came back. By that time, Molly was curled up into Maverick's side, yawning, but instead of reaching with both arms for Deacon as she had been doing all day, she just held out her hand for the milk. Maverick was impressed Deacon had thought to use a travel mug so it wouldn't spill, and Deacon solemnly handed her the mug, which Maverick steadied for her while Deacon went and sat down on the bed.

"Does she have any friends?"

"She played with Augusta's kids a few times," Deacon replied. "I'd been looking at day care for when I start working where Augusta sends hers, but that's too far from here." He blushed. "Not that I'll be here in a month, but I'll have to see where we live."

With me. But Maverick didn't say the words out loud. Despite what he had thought earlier. It was far too soon to voice them.

CHAPTER FIFTEEN

THE BED was cold. Deacon knew why of course before he'd even opened his eyes. He was alone. That thought made him start—*Molly*—and he hadn't even taken another breath before his eyes focused on a sight that made his heart seem suddenly too big for his chest.

They must have all fallen asleep. He remembered thinking he was going to have to lift Molly out of Maverick's arms when she finished her milk, and he didn't remember anything after that. Molly was still asleep. She looked impossibly tiny cradled as she was in Maverick's arms. He had raised the foot support on the chair and tilted the whole thing back so she was snug and safe.

Jealous of a two-year-old? *Am I?* Deacon sighed and snuggled into the comforter, prepared to laze for another minute. Maverick amazed him. He'd coped with everything life had flung his way, and here he was, prepared to step up again. Deacon knew Maverick would have made a joke of that expression. He'd heard him say to Jamie that at least no one could accuse him of having two left feet anymore, but he hadn't said it wanting pity or attention. He'd opened his heart and his arms to them both, and Deacon hoped like hell when this mess was done, Mav didn't decide they were too much trouble and they— They what? Had to move? Or could they stay? Not with Jamie obviously, but he was hoping—

"I can hear you thinking from over here," Maverick mused, and Deacon sat up.

"You had your eyes closed," he accused. "There's no way you could see me."

"I said I *heard* you." Molly stirred, and Maverick dropped a kiss on her forehead just as her eyes opened. "Morning, munchkin. Did you sleep okay?"

Molly started before she woke properly, and her eyes sought out Deacon, but then she yawned and snuggled back into Maverick. Maverick looked over at Deacon. "How about we get Uncle Danny to run you a bath, huh?"

Deacon yawned and shook his head. "She normally has a bath at night. It settles her."

"Uh-huh," Maverick pronounced solemnly. "You might want to change it up this morning." And he opened the blanket he'd covered her with to show the wet stain on his pants.

Deacon scrambled out of bed. *Oh my God.* He was going to *die.* He had completely forgotten to put her Pull-Ups on, and Molly had peed on Mav. "I'll take her."

But Maverick just smiled slowly. "How about you run a bath. I don't think it's gonna get any worse for the next minute or so." He squinted up at Deacon. "Umm, it isn't, right?"

Deacon shook his head violently. "She's usually dry during the day, which is early anyway. I always use Pull-Ups on at night." Then he chuckled and seemed to relax. "I guess it could be worse." He smiled ruefully.

Maverick grinned. "You've had a rough couple of days. Go run the bath. I've had plenty worse."

Deacon ran into the bathroom and found some bubble bath, which he squirted liberally into the running water. In a few minutes, he was back, and Maverick was discussing the merits of chocolate chip pancakes versus ones with bananas.

"Arms up," Mav instructed Molly so Deacon could get her T-shirt off her. The matching skirt had been ditched yesterday. Molly wrinkled her nose when she realized she was wet, but Deacon was quick, and she was soon playing in the bath. He heard the shower come on in Melanie's room and wondered how Maverick was managing. It couldn't be easy, and while he had seen there was a seat added to this shower, he didn't think for one minute there would be in any of the others. There definitely wasn't one in the downstairs, which surprised him, but then, maybe Jamie had been trying to encourage Mav not to just stay downstairs.

He heard the knock at the bathroom door and looked up to see Jamie smiling and balancing on her crutches. "Good morning, Molly." Molly giggled and squirted water out of the empty shampoo bottle. Jamie turned to Deacon. "I'm going to get the elixir of life brewed and be totally graceful and go down the stairs on my bottom."

Molly seemed to notice the crutches for the first time. "Did you get an owie? Uncle Mav got a new one."

Jamie grinned. "I'm not that cool."

Deacon held out a warm towel and helped Molly stand. "Pancakes?" she asked brightly, and Deacon nodded.

"Geraldine from next door is dropping off the booster seat they use for her grandson until you get a new one," Jamie said as she limped out of the bathroom.

Deacon's throat tightened. He'd never had complete strangers helping him, and he buried his head in the towel he was wrapping Molly up in. Molly flung her arms around him. "Pancakes," she demanded.

Deacon had no words, but he returned her hug just as fiercely.

The pancakes were a success. By the time Deacon had found something in the bag Jamie had left on the bed that would fit Molly, brushed her hair, and helped her brush her teeth, Maverick had cooked enough pancakes to feed an army. They were tucking in when Detective Phan arrived along with Loretta, who they had seen yesterday.

Deacon and Maverick left Jamie, Loretta, and Molly in the kitchen to finish up, and they all took their coffees into the living room.

"What is it?" Deacon immediately asked the second Phan had closed the door.

"We were about to arrest and charge Jared Upchurch with Rachel's murder."

"Jimmy?" Deacon said in astonishment. "Are you sure?"

Phan nodded. "Forensics are very damning. He definitely went near her body."

"And you believe he did it?" Maverick asked doubtfully.

"Honestly? We're not completely sure. I'm even less sure he is competent to stand trial if we get that far, but charging him will ensure he is away from the public. His only relative—an elderly father—died last year. He never graduated high school, and his father worked as chauffeur for the couple who owned the house prior to Mr. and Mrs. Fellhouse."

"How is my mom?" Deacon asked politely, and Maverick glanced his way. It had been the first time he had mentioned her.

"I understand her husband has admitted her to a private clinic, and the doctors have said she isn't ready to be interviewed."

Deacon nodded and didn't ask anything else about her. "Were?" Deacon said. "You said you were going to charge Jimmy. Does that mean you just haven't done it yet or that you have doubts?"

"How much contact have you had with your stepfather?" Phan parried the question.

"Percy?" Deacon asked in surprise. "Barely any, to be honest. He was always absent when I saw Molly except at the trial. Why?"

"Because we got a call from a desk sergeant an hour ago who received a call from a communications dispatcher who recognized the address for the 911 call. Apparently Gemma Pierce, the dispatcher, was the secretary who was paid off to drop the sexual assault claim about Percy."

"She was?" Maverick was stunned.

"Technically she was offered a full college scholarship sponsored by Fellhouse and Hanks, Percy's law firm, except she had never applied for one in the first place."

"Very clever," Maverick murmured.

"And we have a problem with his alibi at the time of the murder."

"Percy's?" Deacon asked.

"Yes," Phan confirmed. "Apparently he left your mom to get the passport and said he had other errands and that he would be back for them. He says he did some shopping, but he has no receipts and doesn't seem to remember any specifics that we can confirm with CCTV. This is a stretch, but if he had assaulted Rachel and she threatened to tell, your current problems would be an excellent smokescreen."

"But he had nothing to do with the other murders."

"I doubt it," Phan agreed. "But we only have you as the connection so far. There is nothing to indicate there is any similarity between the murders. It could be convenience. The housekeeper tells us Mr. Fellhouse knew Jared and likely knew about his fixation with you."

"So we might be back to one person being responsible for Jones and Sara Jeffries and another for Rachel?" Maverick asked.

"Yes, and we need to ask your permission to speak to Molly," Phan asked. "We know she wasn't present, but she spent a lot of time with Rachel, and the housekeeper still thinks there was a boyfriend, which could either be Mr. Fellhouse or someone else entirely."

Deacon shot Maverick a worried glance.

"We wouldn't take her to the station or even talk to her ourselves. You would take her to the child advocacy center where trained professionals would ask her questions. You can watch from behind a screen. You're just not allowed to interact with her during questioning."

"When?"

"Today, if at all possible. We can't hold Mr. Upchurch without making a decision for much longer."

Deacon looked at Maverick. "I think Molly would be okay." And this sounded important.

"We were actually wanting to pick up my truck but weren't sure about leaving the house." Maverick glanced at Phan. "Maybe we can do both together?"

"I know how hard this is." Phan sympathized. "And I know you can't just stop living, but there is still the real risk that someone is threatening you, even if Rachel's murder has nothing to do with it. We're still no further forward on either Jones or Ms. Jeffries."

Stop living? Some days it didn't feel as if Deacon had been living for weeks.

"I can get you a ride there."

"I'm not leaving the house with a police escort," Maverick said with a flash of amusement. "And I'm also not thrilled about Jamie being on her own."

"Okay, how about I drop you off to get your truck, the cops stay here, and I follow you to the advocacy center?"

Maverick nodded and looked at Deacon for confirmation. "Does that sound okay to you?"

Deacon agreed. He was getting a little stir-crazy, and while he would never put Molly at risk, they had to take her out anyway, and one trip with Detective Phan as backup sounded very reasonable.

MOLLY WAS excited, and Maverick said after they got his truck, they might just have to stop for a strawberry milkshake. Molly wrinkled her nose.

"You don't like strawberry milkshakes?" Maverick asked, pretending to be horrified. "I'm gonna have to cancel your cool-kid card."

But Deacon grinned, knowing what was coming.

"Berry for girls. Want chocolate," Molly pronounced, then held both arms up for Maverick to pick her up. Deacon cackled at Maverick's expression.

"She picked that little gem up from Tony, Augusta's eldest. I was hoping she might forget, but I think children are like elephants."

Maverick bent and solemnly picked her up, then kissed her cheek, and Deacon saw his expression turn serious. *Maybe he's more worried about going out than I thought?* Not that Deacon blamed him. It was a wonder he wasn't hiding under the bed himself. It was Maverick, he decided. The air of safety. The strong capability. It lulled him into thinking everything was okay, which in some ways was more dangerous than the threat itself. Deacon took a step to the door after Phan and turned back, wondering why Maverick wasn't following him. Maverick kissed Molly again and then held her out to Deacon. "Here you go, munchkin." But Molly stubbornly refused to let him go.

A flash of something *raw* almost passed over Maverick. Sore, like an exposed nerve, and accompanying frustration, and Deacon immediately understood. Maverick wasn't confident carrying Molly while he walked, and Deacon cursed himself for putting him in that situation. Deacon pretended to cry and sniffed, saying he needed a Molly cuddle at which Molly held her arms out, and Deacon took her. He sent a silent apology to Maverick, but Maverick wasn't looking, and Deacon didn't know what to say.

Maverick was quiet on the way to the dealership but seemed to shake it off between Molly's chatter and the sight of his gleaming brand-new truck waiting for him when they pulled up. Phan stayed in the car while they all got out and spoke to an eager Philip Mathewson, who immediately gave them a child safety seat as a complimentary gift.

Deacon decided it would be wise to wait with the detective while Philip made sure Maverick was comfortable with the controls and knew what he was doing.

Deacon had watched Maverick drive around the back lot with Philip before they had disappeared down the road. When Maverick came back he moved with a confidence Deacon hadn't seen on him before. Philip showed them how to work the DVD in the back and ran to his own car to get a copy of *Mulan* that he kept in there for his sister's little girl so Molly had something to watch.

Molly was charmed.

Deacon put the video on for Molly and firmly got in the passenger side. Maverick ran his gaze over Deacon. "I would understand if you wanted to ride with Phan."

"If I didn't think you knew what you were doing, I would never have gotten in the car with you while you were carrying a gun. I'm confident you know what to do to keep us safe."

Maverick's gaze shot up. "I have a conceal carry permit," he said defensively.

Deacon nodded. "I never doubted you would have."

Maverick was different, Deacon decided, as they followed Phan to the advocacy center. He never took his eyes off the road for a second, but he moved confidently and smoothly.

A bit like he had been in bed. No, very much like he had been in bed, and Deacon moved a little to give himself room. Maverick noticed and glanced over. "You okay?"

And because Deacon didn't want Maverick to think this was about his driving, he put a hand on his knee.

"I was just wishing we had some alone time," he said boldly, realizing it was true. Maverick's lips quirked a little as he signaled and pulled in behind Phan's Saab.

Molly looked up when they stopped. "Milkshake?"

Deacon turned in his seat, and Mav paused the film. "We need to go talk to a nice lady for a few minutes, and then it's milkshake time."

Molly nodded but gripped Deacon tightly and didn't want to walk into the center. Once she got inside—even though she was shy at first—she soon warmed to Callie Ramirez, who was a forensic interviewer and family advocate. Molly played with the dolls and the cars for a long time while Callie and Deacon chatted about lots of inconsequential things, and then Callie asked Molly if she would stay with her while Deacon went to get them all some more juice. It was Deacon's signal to leave, and he got up quietly and took the mugs with him.

By the time he got behind the screen, he was shaking so hard Maverick had to take the mugs off him. Phan looked sympathetic. "I know it's hard, but they're good."

"I looked them up," Deacon confessed, fixing Phan with a hard stare. "This place is usually used for victims of child abuse."

Maverick shot a glance at Phan. That had never occurred to him, even with what they had said about Fellhouse.

Phan shook his head. "All we believe here is that there is a chance Molly saw if Rachel met a boyfriend. We have absolutely no reason to think you have anything to worry about, but there are people we can see to put your mind at rest."

Deacon let out a long breath. He'd never thought it, to be honest, but this place had him questioning everything. They listened while Callie carried on talking to Molly, and they both got the crayons out. Callie steered the conversation around to friends and who Molly liked to play with. In the end, Callie didn't have to do a lot of work. It was clear that the questions were open-ended and that Molly was given lots of opportunities to talk. Molly mentioned the games she played with Rachel, and that she hated having to take a nap, and Rachel would let her color and read stories to her.

Molly was asked if she had ever met any of Rachel's friends, and she told Callie about Jimmy, who brought Rachel flowers. Phan made notes intently as Molly described the pink flowers.

Then Callie asked if Rachel had ever driven a car when they went out, and Molly nodded and confirmed the red color of her grandma's, which Rachel sometimes drove. She was asked if Rachel ever took Molly to meet any friends, and she launched into an account of a playdate.

Then out of the blue, Molly asked where Rachel was. Callie said she didn't know, and what did Molly think. Molly said she thought maybe Rachel had gone to live with her friend.

It took another ten minutes and two drawings before Callie had got Molly to describe Rachel's other friend. The man who Molly had only seen driving away in a *black* car, the same color of the cat that lived next to her grandma's. The man who Rachel had told Molly was a secret.

The man who had just become a likely suspect for the murder of Rachel Mackenzie, and—Deacon couldn't help wondering—Emmanuel Jones and Sara Jeffries.

"I THINK it's milkshake time," Maverick pronounced when Callie finished the session after it became clear Molly was getting bored and they weren't going to get any more information from her. Deacon couldn't help but be glad Molly hadn't seen the man's face. It would be far too much pressure for a description, and he had seen Phan pause when the black car was mentioned.

Was it the same black Charger that had been following him? Black was a common color, and all Maverick would say was he didn't like coincidences. Phan didn't, or perhaps *couldn't*, say anything.

Maverick assured Phan they would return straight home and after confirming the route, left the detective at the center. Maverick drove home, and soon Molly was engrossed in *Mulan* again. Deacon couldn't help obsessively checking his mirrors for the black car. They were about fifteen minutes from home when Molly suddenly piped up, "I need to pee."

"Oh hell," Deacon muttered.

"We're a good fifteen minutes away."

"She won't last that long." He spotted a big Target superstore up ahead. "How about if we go in there?"

"You could certainly do with some clothes," Maverick agreed and signaled to turn.

"Yeah." Deacon picked at one of the only two shirts he had. He squirmed. "I'll have to borrow…."

"I know," Maverick said lightly and parked in one of the family spaces near the entrance. Deacon jumped out.

"I'll see you inside," he confirmed and swung Molly up and hurried inside with her.

Maverick took his time. Patted the leather console and climbed out of the truck, glancing at his phone when he heard the notification beep. It was an email from the Denham Institute, reminding him of his appointment. Damn. He had taken a cancellation because he needed to get his back looked at, and he'd forgotten about it with everything else that was happening.

He didn't like the thought of leaving Deacon, but it wasn't fair to ask him to drag Molly along. Maverick smiled as he walked up to the main door. He liked Molly. Not as much as he liked her uncle, but he definitely had a soft spot for her. Maybe he ought to rethink the apartment idea. Kids needed yards. Trees to climb. Grass to—

He came to a complete stop just as the automatic doors opened. *A yard?* When had this gone from an instant attraction to an instant family? But of course, Deacon was now a package deal. Maverick's lips curved into a slow smile, which widened when he saw Deacon coming out of the bathroom holding Molly's hand.

Molly beamed at him while Maverick grabbed a cart, and Deacon lifted her up and sat her in it. They browsed for some clothes for Deacon, and Molly appointed herself chief decision maker with Maverick and Molly pronouncing thumbs up or thumbs down to all Deacon's choices. It was silly, and they had fun even if Maverick did feel a little like a Roman emperor.

Molly came out of the cart while Maverick paid, and then she was hungry, so they got a quick snack. Deacon suggested she visit the bathroom again—Target made it simple for him to go with her—and they disappeared while Maverick walked back to the electronics area and a very helpful lady picked out some DVDs for his truck that Molly would like. Maverick was the first to admit he hadn't heard of two of them. Then he wandered over to the pharmacy. He was paying when he heard Deacon's panicked shout at the top of his voice. "Molly?" His blood ran cold.

Deacon ran from the bathroom and looked around wildly. "Deacon," Mav shouted and ignored the stab of pain in his back as he hurried over.

"I can't find her. We were washing our hands and about six women all came in at the same time, and it was such a squeeze, and before I knew it, Molly was out and I couldn't get to her."

Maverick snagged the arm of a sales associate as she walked past. "Our little girl just ran out of the bathroom on her own. She's only two."

The woman's eyes widened, and she immediately spoke into the earpiece she was wearing, and a security guard came running over. Deacon ran toward the entrance shouting for her, and within a few seconds, two more people were helping.

"Mav?"

Mav turned when he recognized the voice, and the relief nearly brought him to his knees. It was Molly. Carried by a smiling Charlie in full uniform. She was chatting a mile a minute and asking all about his radio. Another cop followed them both in.

Deacon ran to her and practically wrenched her from Charlie's arms. Charlie smiled at Maverick, and they shook hands. "Look who I found outside?"

"Thank you," Deacon said fervently and clutched Molly.

"No problem," he said. "Not that I wasn't surprised to see her. I was just coming on shift, and I thought you must be inside." He grinned, nodding to the small Starbucks by the entrance to indicate why he had stopped. Charlie turned and shook hands with the sales associate. "All under control now," he confirmed, and everyone dispersed. "Can I get anyone a coffee?"

Maverick chuckled. "Since when?"

DEACON LET them talk for another minute until Molly started protesting at the tight hold he had on her, and Maverick shook hands again with Charlie, and they left. Charlie had confirmed he would be one of the patrol cars on duty outside their house later.

Deacon's hands shook as he valiantly tried to fasten the seat belt, and with a firm hand, Maverick shooed him into the seat and said he would take care of it. Molly was yawning by the time they had set off, and whether she usually napped at this time or not, he thought the excitement of the last few days was catching up with her.

It was catching up with him. What would have happened if Charlie hadn't caught her outside? It didn't bear thinking about. He'd been telling himself they would cope fine, and he couldn't even manage a simple trip for groceries without putting her in danger. What did that say for the future? Deacon shuddered. He would never forget the moment of absolute terror as Molly had slipped out of the bathroom door, and the few seconds it had taken for him to get past the women coming in. He never ever wanted to go through that again.

"We could get a GPS," Maverick said conversationally, "or have a tracking chip installed. An old buddy of mine told me he had an app installed on his daughter's cell phone that told him where she was at all times."

Deacon focused on what Maverick was saying. "What?"

"I guess she's a bit young for a cell phone, though," he added thoughtfully.

Deacon gave a shaky laugh, knowing what Maverick was doing. "I thought I was going to have a heart attack."

"Won't be the last, I'm afraid," Maverick agreed. "You wait till she starts being interested in dating." He scowled. "Of course, that won't fly unless she's at least twenty-five."

Deacon laughed. "You're not gonna let her date until she's twenty-five?"

"Nope," he said and patted his holster comfortingly. Deacon rolled his eyes, then had to blink a few times as the words hit him. *Twenty-five?* He knew Mav had been teasing him to make him feel better, but what if Maverick had been half-serious? That he could see himself still being in their lives when Molly was all grown? His breath hitched, and he turned his face to the window. He wanted that. He wanted that so damn much it hurt.

CHAPTER SIXTEEN

TWO MORE days and nothing much seemed to happen. They'd eaten and talked as much as they could with an audience. Jamie had even gotten some books for Molly because there was no way either of them wanted to risk going out again. They hadn't heard from Phan except through the cops. Mav knew Phan had hundreds of things to do and they had been pretty lucky with all the detective had shared, but the not knowing was driving him crazy.

And not just not knowing about the murders. He was completely confused about his reaction to Deacon. They'd only known each other for days, and that was no time at all to build a lasting or any sort of a relationship, especially with what was currently throwing them together.

The heart wants what the heart wants.

Emily Dickinson. One of his mom's favorite sayings. Not that he'd ever read whatever book she'd written those words in, but his mom used to say that sort of thing all the time. His mom and dad had met on Thanksgiving. She used to be a librarian, and it seemed she always had a book in her hands. His dad volunteered as a handyman at the local shelter, and his mom had been down there donating old library books.

The story went that his mom's car had broken down and Dad had fixed it, but his mom used to say she would swear he put sugar in her gas tank, and his dad would laugh and say she was so sweet it was her that'd stopped the car just like she'd stopped his heart. They'd married four months later.

Maverick swallowed heavily. He didn't honestly know if his skewed view of his mom and dad's problems had sworn him off relationships, poured scorn on the notion of a happy ever after, but he was doing them both an injustice. His dad losing his job hadn't made his mom sick. Pride might have been his dad's worst crime, but what did that make him? A chip off the old block? It was easy to make assumptions and hard to admit he'd been wrong. He hoped his dad knew that and his mom and dad were together now. It was a nice thought.

The house was quiet. The sofa was as comfortable as it had always been, and for the past two months that had suited him pretty well. He hadn't gotten much sleep last night—or not until he had a little person use him as a pillow—so why in the hell was he still awake at fucking 3:00 a.m.?

For like a millisecond, he wanted a drink, but then he remembered the responsibility he carried, and the longing for a whiskey was replaced by a longing for something else. Some*one* else. He was half-hard simply thinking about Deacon.

He stilled at the noise in the hall, and then the door to his room pushed open and Deacon stepped cautiously in. The smile he got when he lifted his arm to encourage Deacon to lie down with him was worth every second of his sleepless night.

"Molly woke up a little bit ago. I think she might be starting a cold, but she's gone to the bathroom and had some water, and she went out again like a light. I don't think I'll hear anything else from her until breakfast time." Deacon snuggled in next to Maverick. "You're like a space heater."

Maverick smiled and rubbed his hands over Deacon's chilly arms. "I think you need a blood transfusion. It's been eighty degrees out there today, and it hasn't dropped that much." June in Atlanta was often hot.

"Maybe that was an excuse," Deacon admitted into Maverick's neck after another minute. He raised his head. "Maybe I missed you?" His gaze dropped to Maverick's lips, and the last question became obvious.

"Yes," Maverick answered with a groan and took Deacon's lips, his desire and his erection flaring to life.

Deacon broke off. "Wait," he said and stood up. He pulled the blankets Mav had thrown off and the cushions and arranged them on the floor. He lay down on them and patted the floor next to him invitingly. Maverick was happy to oblige and slid to the floor, pushing his prosthesis out of the way.

Deacon's eyes darkened. Mav could make out the colors from the light spilling in from the hallway. "I brought the lube with me," Deacon said as Maverick pulled him close.

Maverick nuzzled his neck. He'd bought lube and condoms from Target after he'd gotten the DVDs for

Molly, but he wasn't going to put pressure on Deacon by telling him that.

Deacon whimpered as Mav shucked his shorts down, and his thick erection was visible against his belly. Deacon took hold of him instantly. "You have no idea how many times I've looked at you today and wondered if you had anything on under your pants."

Mav groaned and caught Deacon's lips, sucking the bottom one between his own, then clamping his mouth over them both and ravaging them. His hands slid up Deacon's chest, and he cupped Deacon's throat, curling his fingers around the back and applying a little pressure with his thumb to the front. Deacon's cock jerked.

"Why is that so hot?" Deacon asked, whimpering and squirming to get closer.

Mav let his hands roam and soon found Deacon's nipples. The gasp he heard from the slight scratch of his nail on the hardening nub was very satisfying. "I would love to see you with these pierced."

"Oh," Deacon moaned again. "You're gonna make me shoot when you say things like that."

Maverick grinned. He loved the sexy way they talked last time and the effect it had on Deacon. "We can't have that," he said, licking from the hollow in Deacon's throat and up to his chin. Deacon shuddered and chased Mav's lips with his own. Mav broke away and bent his head to Deacon's nipple now he knew the effect he would have. He moaned as Mav fastened his lips on it and swirled his tongue, but when he bit down, Deacon's eyes flew open. "I'm gonna—"

"No," Maverick ordered and clasped the base of Deacon's cock as it throbbed. He'd never dominated, especially during sex, but he'd never had a relationship before, and whatever was happening, it was definitely a relationship. Maybe that was what made the difference.

"You can't do that," Deacon ground out.

"No?" Maverick said innocently. "Says who?"

"Torturing your boyfriend is wrong on so many levels." Deacon fisted his hands, and then he stilled, realizing what he had said. The question in his eyes was obvious.

"We've known each other for only a week," Maverick agreed and smoothed the blond hair out of his eyes. Deacon closed them as if not wanting to face whatever Maverick was going to say next. "And I'm not a good boyfriend prospect." But he wanted to be so very badly. "I was maybe a bottle away from being an alcoholic. My body's broken. I haven't got a job, and I sleep on my sister's couch."

And there wasn't just the two of them anymore.

Deacon opened his eyes and gazed at Maverick. "I have no money, no job, and I don't even have a sister to lend me a couch. I'm also responsible for a two-year-old who will have to come first for the next twenty years."

"As she should," Maverick agreed solemnly.

"And I have a crazy man maybe coming for me after murdering other people."

"Okay," Maverick said in mock seriousness. "That trumps sleeping on my sister's couch."

"That trumps everything," Deacon hissed. "You are at risk being with me, and the only thing that's keeping me here is knowing Molly is safe."

"The only thing?"

Deacon's beautiful blue eyes swam with tears, and he shook his head. "No, I didn't mean that. I meant that caring about you means not putting you in danger, which means I should go check into a motel, but Molly—"

"You're not going anywhere," Maverick said, a warm glow filling him at Deacon's admission. Maybe Emily Dickinson knew what she was talking about. He brushed a kiss on Deacon's soft lips. "If I think Jamie is at risk, I know she has a ton of cop buddies that would either move in here or take her to theirs. We can both talk to her tomorrow and see what she wants to do if it will make you feel better. But—" He was helpless not to grab another kiss. "—you stay with me wherever you are, and I don't mean only because of the murders."

Deacon stared into Maverick's eyes. "What are you saying?"

"I'm saying I understand we've only just met. You're worried physical attraction—no matter how good—" He smiled. "—isn't enough for a forever relationship, and you have to think about Molly."

Deacon gazed at him. "So when we're not fighting for our lives, you think we should date?"

Mav chuckled. "We can date. So long as it involves sleeping in the same bed."

"That is not what you just said," Deacon protested.

"It isn't?" Maverick teased. "I like the idea of candlelit dinners, maybe a movie."

"No, I mean sleeping in the same bed."

"You don't want to sleep in my bed?" He feigned mock outrage. "Whose bed do you want to sleep in?"

"Well, my own."

"And there's not room for me? I mean, I'd take the floor if I had to, but it's hell on my back. You gotta think of that."

Deacon shook his head. "You're impossible."

Maverick nuzzled the side of his neck, and Deacon tilted his head to give him more room.

"I think you like my brand of impossible," Maverick declared and moved to his lips.

Deacon moaned into Mav's mouth, then eased back. "I want you inside me so very badly," he whispered.

Mav smiled. "Fuck, yeah." Deacon passed him the lube, and Mav was generous with it. There was no way he was going to hurt Deacon. He gently inserted a lubed fingertip into his hole, just barely past the first knuckle, and groaned as the action seemed to send a bolt of heat right to his own cock. He rubbed it against Deacon's thigh, knowing it wouldn't take much. He eased his finger in and out and palmed Deacon's sack at the same time, wishing he had two hands free. Another time, he would get Deacon to sit astride him, and that thought nearly took his head off.

"Oh fuck," Deacon uttered.

"I've never heard you swear."

"Molly will—" But the rest of the sentence was swallowed with Maverick's lips. Mav rolled onto his back and brought Deacon with him, kissing him fiercely until Deacon sat up, reaching for the lube and condoms. He was quick. The deft hands. The light touch. So much more erotic than pressure could ever be, and Mav strained toward him. Deacon kneeled up and positioned himself.

"Have you ever done this?"

"I'm not a virgin." The words were a little defensive.

Mav smirked. "No, I guess you wouldn't be." Sex, drugs, and rock and roll? Mav hated that fucking stupid saying. "I meant rode someone."

Deacon's sharp inhalation was as good of an answer as he needed.

He shook his head. "But I want to see you, and this way I can control how slow I go."

It was a good idea in theory, and Maverick steeled himself to stay still when every cell in his body wanted to thrust into what he knew would be glorious wet, tight heat. He swallowed and watched—unable to take his eyes from Deacon for even one second—as he lowered himself slowly, inch by incredible inch. Maverick saw the discomfort register, and he opened his mouth to tell him to stop, but Deacon's eyes quickly held wonder, then heat. They burned—he was sure—with the same intensity that was licking at him.

"You are so incredible," Mav said, awed with the level of trust Deacon was showing. Mav must have moved a little because Deacon splayed his hands over Maverick's chest, but he moved back. A tiny thrust of his hips that begged Maverick to copy it. Deacon lifted slightly, and Maverick's hands supported his hips to make the descent slow and easy. He wanted to say something, anything. Something meaningful. But the words that were on his lips, Deacon wasn't ready to hear.

"Faster." Deacon threw his head back.

"Touch yourself," Maverick ordered, and Deacon's hand curled around his dripping cock. Soon Maverick was thrusting into Deacon, and Deacon was controlling nothing. The sounds spilling from his lips were the most eloquent Mav had ever heard. Need drove them both. Their bodies joined and writhed in moves both unscripted yet seeming like they had practiced them all their lives. Deacon arched and pumped his hand one last time, his head thrown back and his mouth open in the same bliss that was pounding through Maverick until he collapsed forward, and Mav caught him. He would always catch him.

"Give me a minute," Deacon whispered in a hoarse voice.

I'll give you forever. It had been bull. Every word from Maverick's mouth earlier. Insta-love was crap manufactured for books and TV, but every teasing assurance Maverick had given him about taking their time had been a lie. He wanted this man, period. In every way he could get him. Cass would be laughing hysterically at him. Cass had known he was gay and didn't care. He used to waggle his finger at Maverick when he had rolled his eyes every time Cass fell in love, which seemed to be every time he went home on leave.

"Don't mock true love," he would say. "It'll come for you, and when it does, karma will bitch-slap you so hard you won't know which side is up."

And Maverick smiled, letting the furious pounding of his heart laugh along with the echo of his friend.

BREAKFAST WAS a quiet affair because Molly woke up with a temperature and a runny nose. So instead of playing with what seemed almost daily deliveries of toys from Jamie's friends and neighbors in a corner of the dining room, she snuggled up on the sofa and worked her way through the DVDs Maverick had bought at Target. Jamie, Deacon, and Maverick sat at the table to plan what they were going to do. Close enough to see her but far enough away she wouldn't pick up on what they talked about over the noise of *Cinderella.*

"In less than a week, Melanie will be home," Mav pointed out when Deacon mentioned moving to a motel.

"And she stays at Harvey's," Jamie confirmed. She put her hand up to halt any protest. "I'm safer here. You two are safer here. We can always look at this again in another few days if they haven't caught the *bastard*"— she mouthed the word—"but...." She nodded at Molly. "She can't live in some motel."

"The cops got extra time to interview Jared, but doesn't that run out today?" Deacon said. Phan had told them this morning.

Jamie took a sip of her coffee. "Which raises concerns for his safety more than for any other reason. The physical evidence shows he touched Rachel's body. He's traumatized, which can easily be explained from finding her. But no one thinks he's capable of killing her, and while we can't make assumptions, even if he murdered Rachel, no one believes it was possible he killed the other two." She took another gulp of caffeine. "Meaning that, either someone else murdered all three people, or Rachel's murder was a coincidence and didn't have anything to do with Jones or Jeffries."

Deacon wrinkled his nose, and Mav knew what he meant. It seemed too much of a coincidence. Mav had already told Jamie about Percy's missing alibi.

"The cops are still keeping a very close eye on Fellhouse," Jamie said.

"Don't you think if he had an alibi, he would say so since people are looking at him for a possible murder?" Deacon asked. "And what about the black Charger?"

"They're looking through Percy's DMV records."

Maverick leaned forward, wrapping his hands around his cup. "And they still haven't found any family for the original girl that died? Shelley Young?"

Jamie shook her head. "No. She apparently grew up in foster care. Moved cities a lot. I'm told they found an ex-boyfriend who split up with her nearly five years ago. Said she was in love with the idea of a soldier, but she couldn't cope with the separation. They separated when he got deployed, and he was in Iraq when she was killed."

"So we're no further forward?" Deacon asked and looked over to where Molly was. She noticed and looked at Deacon. "Pee-pee?"

"Come on, princess," Deacon said gently and held his hand out. He knew Jamie had spoken to her pediatrician about Deacon's concerns, but they weren't leaving the house at the moment, so no appointments.

Molly nodded and scrambled off the sofa. They both disappeared to the bathroom.

"Deacon says she asks, but he doesn't know if she actually wants to go or because he makes such a fuss of her for asking."

"He's worried, but kids bounce back, and it doesn't seem like she witnessed any violence," Jamie said. "And he's doing incredibly well with her. Melanie was three before she would even try the potty."

"I know. He told me you two had talked. Thanks, sis." He shot his sister a grateful smile. "He's concerned—we both are—what will happen if everything quiets down? Not that I'm wishing for anyone else to be hurt," he said hurriedly.

Jamie leaned forward, dropping her voice. "Between me and you, they think this is escalating. I don't think this is going to go on forever."

That's what he was afraid of. He took another few sips of coffee and listened to the giggles coming from the bathroom.

"You have so got it bad, brother." Mav focused on Jamie, but he didn't deny it. She stretched out her hand and took his. "I can't tell you how pleased I am."

"What if I'm not enough?" Maverick burst out, surprising himself because that wasn't what he was going to say.

Jamie frowned. "I know I'm biased, but you are one of the gentlest, kindest men I have ever known."

Mav shook his head. That wasn't what he meant.

"Oh please," Jamie said in disbelief. "You really think Deacon is that shallow?"

"I—" But no, he didn't. And he knew what they'd said earlier, but the fact was Deacon was scared for his and Molly's lives, and no one knew how he would feel when this was over.

"I saw the email from the Denham. You have an appointment at 3:00 p.m. today."

Maverick raised troubled eyes. "How do you know?"

"Because when you first applied, you copied me so I could take you to appointments."

He had. "I can't possibly go today."

"Go where?" Deacon asked, coming back in with Molly, who promptly raised her arms so she could sit on Jamie's lap.

"To the Denham Institute to have his prosthesis altered and see if he needs gait training," Jamie promptly supplied, ignoring Maverick's glower and taking Molly.

"You can't miss that," Deacon agreed. "A back massage will only relieve the pain temporarily."

"Does your back have an owie?" Molly piped up, obviously listening to what they said and making the connection.

Mav chuckled. "No, Molly. Uncle Danny made it all better—" He clamped his mouth closed.

"And you say I have no filter?" Deacon mumbled.

Mav ignored Jamie's delighted grin and waved his hand like it wasn't important. "I can go next week."

"This was a cancellation, and the next appointment they offered you is over a month away."

"You need to go, and Molly's not well enough to go out. We'll be fine here. This is important," Deacon said.

"So are you," Maverick stressed and watched Deacon's eyes soften. "How about we ask the cops to come inside?" Jamie suggested. "Keith's been going to call around for a coffee. I'll call him now." And she reached for the phone.

Deacon stood and put his hand out to Molly, who climbed off Jamie's knee. "I wish I could go with you, but we'll be fine."

Jamie put down her cell. "It's arranged. Either Keith will come himself, or he will make sure one of the cops we know will be here." Maverick still wasn't happy, but Jamie patted her hip, and Maverick understood. Jamie's Sig wasn't in the safe any longer.

The knock at the door stopped all conversation, and Maverick opened it to Detective Phan. Maverick eyed the older man critically. His weathered face seemed to have more lines on it than the last time Mav had seen him. He showed Phan into the kitchen, assuming he wouldn't want to talk in front of Molly. After a few seconds, Deacon joined them.

"I have some questions," he said unnecessarily and accepted the coffee Deacon handed him. "We have spoken to the Fellhouses' housekeeper—Mrs. Gladys Taylor—some more, mainly about the possibility of the boyfriend, and she remembered something else. We've been looking at Rachel's social media, and she was very active on something called Date a Hero."

Maverick nodded. "I've heard of that. It's a kind of pen-friend thing. Anything from simple letters to comfort packages."

"No." Phan shook his head. "That's Support a Hero. This is for military singles to hook up with men and women back home usually, but sometimes in the country they are deployed in."

Maverick shrugged. He'd never taken much notice of it. Heard his friends mention it occasionally. "But Jared wouldn't be on that, surely."

"Jared Upchurch didn't even have Wi-Fi on his cell phone," Phan said dryly. "We have, however, traced a cousin of his who lives in College Park, and apparently, it was her daughter who was the fan of Six Sundays whose mom made her throw away all her posters when—" He paused and glanced at Deacon.

"When I fell from grace?" Deacon laughed humorlessly.

Phan nodded. "Anyway, Jared was visiting with his dad, and Jared asked if he could have everything. Cindy Upchurch was fine with it. She says Jared's mom had a very difficult home birth and there was a lack of oxygen to the brain, causing developmental problems, something forty years ago they couldn't as easily have handled. She also says there's no way he is capable of this and that she's offered him a home, but he wanted to stay at his house. If the doctors decide he's okay, she is still happy for him to live with them."

"That's a big vote of confidence," Maverick pointed out.

"We just wondered if at any time you'd seen anything, or Rachel had said anything to you?" Phan looked at Deacon.

"You have to understand, I only saw Molly three times including the day I went with Mav. Rachel was always pleasant, but the only time I saw her without my mom being there was when we went upstairs." He looked at Maverick.

"And can you identify any of the men she talked to on these apps?" Mav asked.

"We're going through them, but some of these go back three or four years." Phan hesitated.

"What?" Maverick asked. There was something else.

"We're not sure whether this is a huge coincidence, but Shelley Young was also a member."

Deacon gasped. "That's an awful lot of coincidences."

"We have as many people as we can trawling through both sites and both girls' online histories. We're hoping we might find something. I knew it was a long shot that you might have spoken to Rachel, but it was worth asking."

Maverick showed Phan to the door.

"I hear you had some excitement yesterday. Sergeant Docherty told me Officer Chaplin saved the day." His smile was sardonic.

"Yeah, it's so damn lucky that you cops run on coffee."

Phan chuckled. "You don't do so bad yourself."

"I have a clinic appointment this afternoon," Mav said, still unhappy and part of him hoping Phan was going to tell him to stay at home.

"Refit?" Phan glanced down. "Is your residual bothering you?"

Residual? "You know someone?"

"My dad," he said. "Although it was phantom pain with him. Kept him awake nearly every night."

"Did he serve?"

"He did, but it was smoking that ruined his health. Clogged arteries. My mom wanted him to have it amputated a year before it actually happened. He'd gotten an ulcer that just wouldn't heal. Of course, that's over fifteen years ago." Phan met his gaze. "I'm glad you're not letting it defeat you. Takes some guts."

But Maverick had nearly let it win. "Jamie's colleagues are going to cover the house while I'm gone."

Phan arched an eyebrow. "And I'm assuming you've got a concealed carry permit for whatever's strapped to your hip?"

That made Maverick smile. He didn't think the detective missed anything.

CHAPTER SEVENTEEN

MAV HAD to be honest: he had missed driving. He supposed some shrink might say he liked being in control, and while a lot of that was true—he'd certainly hated being a passenger—he missed his own company as well. It had seemed like driving was always the time he could clear his head, gather his thoughts, make decisions. It had taken him the trip from Atlanta to Las Vegas when he graduated Georgia State thirteen years ago to decide on wanting to fly helicopters. Cass had convinced him to join the Air Force ROTC while in college. Cass came from a huge military family, unlike Maverick, and it had been all Cass had ever wanted to do. Although, to be honest, Maverick hadn't taken much convincing.

And Cass had been right. He'd had the best twelve years of his life and been bitter when it ended right up to last week. When he'd decided he wanted something more than flying helicopters.

If he was honest, he wasn't sure about the whole bodyguard gig, though. And he still missed flying helicopters. Flying anything.

It took Maverick more than an hour to navigate traffic, and he was relieved when he pulled up. He found a parking space quite close to the outpatients' entrance luckily, and still managed to be early for his appointment. A very nice lady called Martha Gregson showed him to a seat in the waiting room, and he pulled out his phone, smiling at the text.

I told Molly you r getting a new leg, and she wants to know the colors.

Maverick chuckled. *Let me guess? Pink?*

Don't b sexist, Deacon scolded. *I like pink.*

Purple?

May b. Where r u?

Waiting room.

Wish I was 2. Txt me when u r coming home xoxo

Coming home? He liked that idea. He liked that idea very much.

He glanced up as a man sat down in a chair next to him and nodded a hello. "Alan Marsh."

He returned the handshake. "Maverick Delgardo."

"What's the wait like today?"

Mav shook his head. "Sorry, first time."

Alan smiled. "They're pretty good, but I've got a flight out of ATL tonight, and I was hoping to be quick."

"And you don't want to miss it." He sympathized.

Alan grinned. "I wouldn't miss it. I'm flying the damn thing."

Maverick's ears pricked up, and in fifteen minutes, he found out that he could easily be a commercial pilot if it was what he wanted to do.

And he suddenly wanted to very much. The only person he wanted to protect was the one sharing his bed.

"I'll be blunt. Their main concern is to be sure your residual's not gonna slip under pressure, but this place is the best. I see Dr. Patel, and he's incredible."

"Mr. Delgardo?" A man in scrubs stood in front of him.

Alan chuckled. "You have to be gentle with him, Ray. He's already had one shock since he got here."

Another hour and Mav was ready to collapse. He had walked, run, balanced, and stretched.

"The problem is your liner," Dr. Patel pronounced. "You need a polyurethane one to make the pressure in your socket more evenly distributed. It performs best with vacuum suspension and the amount of scarring on your residual. It works better with a TSWB."

Mav looked blankly at Dr. Patel.

"A Total-Surface Weight-Bearing socket," he explained. "You already have that, but I don't understand why they didn't follow through and change your liner."

Mav squirmed. "Actually, they might have mentioned that." But Mav had expected an instant solution and gotten frustrated and angry. Then he'd left and run home to hide.

"It's also good for those patients who expect to return to high activity," Ray put in. "And assuming that's the case, we've got to work on those glutes of yours."

Dr. Patel grinned evilly.

"So leg raises with resisted side walking bands around the knees," Ray continued cheerfully. "Anything designed for hip strengthening."

"I don't know how you're walking without a cane," Dr. Patel murmured.

But Mav did. Troy would have called it bloody-mindedness.

Mav was another two hours, but he had a plan by the time he was through. He sat back in the waiting room while the receptionist dealt with another patient and realized with a guilty start he hadn't given the problems at home a thought for at least the last hour. But to be fair, the physical therapist had put him through the ringer.

He didn't mind in the least sitting down for another few minutes while he waited for his next appointment to be scheduled, and pulled out his phone. He had another half-dozen texts from Deacon and smiled, but then before he read through them, he saw a missed call from Troy. The receptionist asked him if he minded waiting another few minutes while she dealt with a cancellation, and Mav told her it was no problem.

The thought of getting his life back was the biggest high he had ever had, and he just wanted to sit and bask for a few minutes. Then he felt a twinge of guilt because he had been gone so long, but he knew Deacon was fine. He had half of the APD watching out for him.

"Mav?"

Maverick's eyebrows rose even though Troy couldn't see him. Troy never called him by his name. *Ugly fucker* or *wanker* were two of his favorites. Not that Mav minded. One night over the usual too many beers, Troy had insisted it was a term of endearment where he came from. Troy also confided he loved Maverick and would happily *shack up* with him except there was the slight problem that Mav was a guy, and the bigger problem—in Troy's drunken opinion—was he couldn't cook for shit. Mav smiled at the memory and decided then and there he would start visiting with some of his old buddies. Getting his life back meant going out with friends, right? And seeing as how Mav was now the designated driver for the rest of his life, he would also be the most popular guy around.

"You got some help for me?"

Troy chuckled and said he had and was going to text him a couple of names and phone numbers. "Did you say you spoke to Charlie? We will have to get together."

"Yeah, not to hang, though, because of everything that's happening."

"And he seems okay?"

Mav frowned. "Yeah, why?"

"Because one of the names I just gave you—Neil Patterson—became a reservist at the same time as Charlie, and he wondered if Charlie was okay after everything that went down."

"I have no idea what you mean."

There was a pause. "I didn't know either," Troy admitted, "or I would have reached out. I don't think he ever told anyone, but some people become real closed off when they leave."

Mav knew it was a dig at him, and it was true. "Closed off about what?"

"Did you know why he became a reservist?"

"From what I understand, he had a girlfriend who hated him being deployed." Not that that in itself was unusual. Separation was shit on the families.

"Did you know she died?"

"Fuck, no," Mav said. But Charlie had mentioned going for a beer and catching up. Something else Mav hadn't done. "But thanks for the heads-up. I'll reach out—"

"As soon as you aren't trying to put down a crazy," Troy finished. Mav could hear the smile in his voice, and he thanked him for the names and the info about his friend. Troy told him to stay safe, and he hung up.

Mav glanced over to where the receptionist was still on the phone and thought about Charlie and what a crap friend he'd been. He'd had three months he could have reached out during, but he'd just buried his head in a bottle of Jack and felt sorry for himself. He was pathetic. It was shit Charlie had given up doing what he loved for his girlfriend and lost her anyway. It was a shame he hadn't met her on one of those dating things Phan had mentioned. Maybe if she had wanted to date a soldier in the first place, she would have been more accepting of him having to do his job. Cass used to talk about Date a Hero, or whatever it was called, all the time.

Although, actually, now he thought about it, Cass only talked about it when he was teasing Charlie.

For a heartbeat, every drop of blood in his veins turned to ice.

Charlie.

No. He shook his head. That was impossible.

Charlie was a friend. They'd hung out. Gotten drunk. Charlie had been tight with him and Cass.

Or had he? It had been him and Cass against the world. Charlie had always joined in, but they hadn't been as close. If Cass and Charlie had switched places and Cass had gone home, he would have been the first person Mav would have reached out to in the hospital. Cass wouldn't have left his side. Charlie had never even been to visit. All this time Mav had been berating himself for not reaching out, but Charlie had never done so once. They'd exchanged one fucking email. Cass would have beaten down the door to his hospital room.

With a shaky hand, he checked his phone and called Deacon. After a few rings, it went to voicemail. He breathed his panic out and dialed Jamie. When that also went to voicemail, he dialed Phan. The detective answered on the second ring, although Mav's heartbeats were so loud in his ears it was a wonder it didn't drown everything else out.

"Phan?"

"Delgardo?" Phan's tone was sharp. He had heard the panic in Maverick's voice.

"Do you know what cops are guarding Jamie and Deacon?"

"I'm not sure, but it will be one of the regulars.... Hang on. I'm actually with Sergeant Docherty." There was a minute's silence. "He sent Officer Chaplin—"

Maverick didn't know how his shaky legs held him. Ignoring the questions of the receptionist as he tried to move as fast as he could out of the building and toward his truck, he clutched the phone tight while he stumbled over the words. "Charlie used Date a Hero all the time. He left the Air Force because his girlfriend didn't like him being deployed. When I saw him for the first time, he said they had a bad breakup, but his lieutenant just told me she died, and he said his cousin had offered him a place to crash. He doesn't like *fucking coffee*," Maverick yelled and nearly wrenched the truck door open.

He heard Phan issuing rapid-fire instructions to his team.

Maverick ignored the seat belt and started the truck, then peeled out of the parking lot.

"What type of car does he drive?" Maverick gripped the phone and wondered how his heart was still beating. There was another silence while he knew Phan was searching.

"We checked the registration of black Chargers in Georgia, but not... *shit*. It's registered in Ohio."

"What is?" Mav ground out.

"A black Dodge Charger," Phan said, and the phone went dead.

MOLLY HAD dropped to sleep, and Deacon turned down the TV. Jamie's neighbor had come through for them again and brought some Infants' Tylenol. Her fever was better, and Jamie didn't seem worried, so he wasn't. He missed Maverick. He was surprised to admit how much he actually missed him.

"Can I get you a coffee, tea, sandwich?" he asked Jamie after checking Molly was okay.

"A bottle of water?" Jamie followed him into the kitchen and sank back down. "And a couple of ibuprofen from the top cupboard?"

Deacon got them both and sat down opposite Jamie. "How old's your daughter?"

"Seventeen," Jamie said fondly, following Deacon's gaze to one of the million photos of Melanie that Jamie had around the house. "She's such a good kid."

Deacon nodded and sipped his own water. "She has a good mom."

Jamie smiled. "Actually, I wouldn't mind an unbiased opinion."

"Of course," Deacon assured her, wondering what Jamie was going to say.

Jamie sighed. "I heard from her dad last week. He called me a few times, and I ignored it, so he emailed me."

Deacon waited. Mav had mentioned he'd had a midlife crisis but no details. Not that he would have expected any.

"We had—I thought—a happy marriage for twenty years. I left the force five years ago when the law firm he worked at closed. Simon was fed up of dealing in boring corporate law as he put it, and he had a colleague who had successfully become a process server. Nothing exciting. He pulled me in with my experience and contacts, and we did okay for a few years. Then he got the idea of expanding. Mav was home on leave, and he was ready for a change, so one night over too many beers, they planned the whole thing. He investigated licenses, got business cards printed, and met Terry Samuels—a twenty-four-year-old gold digger—whose aunt needed some help with a divorce."

Deacon winced, imagining what was coming.

"A month later, he was gone. He emptied our savings, Melanie's college money account, and the money he'd been left by his father, and last week, I got an email saying he knew he had been the biggest old fool on the planet, and he's sorry. He says the college money is back in the account, and most of our savings."

"But it's not about the money, is it?" Deacon said gently. "It's the trust."

Jamie pressed her lips together for a second and nodded. "He didn't just take eighty thousand dollars; he took my dignity. And he didn't only betray me; he betrayed our daughter. And I'm not sure that's forgivable." Deacon reached out across the table, and Jamie clasped his hand. "What do you think I should do?"

"I'm not sure I'm the right person to ask."

Jamie fixed her steady brown-eyed gaze on him, and in that second, she looked so much like her brother,

Deacon's heart hurt. "You were betrayed by someone close to you, and even though you only mentioned her once, I think if you had the chance of a relationship with your mom, you would take it."

Would I? "I don't know. You're right, I've been thinking about her, but what if I miss the idea of what I think our relationship should be, not what it actually always was?"

Jamie's eyes widened. "That's pretty insightful."

He shrugged. "I think it was losing Molly that made me question everything. It takes a lot to put someone else first all the time even if what is best for the other person isn't what's best for you. Parents all over the world do it every day."

"And quite a few never do."

Deacon gave a wry smile. "None of which answers your question, though. What do you think Melanie would want?"

Jamie chuckled. "I think she took it worse than me at first. She misses her dad because they were always close, but she'll be off to college soon, and I would be making a very big mistake to take him back for anyone else but myself."

Sensible lady, Deacon thought. "Why don't you date?" he asked, remembering what Maverick had said.

"You mean movie nights and necking in the back row?"

Deacon joined in with her laughter. "Make him work for it. See how serious he is. That way you can take your time and—"

"Decide if I love the man or just the idea of not being on my own?"

"Now who's being all perceptive?"

They both looked up at the knock on the door. "That'll be Keith," Jamie said, and Deacon stood up.

"I'll let him in."

"And I'll put the coffee on."

It wasn't Keith. It was Charlie, and Deacon smiled as he let the cop in. "You on bodyguard duty?"

Charlie nodded. Deacon looked behind him, but he was on his own. "No partner?"

"The department can't afford two-person rides mostly," Jamie said from the kitchen doorway. "They're more likely to send two cars if they needed it."

"Oh," Deacon said in surprise. "I thought that was your partner you came into Target with?"

Charlie shook his head. "Where's the girl?"

The girl? He said that like he was asking where the suspect was. "If you mean Molly, she's asleep on the couch," Deacon said, probably more sharply than he intended.

Charlie had the grace to flush. "Sorry, I was in cop mode there a little. Can you tell me what firearms are in the house?"

"A Sig P328," Jamie replied tiredly and rubbed her head.

Deacon noticed. "Are you okay?" She'd asked for the ibuprofen earlier.

"To be honest, my ankle's bothering me." She smiled. "I'd go lie down, but the couch is occupied."

"Why don't you go up to your room?" Deacon suggested. "It's not like we won't be safe." He gestured at Charlie.

"And Officer Jenkins will be here soon. They got called out," Charlie confirmed.

"See?" Deacon teased. "I'll be perfectly safe."

Jamie nodded gratefully and turned for the stairs.

"Do you mind if I check the rooms upstairs? Then I won't need to disturb you."

Jamie's eyes widened. "Of course, Officer."

Charlie smiled good-naturedly and followed her out. "I know this is overkill, but Mav would have my guts if I didn't make sure you were all okay."

Deacon grinned, understanding the fervor with which Charlie spoke. He wasn't sure, but it wouldn't surprise him if Maverick wasn't Charlie's boss when they were in the military together. He peeked in at Molly, but she was asleep, so he went back into the kitchen to think about what to make for dinner later.

Charlie must have been very thorough up there, because it was quite a few minutes before he came back down. "Jamie's going to try for an hour's rest," he said, quietly coming into the kitchen.

"Would you like a coffee?"

He shook his head. "I hate the stuff, actually. I just drink it with the guys to be sociable. Mav and Cass used to give me grief about it, but the crap they drank was enough to strip your insides."

Deacon nodded and thought he ought to be sociable. This was essentially Maverick's best friend. "What do you think of Atlanta?"

Charlie shrugged. "It's as good a place as any."

"I've lived here most of my life. I guess you got to see lots of places while you served."

"I wish," Charlie replied, and Deacon could hear the bitterness in his voice. "I did basic, and then I only got to see some shitty deserts before I had to leave."

"I'm sorry," Deacon said.

"Why are you sorry?"

Deacon hesitated. "You're right. It's a bit of a trite phrase." This was harder than he expected. "I think Maverick mentioned you had family here?"

Charlie smiled, but there was no affection in it. "I don't have family anywhere, not anymore."

Deacon shuffled a little. Maybe he would go and check on Molly.

"I used to have a son," Charlie said completely out of the blue. "But my girlfriend was no good at taking care of him, so I left doing what I was trained for and came home."

He used to have a son? Crap, what had happened? Did Mav know this? Deacon knew he should ask a question, but he didn't know where to start. "How old?"

"One. He was murdered."

"Murdered? Oh my God, I am so sorry." It was unimaginable. "Did they…?"

"Catch the guy?"

Deacon nodded. Not sure he wanted to know, and not sure how to deal with the way the conversation was going.

"He will be punished soon."

Deacon shivered. That wasn't what he had asked. He stood up, needing to say something but not sure what. "I have tea if you want some."

Charlie laughed. "Tea? The great Deacon Daniels is offering me tea?"

Deacon frowned and took a determined step toward the kitchen door, but just as quickly, Charlie rose and blocked him. "I have to check on Molly."

"She's fine," Charlie said. "I checked before I came in here. Sleeping like a baby. They both are."

Deacon swallowed. He suddenly didn't like this at all. "Then I think I may go join her. It's been a difficult few days."

Charlie nodded, but he still didn't move. "My girlfriend died as well."

Deacon froze.

"She was run off the road. Never stood a chance. It was a complete joke. Only a jo—"

Deacon lunged, but he wasn't fast enough, and he definitely wasn't strong enough. He struggled even when Charlie's large hand covered his mouth, and when he felt the needle pierce his skin, he fought like a madman. But his arms were so heavy, and his legs didn't seem able to hold him up.

"Now the joke's on you." The last thing he heard was Charlie's laugh.

CHAPTER EIGHTEEN

LIGHTS AND sirens.

It had taken Mav over an hour to get back, and he still wasn't sure how he'd done it without wrecking his truck or getting pulled over. His heart nearly fucking stopped when he saw the ambulance, and he braked, uncaring who or what he blocked and scrambled out of the truck. Someone tried to put a hand out to stop him thundering forward, but luckily, Phan saw him before he took anyone out.

"Jamie's okay," Phan started as he just about stopped breathing when a stretcher was pushed out of the front door. A paramedic followed with Molly bundled up. Mav glanced behind them wildly, willing to see a third.

"Deacon?" he yelled, but Phan reached him before he got inside.

"Jamie and Molly were both drugged. I'm sorry. Deacon is missing."

Mav's heart thudded painfully. "Fuck." He wobbled and put out a hand to the doorframe.

"Come with me to the hospital," Phan urged, "and we'll tell you what we know." Maverick started to follow the EMTs to check on Jamie and Molly, but they were too quick for him. "We got here ten minutes after you called me," Phan continued, "at the same time as Officer Samson, who had been called out for a house fire—arson—literally around the corner. The house was empty, but the caller said three people were trapped. Chaplin told Samson he would be okay, and he should leave him."

Mav tried to clear his throat. "A diversion."

"Did he know you had an appointment already?"

"No."

"So he decided as soon as he found out about my request for extra back up."

"And it's definitely him?"

Phan nodded. "On the way, I spoke to the next of kin that's supposed to live here. The cousin?"

Mav ignored the pain in his leg and kept up with Phan toward his car. The ambulance drove off with sirens and lights blazing. Then he realized Phan was waiting for an answer. "Yes."

"It was actually a school friend, but he told us that Charlie confided in him once over one beer too many that he was here because his girlfriend and baby were killed in a car accident. He and Shelley didn't exactly have a stable relationship. Finding out about the child was what probably pushed him over the edge. I know this is small comfort at the moment, but it was only lack of opportunity that stopped him going back for Molly. The neighbor saw him helping Deacon into the car. She said he seemed unwell, and Charlie had his arm around him. When she came out to ask if everything was okay, he said Deacon had just had some bad news and he was taking him downtown.

"He told the neighbor Molly and Jamie had already left. He said his colleague would be by to check on the house and would she tell him they were safe." Phan shook his head. "She lapped it up. Never occurred to her to ask why he didn't radio it in."

"Cops tend to be believed," Maverick whispered. He'd believed him. Trusted him. Fuck, he should never have left them. "Can't you track the patrol car, though?"

"Ditched within five minutes, but we've got people checking CCTV for the Charger."

Maverick moved restlessly. He needed to do something.

"There is nothing anyone can do until we have somewhere to look. We're hoping Jamie or Molly might have heard or seen something."

Mav was never going to let Deacon out of his sight again when he got him back. And it would be *when*. He was going to tear up Atlanta until he found him.

It was amazing what a blue flashing light could do. They made it to the emergency room in half the time it would normally take, and they were both immediately shown into where Jamie was. Molly had been taken down to pediatric ICU to be on the safe side because she hadn't come around as fast as Jamie.

Jamie was sitting up in her own cubicle with a nurse checking her vitals and a doctor writing a report. She blinked back tears when Maverick came in. "How're Molly and Deacon?"

"Deacon's missing."

Jamie blanched. "And Molly?"

"You tested positive for ketamine," the doctor confirmed. "Intramuscularly, it would start to work in around three to five minutes. Molly was also given a dose, which is why she's in ICU."

Jamie's hands flew to her face. "Is she okay?"

The doctor nodded. "We need to keep a closer eye on her. There is no antidote for ketamine, and she's still very sleepy."

He needed to go see her, but Maverick was torn between that and going to find Deacon.

"I am so sorry." Jamie gulped.

Mav rushed to her side. "It wasn't your fault." *It was mine.* He should never have left them. He'd spent three fucking hours congratulating himself on getting his life back when he was putting Deacon's at risk. And Jamie's. The thought of her ending up like Rachel made him want to throw up. And for a second, all he could see were blue eyes, and he fished in his pocket for his phone. There were a few more funny messages from Deacon relating Molly's comments about his leg, but the last one killed him.

"Don't feel you have to rush. We're safe. Charlie arrived."

It had been timed nearly three hours ago. "I got a text from Deacon at two forty this afternoon saying Chaplin had just gotten there."

Jamie glanced at Phan. "He said Samson got called away."

"Arson attack three streets away. Likely staged, but the house was empty."

Jamie breathed out a sigh of relief. "Small mercy."

"Can you tell us exactly what happened?"

"He followed me upstairs. Said he wanted to check all the rooms, the windows. Said he didn't dare leave anything to chance because of you," she whispered, glancing at Mav.

"He put his head into the bathroom, and I took my gun and holster off and turned to walk to the safe. Molly," she added, and Maverick understood. She couldn't run the risk of Molly being anywhere near it if she came upstairs while Jamie was still asleep. "He overpowered me as soon as my back was turned. Injected me in my neck. If I hadn't had the cast on, I might have stood a chance."

"We also think Chaplin might have been trying to grab Molly yesterday at Target. It's completely out of his way between his apartment, headquarters, or your house," Phan said.

"But there was another cop with him," Maverick said in confusion.

"No, that's the thing. We contacted Officer Lee, who was actually on his way to start his shift. Apparently, Chaplin was just exiting Target and walking Molly to his patrol car when he saw the other cop pull in. Then a security guard ran over to him to tell him Molly's family was inside. When he got inside, I understand he pretended like he'd seen her outside and carried her back in. According to Officer Lee, that's not the case at all, but as he doesn't work with Chaplin, Lee wouldn't have thought there was anything wrong. We're checking the cameras, but we think he scooped Molly up as she came out of the bathroom. It was likely he was following you."

Jamie dropped her hand and looked at the doctor. "I want to go sit with Molly."

Maverick silently thanked his wonderful sister.

The doctor started to argue. "Ms. Stanton—"

"When Molly wakes up, she will be terrified. I'm going to stay with her until you find Deacon." She looked at Maverick. "Go bring him home."

Gladly. But where the fuck do I look?

The doctor capitulated at Jamie's insistence, and she was wheeled to the pediatric ICU.

"So where do we look first?" Maverick asked and put a hand up when he knew Phan was opening his mouth to object. "Either I come with you, or I go looking on my own. Which would you prefer?"

Phan sighed and muttered something that sounded like "stubborn bastard" but got on his cell phone as soon as they left the ER after explaining he was posting guards on the miniscule possibility Chaplin might try and snatch Molly again. "I'm not taking any chances," he said as they walked to the car.

"I'm assuming his apartment is empty?"

"The cops have it secured, but I want to swing by and take a look myself." Phan gazed at him sternly. "If I tell you anytime to stay in the car, you do it without question, or I will lock you up."

Maverick was making no promises. Ignoring his back, which now throbbed persistently, he did his best to keep up with the detective. The apartment was small, clean, functional. Not that Mav would have expected any less. Neatness was ingrained in basic training, and some never lost the habit.

"There's nothing," Officer Deene confirmed while Phan walked around. Maverick had been ordered to stay at the door, and Phan had put on gloves before he walked in.

Maverick didn't especially mind, because apart from the bedroom, it was one room, so he could pretty much see everything. Phan picked up a photo and showed it to Maverick.

It was the same one Jamie had. The one of the three of them in their flight suits. Maverick was glad Phan didn't expect him to comment. Officer Deene came out of the bedroom, holding a box of gloves. The type you found at the dentist. "I don't know if these are significant. Cops sometimes have them."

"Charlie was allergic to latex," Maverick offered.

Phan nodded. "Which may or may not explain the nitrile gloves found in the Emmanuel Jones crime scene. They weren't burned properly. Nitrile is latex-free, but it could easily be a coincidence."

Phan agreed there was nothing to see—not even a laptop—and they left to go to the station. Once there, Phan allowed him to come into the small conference room. Maverick ignored everyone's surprised looks, but he recognized Keith, who immediately asked how Jamie was, and the younger detective—Wright—who had accompanied Phan the first time he had come to Jamie's house. There were two other people, who Phan introduced as Detectives Malwecki and Smith. They had worked the Rachel Mackenzie murder in case it was decided it wasn't linked to the other two.

"I don't need to spell out that Delgardo is known to the suspect and intimately involved with the kidnap victim, Daniels, and therefore in a compromised position. However, he is also the closest thing we have to an authority on Hunter Chaplin, and we may need his input." The other detectives gave Maverick a skeptical look but held their tongues. Phan noticed. "It was Maverick who put together the connection with the dating sites and ultimately may have saved a two-year-old from also being kidnapped."

He'd been thinking about that. The dating sites and trying to remember every teasing conversation between Charlie and Cass about them, which he'd always ignored.

Malwecki spoke. "We have CCTV sightings of the Charger crossing the I-75 just past a Walmart Supercenter, then also passing Woodland Square Mall on Johnson Ferry Road heading toward East Cobb, but nothing from the Target that overlooks Roswell Road. There is one camera that's faulty, so we can't absolutely say he didn't arrive at East Cobb and turn east, but the camera a mile farther on shows nothing. He could also have stopped anywhere after Woodland Mall. It gives us, at best, an area of five square miles and a dozen places he could have hidden the car."

Phan sighed. "Then I want patrols searching the area." He stared at the map on the computer screen Malwecki had. Keith tapped an area. "There's a big self-storage area. We've contacted the manager, and he's meeting officers there. There's no records of Chaplin taking one out."

"Check his friend's name and any name you have come across in our investigation," Phan added. "Especially the girlfriend."

"And Enzio Castille," Maverick suggested. It would be beyond sick to use Cass's name, but then he guessed Charlie was beyond sick.

"There's a unit registered to a Mirabelle Castille," Detective Wright reported from where he was sitting in front of a laptop. Maverick closed his eyes in disgust.

"That is Cass's twin sister. Charlie had a thing for her at one time too, but Cass told him if he hurt her, he would break his legs. None of us thought Charlie was serious, because just after that, he started dating someone else. It may have been on the Date a Hero site."

Everyone left except Phan and his partner, and Maverick of course. "Anything else you can think of?" Phan asked.

"The dating site," Maverick said. "I'm sure Charlie mentioned a few other names, but I didn't take much notice."

Detective Wright pulled the laptop toward him, and his fingers flew faster than Maverick had seen in a while.

"He's not just a pretty face," Phan said wryly. "He should be in cybercrimes, but he gets bored."

And he must clearly be older than he looked, Maverick thought.

"Okay, I'm on as Hunter Chaplin, but his search list is huge, spanning at least four years."

Wright rattled off various names, but Mav shook his head in frustration.

Wright's fingers were quick. "I'm checking the women who listed Atlanta as their home city." Wright clicked some more keys. "Amanda Robertson?"

"I have no idea. We used to ignore him half the time."

"There is only an Amanda or Mandy Robertson who lists Atlanta as her home city. Let me get the IP address, then…."

"Don't do anything to make the search illegal," Phan cautioned.

"No need." Wright angled the screen to show the profile picture of a pretty brunette standing in front of a bar. "Mandy's." The bar's name was clearly visible, and he went on another screen.

He wrote down an address. "There's a bar in East Cobb owned by a Joshua Robertson, fifty-five years. Anyone want to bet me he named the bar after his daughter?"

Phan snatched the note. Obviously, there were no takers.

A WHIMPER. Deacon was conscious before he realized the sound had come from his own throat, which was cracked, dry. He couldn't swallow because something was in his mouth, and it was cold. Silent and very cold. With more courage than he ever thought possible, he opened his eyes, but the dark was so complete, it was as if they were still closed. Nausea swamped him right on the heels of panic, and his nostrils flared as he tried to take deep breaths. If he vomited, he might choke, and he had no intention of dying today.

He had Molly, and she needed him.

He hoped he had Maverick.

Deacon shivered and couldn't help the moan as his bands tightened. It felt like his shoulders were being pulled out of their sockets, and the stone floor was so cold. Maybe if he tried to sit up? He was lying on his side, and he did his best to shuffle, but with nothing for purchase, it was impossible. He couldn't even straighten his legs. It was like he was hogtied.

The light that flooded the space made him jerk in surprise, and he watched, desperately trying to bank down his fear as first black boots, then the rest of Chaplin came into view as Chaplin jogged down some stone steps. Deacon was in a cellar of sorts, but he didn't dare look around and belatedly wondered if he should have tried to pretend he was still unconscious.

It was far too late anyway, because Chaplin's green eyes had fixed on his own as soon as Deacon had seen him, and Deacon didn't dare look away.

"Good, you're awake," Chaplin said, like this wasn't some sick version of normal and he was just shooting the breeze.

Chaplin—he refused to think of him as Charlie—bent down and tugged at Deacon's ties. Deacon tried to swallow the gasp of pain, but as he couldn't close his lips, a small grunt escaped them. Chaplin's gaze rested on his again, about the same time as Deacon heard a noise, and hope flared for a giddy second until he saw the needle Chaplin pulled from his pocket. He tried to move, tried to struggle, but it was impossible. It took Chaplin barely five seconds until he jabbed it straight into Deacon's neck.

"Struggle all you like. You can't be heard in here, but I will be missed until we close, so I need you quiet for another hour, that's all. Ket doesn't last long, unless I gave you too much." He smiled, but the cold still in his eyes made Deacon shiver. "Or unless your body mass is too small to metabolize the dose safely."

It took Deacon a second because his vision was already blurring. *Molly?* He knew that was what Chaplin meant when he watched the horror wash over Deacon.

"It would be fitting payback. You took my child. He died in agony."

But Deacon couldn't reply. He could barely see. He tried to dredge up coherence and keep his eyes open.

But it was no use.

THE NEXT time Deacon woke, he wasn't gagged, and he tried to lick his dry lips. The sound of breathing made him wrench his eyes open. Chaplin was so close, leaning over him, holding the rag he had just removed. Deacon recoiled, but Chaplin's sharp backhand nearly put him out again. He bit back the pain as his arms were yanked forward, and he was cuffed. He was also sitting up, but still on the hard concrete floor and shivering.

Molly. The last thing Chaplin said slammed into Deacon's brain. "Molly?" He croaked the name as a question.

"She's awake, so I understand. Not that it's of any further concern of yours."

He tried to think. Deacon glanced around. He'd been right about the cellar, and there was a strange sweet smell in the air he wasn't sure about. Where the hell was he? He had no idea how long he had been unconscious. Chaplin sat back on an upturned crate, the kind bottles…. He was in a *bar*. He was sure he was. He couldn't see any evidence of it, but Noah's uncle from college had a really old bar, and Noah had shown him around. That's what the smell reminded him of.

There was no point asking why he was here. He knew that. "I didn't know."

Chaplin's eyes glittered. "It doesn't matter. You were still the reason he died."

Which was true. Chaplin was only saying what Deacon had told himself for weeks. "Yes," he acknowledged. "But that isn't Molly's fault."

"You can't stop me." Chaplin ignored him. "I was originally going for a new life. I have money, identity, but you hooking up with Maverick makes it impossible."

Deacon swallowed. He'd watched as many cop shows as the next person. Wasn't it worse if they thought they had nothing to lose? "Why?" Maybe he should try and get him talking. Give them a chance to find him. If they even knew where to look. He had no idea where he was. "There are a ton of countries in the world you could go to."

Chaplin moved fast, and Deacon instantly realized it had been the wrong thing to say before he was yanked forward by his hair. Tears stung his eyes.

"This is my fucking country," Chaplin snarled. "I *fought* for this country. I was prepared to *die* for it. You don't get to sit there like the leech you are and tell me I have to go somewhere else." He shoved Deacon away from him in disgust, and Deacon fell back, crying out at the sharp pain as the back of his head connected with the stone wall he had been leaning against. Deacon closed his eyes against the burn in them but opened them as he heard Chaplin moving something.

He lifted two jerry cans from the corner and set them next to him. Deacon didn't so much as take a breath. Chaplin was going to torch the place, torch him. He was helpless to meet Chaplin's eyes when he saw him looking, and his lips parted as if he was going to scream at what he saw in them, but he didn't seem able to make a sound.

All he could think of was what Chaplin had done to Manny and Sara Jeffries. And Sara Jeffries had still been alive while she burned.

CHAPTER NINETEEN

"EVERYTHING'S CLOSED up," Keith confirmed as he ran back to Phan's car.

Maverick had gotten out, unable to keep still. He'd thought for a second Phan would never let him come, but the fact remained that unless they had luck with Charlie's ex-girlfriend Mandy, he was still the only one who had a chance of talking to him. He had no idea what to say, but he'd been quick to point out they might need that advantage.

Phan hadn't bothered with another warning for him to do as he was told. Mav thought he knew by now if Deacon's life was on the line, Maverick would do whatever it took. They'd even tried getting Maverick to call Chaplin's phone a few times. It was turned off, presumably so he couldn't be found.

Maverick looked as APD officers hurried over with a middle-aged man and the young woman—Mandy—from the photograph. He assumed the man was Joshua Robertson, Amanda's father, and the owner of the bar.

Phan shook hands and was wary with the details, just saying there was a chance he was holding someone hostage in the cellar. Amanda looked horrified. "Hunter helped me close up. He used to come by for a drink last thing, and he'd help. I thought at first he wanted to date again, but he never made any move on me." Tears filled her eyes. "I felt sorry for him. I thought he was lonely."

Joshua put an arm around his daughter. "Makes me feel sick of the thought of going home early and leaving them here, but Mandy's mom has got MS, and she's going through a flare-up. Her sister stays with her, but it always helps if I can get home sooner."

"And did you speak to Hunter before you went home?" Phan asked.

Amanda nodded. "I'd lost my keys, so Ricky, our other barman, locked up, and Hunter drove me home."

"You lost your keys?" Maverick asked sharply.

Amanda and her father looked at him as if just noticing he was here. "I called Dad to let him know, but the takings were already in the safe, and he said they'd probably turn up in the trash where I'd dropped them by mistake in the morning."

"But you assume Hunter has them?" Joshua Robertson asked Maverick.

"I would say that's likely," Phan acknowledged.

"How did he get someone in there without anyone noticing?" Phan asked Robertson.

Amanda put her hand to her mouth. "The old cellar. The outside trap was damaged, and he said it was a security risk. He brought a toolbox from home and was going to repair it. He backed his car around to where it is, and that's at the opposite end of the parking lot."

"We don't use the cellar anymore for storage," Robertson added, "but he's right, if someone got in there, technically they could have access to the place."

Maverick's hands tightened into fists. He probably had Deacon in the car and moved him when Amanda left.

"Can you go through this plan of the building, sir?" Phan spread out a copy he had just been given of the layout.

Mr. Robertson peered at them and pointed out the cellar accessed from the trap door. "We stopped using it when I did the remodel three years ago, and the inside door to the cellar is always secure."

"Is there a key to it on Amanda's bunch?" Phan asked.

Amanda nodded. "I think so. I have a ton of keys on there I never really use, so it's quite likely."

Phan thanked him and passed the plans to the SWAT commander. Mav tried not to think about what might happen if they tried for a breach. He didn't see anywhere on those plans the cellar could be easily accessed from, but he knew they would also be trying to see if they could get listening devices anywhere near.

"He was always so considerate," Amanda whispered. "And he even texted me tonight to say he got home safely."

Maverick's ears pricked up at the same time as Phan said, "Can I see your phone?"

It was a different number. A throwaway they didn't know about. "He told me his phone had broken and he had to wait three months until his contract finished to go with another provider."

Robertson hugged his daughter. "I understand you guys have to do whatever, but I really don't want her here while you do it," Robertson said grimly, and Phan nodded, beckoning to Officer Deene.

"Can you please accompany the Robertsons home and stay with them until you hear from me." They turned and left.

"Kim?"

Maverick turned to where Detective Wright was, and Phan walked over to him. "What have you got?"

"CCTV of the Charger stopping at Home Depot early this evening. I made a phone call, and according to the receipts, he bought a heavy-duty bolt and padlock—"

"The trapdoor," Maverick said.

Wright shot him an uncomfortable look.

"What else did he buy?" Phan asked.

"Some cheap barbeque accelerant and a gas lighter. We then have him stopping at a Mobil station twenty minutes later and filling two jerry cans with gasoline."

Maverick took an automatic step forward to the bar, and Phan grabbed his arm. "I can't let you go in there." Maverick watched as two armored vehicles pulled up and SWAT climbed out of each one.

"You're going to kill him."

Phan shook his head. "We are hoping he comes peacefully—"

"I don't mean Charlie," Maverick nearly shouted, and Wright, Smith, and Malwecki all fell silent. "Chaplin's in there with fuck knows how much firepower and nothing to *lose*. He has Deacon. Chaplin's a cop. He's going to know every scenario, and the likelihood of any of them, including him getting away, is less than zero."

The pained acceptance in Phan's expression gave him no comfort. He didn't want to be right. He watched Phan order officers to surround the large parking lot. The bar used to be some sort of hotel. It was popular for weddings and other parties on weekends, but half of it was closed down during the week. Soon the whole area was cordoned off, lights were erected, and the place was surrounded. They knew Charlie had to be in there because the black Charger was around the back.

Another man in a suit got out of a car and walked briskly over to Phan. "Have we made contact?"

Phan shook his head. "We could use a megaphone, but we think he might have a cell phone we can use."

The man nodded and looked at Maverick, then inquiringly at Phan. Phan made quick introductions. "Phelps is one of our most experienced hostage negotiators."

Phelps gestured for everyone to be quiet and pressed the button to connect. It was answered with silence. "Mr. Chaplin, this is David, and I'm a negotiator with the police. I want to check if you are both okay and if you need anything down there?"

Everyone heard the laugh. "Don't bother. We're not going to be here long enough to need food, and if you send in SWAT, I will just blow everything faster." The line went dead.

"I'll try again in a minute," Phelps said confidently. "They often threaten the worst scenario right off the bat. Most people don't actually want to die; they're looking for a way out."

"Let me talk to him." Maverick held out his hand for Amanda's phone. Phan hesitated. "You have nothing to lose either," Maverick said. He met Phan's gray eyes. "Please," he whispered. "I might be the only one he will listen to."

Maverick could count every one of his thundering heartbeats until with a nod he got a tiny glimmer of hope.

He was all in.

Whatever it took to protect Deacon, he would do. For the first time in the seven months since he'd woken up in that fucking hospital, Maverick had found something—*someone*—worth fighting for. Deacon had saved him. In a few short days, he'd gone from the same future as his father to the possibility of actually being a father. And he wouldn't have ever been able to do it for himself, because he'd needed something else to care about. Someone else.

Even if Deacon didn't want him. Because right at that moment, he couldn't think about that. He'd had one thing to do in return for getting his life back, and it had been to protect Deacon. He had failed spectacularly, but if this was one more chance, he would give it everything he had.

He had the cell phone in his hand a moment later, and Detective Wright hushed everyone. It was easy to press redial, but he found Hunter's name in her contacts just to give him a second to steady his breathing. He pressed the button, willing his hands not to shake and praying with everything in him it was answered.

It connected, but Charlie didn't say a word. He wasn't stupid, and he would assume it was the cops trying again.

"Charlie," Maverick clipped into the phone, completely amazed that his voice sounded calm when everything inside him threatened to break apart.

"Well, well," Chaplin answered after a few seconds' silence. "What can I do for you?"

It was time to lay it on the line.

"You have something that belongs to me. What do I need to do to get him back?"

DEACON HAD gone from shivering violently to being in danger of falling asleep. He jerked in pain as Chaplin kicked him. "I know you're cold, but don't go falling asleep." he smirked. "Things will heat up real soon."

Deacon didn't have any spit left in his throat to swallow down his fear. "Tell me about Shelley."

Chaplin put his head back and laughed. "Keeping me talking's not going to help you, but just for the record, she was a fucking psycho."

"What?" Deacon couldn't help the involuntary exclamation.

"It was Jason who didn't deserve to die. She got exactly what she asked for, and if she didn't die then, when I found out what had happened, I would have shot the bitch myself."

"I'm sorry," Deacon offered, but there was nothing he could say.

"You will be," Chaplin confirmed, and Deacon shivered again. Not because the words were delivered with menacing intent, but because they were implacable. No way out. He watched as Chaplin stilled a fraction before Deacon heard something from upstairs as well. Chaplin swung around so fast, and everything in Deacon froze as he saw what Chaplin held in his hand.

A gun.

Deacon tried to tell himself it made sense. That seeing Chaplin holding it didn't mean he was going to die right that second. He still had time. Time to be with Molly. Time to be with his new friends. Time for a new career.

Time for a new love.

Maverick. Time to be with him. Maverick had laughed and said they could date. Then he'd stared at him with those sexy brown eyes and said it was okay so long as they slept in the same bed. Even if Mav decided in the end that Deacon was too much trouble, he desperately wanted the chance to find out.

Deacon's lips parted to take a breath, but the shrill sound of a cell phone nearly stopped his heart. Chaplin didn't jump. He looked almost resigned as he reached into his pocket with his other hand and pulled out the phone. A small smile played on his lips when he read the number, and a little hope seeped into Deacon's mind.

Chaplin answered it without saying a word. Deacon knew it was the cops, and a little bit of him died when Chaplin made it clear he wasn't interested. Chaplin turned away, listening again for sounds from upstairs. The phone rang again before he said anything. Chaplin answered, and his eyebrow raised sardonically. "Well, well. What can I do for you?"

Who was it?

Chaplin pressed the speaker button, and Maverick's voice rang out loud and clear. "You have something that belongs to me. What do I need to do to get him back?"

"*Mav?*" Deacon whispered, but Chaplin raised his gun, and Deacon clamped his lips closed. Mav meant him. Deacon belonged to Mav, and everything in him wanted it to be true.

"Deacon?" Maverick asked sharply. He didn't think Mav would have been able to hear him.

"I have my Glock 22 pointed right at his head and enough gas to light this place up so it can be seen from space. He took everything from me. Why in hell would I give him back?"

There was silence. Then Maverick spoke. "You took an oath."

Chaplin scoffed. "To protect and serve?"

"Not that one," Maverick insisted. "The one we all said over ten years ago. The one Cass, you, and I all recited ready to die for what we believed in."

"I—"

"To obey all officers, Private."

"You're not my lieutenant any longer," Chaplin said, but even as he said it, Deacon heard something in his voice. *Longing?* Did Chaplin still want the career he had been forced to give up, or was it about something else? Maybe he still wanted the family he had surrendered with the expectation of making another? Maybe the first time he had thought he belonged anywhere was with Cass and Maverick. And he had been forced to let that go.

It would never excuse the deaths he had wrought, but in a way, Deacon could almost understand it.

"You can't give me anything now, Mav," Chaplin said. "I don't have anything I want anymore, and I'm not stupid. I know I've got a needle with my name on it waiting for me out there."

Because Georgia still had the death penalty. Deacon's heart sank. What had he said about being without hope?

"Then if you've nothing to lose, we can talk face-to-face. You explain it to me so I understand. You owe me for Balcad."

Chaplin shook his head. "You taught me better than that, Mav. I know you're going to come in here intending on doing a sight more than talking. You were always the strongest out of the three of us. Faster."

"I am unarmed."

Deacon's heart sped up. "No, Mav—"

Chaplin's gun was at his temple faster than he got out another word.

There was a silence, and Chaplin smiled. "You come to the door," he said into the phone. "You have three minutes because that's how long the fuses are. I will light them before I walk to the door, so if I'm not in time to run back and put them out, the place blows. And none of the APD out there will get near enough in time, so don't bother trying to rush me." He clicked the phone off before Maverick had time to answer.

"I CANNOT possibly let you go in there," Phan said before Maverick had even had a chance to process it himself. Maverick quietly held out the phone.

"Do you have a better idea?"

Phan opened his mouth and closed it.

"Sir?" Detective Wright asked incredulously. "You can't really be considering this."

Phan just stared at Maverick, and Maverick held his gaze, calmly like he had all the time in the world, not like his life was about to implode.

"It will be your job," Wright added.

"And if we do nothing, it will be Daniels's life." Phan turned to Wright, and the other detective shut up. "He's right, though," Phan continued, glancing back at him.

"As are you," Mav replied.

Phan turned to the sergeant standing next to him. "Have we got anyone with us who can take the shot if you get a chance?"

"No," Maverick burst out. "You heard what he said. He has fuses…."

Phan shook his head. "I think that's a bluff. He didn't buy any. If he needed the lighter fuel, it makes sense he would get the fuses at the same time. He's not used fuses in any other fire, and they are incredibly difficult to time unless you happen to be an explosive expert." Phan arched a brow. "I take it he wasn't?"

Maverick frowned. "He was an avionics specialist."

"And nothing in his APD career either," Phan confirmed.

"But that's a huge risk."

"So is letting a civilian go into a situation like this, but at the moment, I have no way of luring him out. We can let the SWAT team go in, but I understand from Robertson the trapdoor has a good thirty feet of passage before the cellar we think he's in. We wouldn't have the element of surprise, and Chaplin, with nothing to lose, could take out more people along with himself and Daniels. At the moment, all I have is the chance of him coming to the main door to let you in. Now get a vest on," Phan instructed, and turned to another man standing by quietly, who Maverick noticed was in full tactical gear. The SWAT leader, he would guess.

Maverick was determined the cop who handed him the vest wouldn't see his hands shaking even if this time it wasn't because he desperately wanted a drink. He strapped it on, only half listening to the instructions the negotiator was rapidly firing at him. Then everything seemed to drop quiet again as Phan met his gaze.

"This has one objective. We want a shot. Rawlings is an ex-Special Forces marksman. All I need is for you to create the chance."

"Can you do that? Aren't you supposed to talk him down?" Maverick asked doubtfully, even though if he had a gun, he would pull the trigger to protect Deacon himself.

"I can't." Phan nodded at the guy in tactical gear talking to another two men dressed in the same way. "But they can. He has made it clear he intends to kill himself and his hostage. They have the green light."

Deacon. Every memory ran through his head like a film show. The day he had done the massage. *A slow kiss.* When Molly had peed on him and Deacon had nearly gone purple in embarrassment, and when Jamie had deliberately tried to tease him and he hadn't been fazed at all.

"Are you ready?"

Maverick nodded.

"We're trying to get listening devices, but the cellar is making things difficult. Try and get him to talk as much and as long as you can to give us time. Anything you can think of to delay him, do it."

"I understand," Mav confirmed grimly.

"Then just do what we need. Don't be a hero."

A hero? Maverick was anything but.

CHAPTER TWENTY

MAVERICK STARTED walking across the yard toward the main door with his arms up. It was awkward because he wasn't as easily balanced with his arms raised. When he got about ten feet from the doorway, it opened just a crack, and he stopped. "Charlie?"

"No, it's me." Deacon was framed in the lights from all the headlights behind Mav.

"Deacon!" Maverick yelled as his heart thudded, knowing the sniper he had seen would have a kill shot trained on whoever opened the door.

"I've been instructed to tell you unless you come inside, I will be shot in the head. He is standing behind the door."

Mav took a step and heard the croaked "Stop," and knew the word had been forced out of Deacon. Mav froze. In his mind's eye, he could see the sniper looking for an edge. Deadly force had been approved.

"He says you are to... take your leg off."

Mav jerked in shock. "What?"

"Take your leg off. He doesn't trust you."

Mav's jaw dropped. "But—"

"He says." Deacon swallowed, and Mav knew the words were being wrung out of him. "He says you have to crawl."

And in that second, Mav understood how arrogant he had been. How filled with so much conceit... it sickened him. *Don't be a hero.* But he'd thought he would be. In his head, he had decided he could save the day. He'd completely made the wrong call, and the urge to vomit nearly overpowered him. Somewhere, wrapped up in such giant hubris, he had separated the friend he had flown with from the man who had brutally murdered three people and was planning on a fourth.

The fourth who meant everything to him. For a second, Mav was dizzy with the knowledge that his egotism might cause Deacon's death. He should have left it to people who knew what they were doing. But without another word, he dropped to the dirt, rolled back his pants, pressed the button to release the suction, and pulled off his leg. He didn't throw it, but he was so fucking tempted.

Mav didn't give Chaplin the benefit of so much as a look to show his humiliation. He would crawl. He didn't care. If taking this pound of flesh from Maverick soothed the beast in front of him, he would do whatever it took. The ten-feet gap seemed to yawn wider, but then he was there, and the firm grip on his wrist pulled him through, and the door closed behind them.

And not one single shot had been fired. Charlie had been so clever, and Maverick hadn't. Mav heard a sound that made his heart stop. A whimper. His eyes focused in the semidarkness and connected with Deacon's, but before he could say a word, a Glock 22 was roughly shoved at Deacon's temple, and Mav finally looked at Chaplin. He wasn't Charlie anymore. He didn't deserve the reminder. The affection. "Why?"

"You know why," Chaplin retorted. "You said you would always look out for us."

"Don't try to make out that this was ever about me."

For a second, neither of them seemed to breathe, but then Chaplin smirked. "You're right. My life isn't yours anymore."

"It never was."

"And yet once upon a time, you would have died for me," Chaplin mused. "Now you're too busy to even make a phone call."

"I was busy doing nothing except having my own pity party."

He heard the short laugh. "How many guns did I have trained on the door?"

"A few," Mav acknowledged, knowing to admit anything less would be pointless and whatever chance he had of any sort of trust would vanish.

"And you were supposed to draw me out?"

"Of course," Maverick acknowledged, again, knowing there was no point in arguing. It had been a dumb idea.

"I haven't lit a fuse. I don't have any."

Maverick's heart jumped. "But you've still got the gas, huh?" His eyes flicked to the gun.

"Don't even think about it, or your boyfriend burns while he's awake to really enjoy it."

It was like a switch was flicked. How had Mav missed the evil in the voice of the friend he had known? He had trusted Chaplin. He would have guaranteed his loyalty right up to this second. Mav guessed somehow he had still thought of the friend who'd had his back.

Fuck. Was this his fault? No, that was even more conceited, except maybe if he had reached back out to Chaplin when he had called him and been his sounding board, he'd have... *what*? Not made the jump from having a bad day to slaughter anyone who made it so?

"There, I've even supplied the crutch you need." He waved the gun. Deacon never took his eyes from Maverick. Sad eyes. Eyes that seemed to ask why he had come. And Mav wanted to ask him how he could ever think Mav wouldn't, but the silence remained. The question and the answer were far too private.

Chaplin wouldn't take that from them as well.

"What's Balcad?" Deacon asked.

"Still trying to keep me talking?" Chaplin laughed shortly.

"Balcad is a town near Mogadishu and—" The gun pressed against Deacon's temple shut Maverick up.

They made a pathetic group walking back to the cellar. Deacon was Mav's crutch, and Chaplin's gun the motivation to keep them moving. He waved them both to the cold cellar and sat down on an overturned crate. He even lowered the gun, but Maverick knew it would barely take him a second to lift it and fire, and Mav was in no position to rush him. He couldn't even stand. Chaplin had been very clever.

"So now what?" Maverick ground out, taking a look around the room. Empty but for an old sink in the corner and the gas cans.

"I never wanted you involved," Chaplin answered.

"Then why?" Maverick asked. "Deacon had nothing to do with Jones's decision. The man was an imbecile." *Who didn't deserve to die.*

"So he insists. Have you ever seen him on stage?"

Maverick shook his head, wondering why the sudden change of subject. Apart from the few seconds he'd seen on TV when Jamie and then the reporters had shown him, Six Sundays had never been on his radar.

Chaplin smiled then fiddled with his phone. He turned it so Mav could see the screen a second before Deacon's voice seemed to fill the quiet of the cellar. It was "Only a Joker." The song that had been their number one. But even as he listened and knew the singing was good, all he heard, all he saw, were the deaths surrounding it. Something made him glance at Deacon just in time to see a single tear fall.

"Turn it off," Mav ground out and reached for Deacon's hand. The desperation and the apology were clear in Deacon's gaze. *It's not your fault.*

"So you see, shake a bit of ass, throw a kiss, and he had the girls eating out of his hand. They didn't even care he's gay." Chaplin shook his head as if that was baffling. "I mean, what's with that? Do they think love will make him straight?"

"It's an innocent fantasy," Deacon said. "And I doubt very much if there's anything sexual in it. They're kids," he said, and Maverick could hear the disgust in Deacon's tone and wanted to tell him to shut up. He squeezed Deacon's hand in warning, but it was too late.

"Kids?" Chaplin jumped up. "Shelley wasn't a kid. She *had* a fucking kid."

"You also said she was ill."

Chaplin stared at Deacon. "I think I actually called her a fucking psycho, but none of that excuses what you did."

"He didn't do anything," Mav said, trying to be reasonable and wishing he had listened to the negotiator so he would know what to say. "And you have me now. We don't need him."

Chaplin scoffed. "I don't *need* either of you."

Which was what Maverick was afraid of. If Chaplin lost all hope, he would kill them all. "Why don't you use us as a bargaining tool?"

Chaplin shot him a derogatory look.

"No, I mean it." He waved at himself. "I'm no threat to you. Tell them if they provide you with a truck, you will let him go. You can use me as a hostage."

"Or I could do it the other way around."

"You could." Maverick could almost hear the hammering of his heart. "But Deacon would need tying up to immobilize. I can't run anywhere." He could see Chaplin consider it for a second. "And you've ruined his life. What better way to punish him than to make him live as a nobody?"

Chaplin still didn't dismiss the idea.

"It's the only way you are going to get free. I'm sure you have money stashed." He'd seen the tiny apartment and knew Chaplin had never been out of work. He had money, Mav was sure of it. A flicker. A flicker of something in Chaplin's eyes. It was hope. He was sure it was hope. Chaplin fished the phone out of his pocket. "Seven missed calls," he mused. "I am popular."

He met Maverick's gaze. Whatever Mav said, he never thought Chaplin would go for it, and he knew he would have multiple guns trained on his head as soon as he appeared, but they wouldn't have a clear shot.

"So what if I do get out? What then?" Chaplin mused almost to himself. "Maybe I should ask for a million dollars while I'm at it."

He was fucking with them. Maverick knew it, and his heart sank. He wanted to scream and rail. Shout his frustration and his fear. He had made Mav crawl, but if Chaplin thought humiliation would make him what—*less*?

Less determined? Less of a threat? Less of a man?—then he didn't know his lieutenant as well as he thought he did.

Mav would beg if it made the difference between Deacon living and Molly not having someone to take her home. He would do whatever it took. He needed to get the gun. He felt Deacon shiver at his side and put his arm around him but kept his eyes on Chaplin while Chaplin stared back. He needed Chaplin to come to him. He could do fuck-all from where he was.

He saw Chaplin glance toward the gas canisters and lick his lips. Maverick stared at Charlie. He had to think of something. "I spoke to Troy."

Charlie huffed. "He was good. Heard he got a new gig."

"He had a lot of good things to say about you."

"Flattery will get you nowhere," Charlie said sarcastically, but he was still sitting.

Keep him talking. "And we spoke to Mandy outside. She said she was hoping you were going to ask her for a date."

"*It's too late*," Charlie said in exasperation.

"Here? Absolutely," Maverick agreed. "We both know that. But are you really ready to just give up? That's not the Charlie I know. That's not the Charlie who had my back more times than I care to count."

"I'm not that Charlie, Mav. I haven't been that Charlie for a long time," he whispered with finality, and Mav knew it was no use. He wasn't getting anywhere. He was out of options, and if something didn't happen fast, they were going to die.

THERE WAS something wrong. Deacon clamped down on the hysterical laugh that threatened to break free. *Something worse, then.* Maverick's gaze held his.

For once, he wasn't looking at Chaplin. Chaplin moved his head, and Deacon turned to watch. He was looking at the gas cans. Maverick squeezed his hands, and suddenly Deacon understood. Chaplin wasn't going to let them go. He was quite sure Chaplin was insane. Not that sane people couldn't commit murder, but there had been something as he was talking to Maverick. Something missing. And it wasn't just compassion, but that definitely seemed absent. What was Maverick trying to tell him?

He looked at the gun. Chaplin was big. Not as big as Maverick but certainly bigger than him, and most likely stronger. Deacon had never even held a gun, let alone fired one, and the thought he could wrestle a cop for one was laughable.

Except, they had no choice.

Then he heard a sound, they all did, and Chaplin swerved around to the stairs, and in an instant, Deacon was on his feet and lunged. But Chaplin was quicker and the gun in his face was the threat he needed to freeze. There was no other noise, but they had heard something, someone, and the knowledge was reflected in the cool green eyes staring at him.

"Char-lie," Maverick said, but Deacon noticed the fractional gap and knew Maverick was struggling to call him by the nickname.

Chaplin kept the gun trained on Deacon but glanced at Mav. "What's up there, *Mav*? Forgotten my name along with your friends?" He smiled, but the pity and condescension was evident on his face. "You didn't honestly think I was going to fall for your 'let's get out of here' speech, did you? I've planned this for months, and while I love the idea of him living with nothing, I've done that, and it's getting tiresome. He doesn't deserve to live, but for old time's sake, I'll give you a sporting chance. You have three seconds before I pull this trigger. Let's see you try and get the gun from me, huh?"

He couldn't do it; Deacon knew Maverick couldn't do it—it had to be him—and he launched himself desperately at Chaplin at the same time as the door to the cellar nearly exploded. Smoke, a flash of light so bright, and something hard hit him in his gut and he flew back. Shouts and the answering *pop pop pop* told Deacon someone had fired a gun. "Mav?" he tried to call out and shrank back as something out of a nightmare reached for him with big hands and pushed a mask against his face. For a second, he struggled to take a breath, but everything really hurt, and he suddenly wasn't interested in trying for another one.

CHAPTER TWENTY-ONE

THE SAME fucking white chairs.

Maverick had understood what had happened. He thought it likely they were listening, and as soon as Chaplin said he was going to kill Deacon, they had acted. He knew they'd had no choice.

Hearing the footsteps, he looked up immediately, watching Phan as he strode toward him. "Any news?"

Mav closed his eyes and shook his head. Deacon was in surgery, fighting for his fucking life because he'd had to do what Maverick should have done, had been trained to do. Deacon didn't know anything about guns. He wasn't trained to disarm anyone, but he'd thought he had to act because Maverick was too fucking useless to even stand up. When he'd heard the shot, he'd known from the sound it had been a .22. He'd heard them often enough, and he knew what happened even with the smoke making it difficult to see what was happening.

"I was trying to work out how to tell him I knew you would breach, but he didn't understand. He thought I expected him to try. He's gonna—"

"No, he's not." They both looked up at Jamie, balancing on her crutches. Maverick reached blindly for her, and she sank to the chair next to him and put her arms around him. For a second, he soaked up the comfort, but then he drew back. He didn't deserve it.

"This isn't your fault." It was as if she had plucked the words right out of his brain.

"He was one of my best friends," Maverick nearly shouted. "I served with him for five years. How didn't I know? How could I possibly not know?"

Jamie put her hand on his arm. "Because you're not God. I know you think you know everything, but I hate to burst your bubble."

"She's right," Phan agreed. "There were a lot of things we should have picked up on, but hindsight is a wonderful thing."

Maverick shook his head. Deacon had been hurt twice, and both times because Maverick hadn't been able to do his job. He had no business taking this on in the first place.

"We found something else out," Phan said, and Jamie nodded.

"You won't believe what Kim was told."

Kim? He looked at the detective and his sister.

"It was actually Jamie's idea, but I had one of my officers check CCTV. The car that sideswiped her originally was a Dodge Charger, a black one."

Mav looked at them both. "But there's no way he could have known."

"He was in Keith's office when he took my call after Shirley rang me about Deacon. I wanted his opinion. Chaplin was just getting a chewing out for being late, and Keith made Chaplin wait while he did a background check for me."

"He didn't want Deacon to have any sort of backup. We've also got warrants to confirm his IP address. We have all his social media access and can prove he arranged to meet Rachel Mackenzie."

"Is he alive?" In all the panic about Deacon, he had never given the bastard a thought.

"For now," Phan said grimly, and Mav watched Phan and Jamie share a look. Chaplin had been right about that. He did have a needle with his name on it waiting for him.

They all looked up as the swing doors opened and the doctor walked over to them. "Mr. Daniels's family?"

"Yes," Maverick croaked and stood up.

The doctor focused on him. "He's out of surgery and will be taken to ICU. The bullet nicked his left ventricle, so no pulmonary veins, thank goodness, and thanks to the paramedics on standby, his heart was still beating when he got here. I won't lie, he's lost a tremendous amount of blood, but he's been lucky. You will be allowed to see him for a very short period of time once he gets settled, so I suggest you wait here."

Maverick sat back down, and Jamie squeezed his hand. "I ought to get back to Molly."

He'd never asked. "How is she?"

"Bright as a button and wants to know where Uncle Danny is." Jamie pressed her lips together and blinked a few times.

"How about you let me be your chauffeur, and I'll go grab a wheelchair?" Phan said kindly. "You shouldn't be walking on that ankle."

Jamie smiled and acquiesced. Phan walked away. She took Mav's hand. "He will be all right. I know he will. As soon as you hear anything, you tell me. Phan says he will have someone outside of both ICUs all night." She looked out the window. "Day," she amended.

Maverick nodded. He must have been sitting here longer than he thought. After another minute, Phan returned with a wheelchair and a coffee for Maverick.

"Anything you want—food, clothes, a break—the nurses know to call me."

Maverick was surprised, but then, the way Phan had looked at Jamie, maybe he shouldn't be.

It was nearly another three hours before they let Maverick in to see Deacon. His blood pressure was dipping dangerously low, and he was on a ventilator. Mav was nearly beside himself between the real terror Deacon wasn't going to make it and the absolute conviction he was responsible for it. In the end, he was convinced the nurses let him in because they took pity on him, and he hadn't done or said anything to draw attention to the fact he was still sitting there an hour after the nurse had decreed he would be allowed to stay for five minutes.

And held his hand. The nurse had said Deacon was a fighter, but Maverick knew that already. The way he had stepped up for Molly after everything he had gone through showed that. And in the cellar. He had tried to take on an armed cop. A trained serviceman. And he had stepped up because the man who should have done it couldn't do so.

The whole time Mav had served with Chaplin kept running through a loop in his head. The first time they had met. Maverick had just been posted to Iraq that time, and Chaplin was his technician. Chaplin had the experience a junior pilot didn't have, and that's why they had been put together. And he had slotted right in with him and Cass. Five years, they had been together, Iraq twice, home, Somalia. Plus, the rest.

I should have known. And he should have.

"Name's Hunter Chaplin, but everyone calls me Charlie."

And Mav had shaken hands and introduced himself as Delgardo. Charlie's eyebrows had gone up.

"No first name?"

And Mav had blushed or as much as he could do and be noticeable. "It's Mav."

"Mav?" Charlie had repeated doubtfully. "What kind of a name is—" And he'd caught on immediately and laughed. The bastard had laughed until he cried, and Mav had to stand there and take it, and then when he had sobered up, he had put on his shades and said he thought he should be called Iceman.

And he would hum the fucking soundtrack for Top Gun *every chance he got.*

And they had been friends. Friends for life, they always said. Then Maverick had forgotten. And Charlie had killed people.

"Mr. Delgardo?"

Mav looked up to the same doctor who had operated on Deacon. He stood with difficulty. "He's stable and his blood pressure is where we want it to be. I'm not going to take him off the ventilator until tomorrow because I want him to remain sedated to give everything a chance to start healing." He smiled. "You really ought to go home."

"I heard…." He felt useless. "I heard that patients even on a ventilator can hear you."

The doctor's eyes softened. "You weren't talking."

"I was worried the nurses would kick me out if I made a noise."

Dr. Granger—according to his name tag—chuckled. "You can stay, and yes, there are a lot of accounts of people being in comas who have given quite accurate accounts of conversations they have heard, but this is a *medically induced* coma. He is sedated deliberately, and it's not exactly the same."

"Will I be in the way?"

Granger shook his head. "I don't think so, but it's the nurses' decision. I just do as I'm told." He lowered his voice. "I will tell them I have no objection."

At the last second, Mav remembered to thank him and they shook hands.

IT TOOK two days.

Two days of sitting in more white chairs, sometimes by Deacon's bedside, sometimes in the corridor while the nurses saw to Deacon and the doctors examined him. He didn't know what he would have done without Phan, who brought him a change of clothes and kept feeding him. Then yesterday, he had driven Molly home with Jamie, and Loretta had even volunteered to stay for a few days to make sure they were okay.

He'd seen Jamie a few times when Molly had been asleep, but he hadn't been able to face seeing the little girl himself.

He wanted a drink.

He desperately wanted to feel the smooth liquid bathe his scratchy throat.

Just one. He wouldn't do anything to risk his license now he had his freedom.

Just one.

But even as he was saying it, he knew it was a lie.

Then the slight squeeze of his hand took away any thought except the man lying in front of him.

And he opened his eyes. Deacon couldn't talk because of the tube, but they soon dispensed with that, but then what seemed like every fucking doctor in the hospital wanted to see him, and Maverick was back outside. He wasn't Deacon's next of kin, he was told very gently like he was *five* when he made a fuss.

But then another hour and everyone had left, and the nurse came for him. Deacon looked better. All the tubes were out, just the one IV. He had his eyes closed. "He's sleeping, but he's going to be fine," the nurse said and smiled. "We're moving him to a general ward in an hour."

Maverick nodded. Relief flooding him and making him giddy. He was going to be fine. *They* were going to be fine.

"He's been very lucky," the nurse said.

Maverick stilled and turned to look at her. He'd seen her a few times, but not yesterday. "Yes," he said agreeing. Hoping she would elaborate.

She looked at him, probably realizing she shouldn't have said anything. "Well, he's okay now," she murmured and left.

Mav slid down in the chair and took Deacon's hand. He wasn't Deacon, though. He was Daniel, and he wondered what he would want Mav to call him—if anything. Because he'd nearly fucking died, and Mav hadn't been able to do shit about it. He gazed at the limp hand in his larger one, and he suddenly felt big and ugly and so fucking useless.

"Mav?" Maverick turned to see Keith, Jamie's old partner, by the door of Deacon's room. "Is everything okay?" He took in Mav's expression and glanced at Deacon.

Mav nodded, not able to say the lie out loud. "What is it?"

Keith winced, which drew Maverick's attention, and Keith glanced back to the bed. "Out here?"

Maverick caught the nurse's eye to indicate he was just stepping out. She smiled cheerfully, and he knew Deacon would be watched.

"I know you've been a little busy, so you probably haven't heard, but Chaplin was up before the judge, and he's locked up awaiting trial."

Maverick expected nothing less. Keith sighed. "This morning he was shanked on his way back from the shower. He's alive," Keith tacked on hurriedly.

Maverick swallowed and tried to feel a little remorse. But he didn't want him to die.

"He's here guarded."

"He is?"

Keith scrubbed his jaw. "It was too serious for their medics. He had to be operated on. I've kept Jamie up to date, and I'm arranging extra security. I've just come from there—"

"And why are you telling me?" Maverick interrupted, but he had an awful feeling he knew.

"I said I would ask."

"He wants to see me?"

"Some idiot of a nursing assistant told him you were here."

"Why the fuck should I see him?"

"No reason whatsoever," Phan said, joining them and shooting a glare at the sergeant. "And to be honest, I'd rather you didn't."

Mav clasped Keith's arm as he took a step away. "I'll give him five minutes." He didn't owe him squat, but maybe if he listened for five minutes, it would help the guilt. The unrelenting feeling that this was his fault. That he should have known. He had to get rid of it, or they would have no future. He'd even spent the last few hours looking at Realtors' sites while he sat in those chairs. There was a house in the same community as Jamie with a big yard and a tree that was just begging for a tree house.

He would do this and be done. Put it behind him.

"Then I go with you," Phan said. Maverick followed Phan past the three guards into a separate room that was a short five-minute walk away from ICU, which didn't thrill Mav at all, but Phan told him he would be going back to prison tomorrow. He stopped outside the room door while Phan showed his ID to the officer on duty and explained who Maverick was. Chaplin must have heard because he opened his eyes and fixed them on the door. Maverick stared at him for a long moment. If he had looked smug or satisfied, Mav would have turned back around and gone back to Deacon, knowing the only other time he would ever have to see him was when he was tried for murder.

And convicted.

He pushed the door open and took three steps toward the bed. The nurse asked Phan something, and Phan paused at the door. Chaplin was handcuffed to the rails. "I didn't think you would come." He frowned. "Do you need to sit—"

"No," Mav bit out. "I won't be staying that long."

Chaplin nodded. "I just wanted to say something." He took a long breath and glanced at the detective, who was nodding at something the nurse was telling him.

"I'm listening." Knowing what Chaplin had done. Knowing what he had *nearly* done was making Mav's skin crawl.

"I have money."

Maverick frowned. What had that got to do—

"And I'm going to be in prison for either a long time or the rest of my life." A corner of his mouth turned up. "Whichever comes first."

Maverick didn't respond.

"So, I'm never going to spend any of it."

"I don't want it, and neither does Deacon, if that's where this is going."

And Chaplin smiled. He smiled so wide, it made Mav feel nauseous. "Oh no, I didn't mean that. But you do have a choice. I'm told by my attorney I could live for years even on death row. It's very common. What I mean is as soon as I get back there, I will put feelers out—shouldn't take long—to see who knows someone who can do a task for me."

Maverick knew he should walk away, but the dread in his belly seemed to cement his feet to the floor.

"Back to the choice. You walk away from Daniels. You stay away from Daniels, or not only do I make sure he dies, but the child will go too." He closed his eyes. "I'm reliably informed I can get it done for five thousand dollars."

"Get what done?" Phan came up to the bed.

But Maverick couldn't reply. He would be lucky not to vomit what little he had eaten. He simply turned away from the bed and walked away and kept walking.

Phan caught up with him by the entrance doors. "Mav, what did he say? What's wrong?"

"Nothing," Maverick clipped out and hailed the nearest cab. He opened the door and looked at Phan. "It's just been a shit day, and I need a drink."

Fuck, did he ever.

CHAPTER TWENTY-TWO

A week later

"Is THIS seat taken?"

Maverick looked up, ready to belittle the cheesy line, and stiffened in shock. "You can't be here."

Deacon smiled. "My doctor would probably agree," he said, and he beamed at the bartender and ordered a caffeine-free Diet Coke with extra ice and no lemon. "Not that you would know what my postoperative instructions are."

Mav stared back at his drink. At the Jack and Coke. The same one he had been ordering on the hour every hour and leaving untouched for the past fuck knew how many days. He didn't care. "I mean it," Mav ground out. "Please go." His hand shook with the desperate need to touch the one next to him.

"Says who?" Deacon retorted and took a sip.

"It isn't safe," Mav burst out and glared again when he noticed Deacon rubbing his chest. "Shit, Deacon," Maverick moaned in despair. "You can't be seen with me." He'd picked the first place he had seen to rent nearest a bar, and as far from Deacon, Molly, and Jamie as he could get until the trial was over. Then he was going for good, and none of them would see him again. He swiped a tired hand over his face and wasn't surprised when it came back a little wet. He was pathetic. "You should probably still be in the hospital."

Deacon shook his head. "No, I got discharged." He looked at the clock on the wall above the bar. "An hour ago."

Mav's jaw dropped. "Then what the hell are you doing here?" He glanced at the door. "Please, Deacon, just go home. To Jamie's," he added. "You two can stay there as long as you like. You won't see me; I moved out."

"Yeah, I understand, into that rat-infested hovel you call an apartment."

Mav scowled again. It wasn't that bad, and he'd needed all his money to transfer into the account he'd opened for Deacon and Molly. It was never too early to start thinking about college. And how did he know about the apartment? "Phan." Who was now dating his sister. She had finally decided her ex could see his daughter whenever possible but had firmly relegated him to the ex pile.

Harvey Richards seemed to have been relegated to the friend or the "not in this lifetime" pile. And Mav had never been back since the day he left Chaplin and eventually confided in Jamie why. And he'd also pointed out someone couldn't be with them every second of every one of Chaplin's miserable days, and she had understood. But in all the days after, when she had called him, she had never mentioned Deacon once, and it had killed Maverick not to ask.

Which she was probably counting on.

Maverick threw a fifty on the bar and stood up. "Then if you're not going, I will."

Maverick walked out of the bar, closely followed—he knew—by Deacon. He stopped at the sight of Kim Phan leaning on the truck outside. "This your ride?"

Deacon nodded. "I asked him to explain because you might not believe me." And he winced and rubbed his chest.

Fuck. "Get inside the damn car."

"If you promise to listen." Deacon took his hand, and for a second, Maverick wanted him to never let go. He eyed Phan.

"This isn't safe. You know it isn't." Because he knew Jamie would have told Phan.

Phan lowered his voice. "Get in the car."

Mav sighed and did as he was asked, but only because he didn't want Deacon either standing up or visible, and turned to Phan. He hadn't followed Deacon into the back seat. He didn't trust himself to.

"At seven forty-five this morning, guards found Hunter Chaplin bleeding out on the floor of the showers. He didn't make it to the hospital this time. He was pronounced dead on the scene." For a second, Maverick didn't breathe.

"But?"

Phan held up his hand. "And before you ask, my contacts have spoken to Larry 'the King' Ricshon, and in return for certain privileges—a conjugal visit—he has confided that yes, Chaplin did make inquiries about the threat to Molly, Deacon, and Jamie. Unfortunately he picked the wrong person. When Jamie was a beat cop over twenty years ago, she got called to a domestic about a guy who was trying to beat up his wife. Apparently the cop she was riding with said the call from that address came weekly, and they were wasting their time because the wife would never give evidence. Jamie refused to comply and got there just in time to save her life. Larry—seven at the time—was hidden in the wardrobe where his mom had shoved him when Daddy got nasty. Larry has never forgotten it and now considers the debt paid," Phan said. "Of course, all this is off the record. We have no witnesses, and this is pure hearsay."

"So, it's over?" Maverick trembled.

"Yes." Phan had the car moving a moment later.

"Stop," he croaked out.

Phan blew out an exasperated breath. "He's dead. He can't hurt anyone. He didn't put out a contract."

"I know." And Maverick smiled for the first time in over a week.

"Then why am I pulling up?" Phan asked.

Maverick turned to meet Deacon's hopeful gaze. "Because I want to get in the back."

IT TOOK another four weeks before Deacon was well enough to go house hunting. The apartment idea had gone out the window when Mav had shown him the Realtor's listing on the house five minutes away from Jamie with a yard and a tree and—Molly insisted—somewhere for a dog.

"You're going to get her a puppy, aren't you?" Deacon asked in resignation when she was bathed and finally asleep on the pull-out bed in Melanie's room. Jamie and Kim were out on a date, and Mav and Deacon had enjoyed a lazy evening and some quiet time for just the two of them.

"It's a good way of teaching her responsibility," Maverick murmured and nibbled across the bottom of Deacon's jaw.

And they had talked endlessly for the four weeks. Talked about how difficult—how new—their relationship was. Maverick had said he would stay in his apartment because he didn't want Deacon to think his safety ever came with conditions. Leaving the night he had found out they were finally free of Chaplin's threat had nearly killed them both, and it had lasted a week until Molly had burst into tears at bedtime, stamped her foot, and wanted to know why Uncle Mav didn't love them anymore.

Deacon had folded his arms and stared at him with the same challenge in his eyes, and Mav hadn't left either of them again.

Deacon dropped a kiss on Maverick's bare chest. "There was something I wanted to ask you when we were in the cellar with Chaplin."

Maverick's eyebrows rose.

"What was it about Balcad he didn't want you to say?"

"I saved his ass. We were picking up some troops, and he'd gotten drunk the night before. Made a rookie mistake that could have gone badly wrong, but I caught it in time. He could quite easily have been on his way home that time." Maverick smoothed a blond hair away from Deacon's eyes. "Did you hear from your mom?"

"If you count the letter from her lawyer confirming they wouldn't be contesting any custody and she understands that. Apparently the business is sold, and it's likely Percy may even do some time."

"I don't know how she can stay with him after the others came forward." Percy had apparently sexually assaulted two other employees. Phan had shared that tidbit last week.

Deacon shrugged. "She's buried her head in a bottle for years. Why should now be any different?" He slapped a hand over his mouth, and Mav chuckled at his horrified expression. No alcohol ever again for him. What he had now was way better. Deacon blinked up at him. "Did I ever tell you I had no filter?"

"Uh-huh," Mav chuckled and slid farther down in the bed, taking Deacon with him. "I have my last fitting appointment tomorrow and a job interview at three with Delta."

Deacon huffed. "I'm not sure I like the idea of you in that sexy pilot's outfit with all those flight attendants rushing to obey your every whim."

Mav grinned. "Says the man who's just got a narration contract for a romantic suspense novel. Think of all your adoring fans."

Deacon smirked. "I'll be thinking of you when I read it."

"Why," Mav said suspiciously. "What's it called?"

Deacon threaded his fingers through Maverick's. "In Safe Hands."

Mav smiled and bent down to kiss him. "And you always will be."

Enhanced World: Book One

Talon Valdez knew when he transformed into an enhanced human, his life and his dreams were finished. Reviled, mistrusted, and often locked away, the enhanced were viewed as monsters, despised by the public, and never trusted to serve in the military or any law enforcement agency.

Years later he gets a chance to set up a task force of enhanced to serve in the FBI, but with one proviso: each enhanced must partner with a regular human.

Finn Mayer dreamed of joining the FBI from the time he was fourteen and made every possible sacrifice to make it happen, including living with his selfish mother and bullying, homophobic brother and never having a boyfriend. But his undiagnosed dyslexia stopped his aspirations dead in their tracks. His last chance is to partner with Talon, an enhanced with deadly abilities who doesn't trust regular humans with their secrets and wants Finn to fail.

Four weeks to prove himself to the team. Four weeks for the team to prove itself to the public. And when another group threatens their success—and their lives—four weeks for them to survive.

www. dreamspinnerpress.com

CHAPTER ONE

FINN MAYER was so excited, his hands shook as he tried to open the official-looking letter. This was what he'd always wanted. This was what he had dreamed about every day. This was why he did six long years at college while slogging his ass for minimum wage. *Regretfully we have to inform you....* The rest of the words blurred as his heart plummeted. He held the letter out so he didn't get tears on it and blinked furiously. It wasn't possible. He'd convinced himself it would be a conditional offer of acceptance, which was almost a guarantee. He'd just had to get through the poly, the personal interviews when they called him back, and references. What had happened? What had he done wrong?

The screen door slammed, and Finn stuffed the letter in his pocket quickly before his older brother, Deke, saw it.

Deke stood in the doorway, absently scratching his crotch. He was thirty-seven but looked a good ten years older. His balding sandy-brown hair was going gray at the temples. His double chin burst from his collared shirt, just like his beer gut spilled over his wrinkled suit pants. Finn was too distracted to even crinkle his nose in disgust.

The screen door slammed again, and his mom's voice piped up. "Finn, did you start supper?"

"Yeah, Finn," parroted Deke. "Did you start supper?"

Finn ducked his head and brushed past Deke into the kitchen. He knew Deke wouldn't get into anything with him while his mom was there. Not that he was convinced she would care if he did. "I just got in, Mom. I'll start now," Finn said woodenly. He needed to think, but he couldn't disappear until they were eating.

His mom narrowed her eyes and followed Finn with her gaze as he opened the cupboard and took out a bag of potatoes. "Finlay," she sighed disapprovingly. "You know your brother works incredibly long hours to support this family. It isn't much to ask for a little help around here while he's providing a roof over all our heads."

Finn didn't reply and quickly started peeling potatoes. The "incredibly long hours" were a joke. Deke took twice as long to do anything because he was too lazy. Finn knew he and his other two cronies—Albert Crawford, the bank manager, and Desmond Attiker, the local deputy sheriff—could always be found in Alma's Café on Main Street, having at least a two-hour lunch every day. It was pointless to argue anyway, and his mom knew full well half of Finn's wages also went to pay for the upkeep of the so-called roof. The only thing that had stopped him from moving out years ago was the fact that he wanted Deke not to make waves with his application when the FBI did the family interviews, and even the rent Deke charged him was cheaper than getting his own place.

What had he done wrong? He knew he wouldn't have failed the poly. His boring existence contained no secrets to keep. Well, maybe one, but Finn was so far in the closet, he was almost able to pretend it wasn't real.

And Deke would never think Finn had a chance of getting accepted into the FBI, so he wouldn't have bothered trying to sabotage it by giving him a crappy reference.

Finn fisted his hands, the peeler cutting into his palm. It was impossible. They'd made a mistake. Deke couldn't have been right, not now, not after all this time.

He'd laughed hysterically when Finn told him the reason he wasn't joining him at the insurance company Deke owned, as his mom and brother expected, was because he needed to attend college full-time. Deke had insisted college was a complete waste of time and Finn just needed to join the real world, but Finn could think of no greater torment than working with Deke for the rest of what he knew would be a miserable life. There were only so many online courses he could cope with for another reason, which meant he had to be physically present in class at least three days a week. The entry requirements for the FBI were tough, and as law and order, languages, and computer sciences were all impossible for him, the only other recommended professional field they would take from was accounting.

Finn had stacked shelves at the local Z-Mart since he was thirteen. Mr. Jacobson was blind, and Finn had discovered accidentally that he was being robbed by his

CPA. Finn had been asked to copy some papers for Mr. Jacobson, and Finn, quick with numbers, had noticed the discrepancy straight away. Mr. Jacobson was eternally grateful, and Finn had taken over his bookkeeping when he was seventeen, then studied it at college. In return Mr. Jacobson had exaggerated his professional ability on his references.

Mr. Jacobson had recently accepted an offer for his two stores and had told Finn he was retiring. The thought that he had a prospective FBI agent stacking shelves for him for years had always tickled the old man, and he'd been happy to help.

Finn could feel the letter rustle in his pocket as he moved to fill the pan with water. *Ten years.* Ten years since his school had two agents come and talk to their class as part of a college awareness scheme. Cookeville High School, Iowa, had a really low rate of seniors going to college, and the new principal had tried to change all that by bringing in what he thought might be tempting job opportunities.

It worked with Finn. At fourteen he was hanging with an increasingly wilder crowd. His reading challenges just about turned him off school. He was lucky, really. Were it any major city, his crowd would already be doing drugs and probably stealing. It was only the lack of opportunity that kept his nose clean up to that day. He walked out of that lecture theater completely changed. He wasn't stupid, though. His dad was the only one he told, and his dad promised not to mention it.

His dad. The knife trembled in his hands as he chopped the potatoes. Three years didn't dim the memory of him coming home one day to find his dad had finally lost his battle with depression and blown the back of his head off with his old service revolver. Another souvenir he got from the Vietnam War.

He never forgave his mom for her part in it. Every day she was out on one of her committees or seeing her friends. Her hair done, her nails carefully manicured. The cab fares because she never learned to drive and wasn't willing to. It never occurred to her to get a job, to help his dad when he needed a newer power chair. The endless arguments Finn could hear because his bedroom was right next to theirs. How, if his mom could drive, they could start going out together.

He never forgot the last one, though. When his dad quietly asked if the reason they never went out together anywhere was because she was ashamed of being seen with a cripple, as he bitterly called himself.

Finn had held his breath as he lay in his dark room, staring up at the ceiling, waiting for the denial that never came from his mom's lips. The next day he came home early from college because a tutor was sick and found his dad. The powder burns around his mouth, the blood, and brains all over the wall behind him.

Finn nearly threw the peeler in the sink. His mom got out the store-bought pie she purchased that morning. He laughed giddily. He could go rob a bank, take drugs, *have sex*....

Tears sprung to his eyes, and he blinked rapidly so his mom wouldn't notice. No one knew he was gay. No one. Not the FBI because he'd read on an internet forum that, while they didn't discriminate, it could sometimes be the difference between being accepted or not. Apparently it was something guys could be blackmailed over. So he played the game. Took a girl to prom. Had occasional college dates. Nothing serious. No one knew he'd never slept with a guy. No one knew he'd never actually had sex with a girl either. He had plenty of jerking-off material in his bedroom and made sure he had enough copies of female tits in case Deke ever came snooping. His favorites he could pass off as sports magazines. He never even dared get a porn subscription. He was pathetic.

Finn dried his hands and mumbled to his mom about not being hungry. He was going to start right now. He was going to get a decent job, move to a big city, and subscribe to the most expensive porn site he could find.

"Des Attiker told me he had one of those weirdos in lockup today," Deke said as he passed.

His mom made a sympathetic noise.

"Should have 'em put down at birth." Deke took a swig out of the beer bottle he was holding. "There's actually some talk about them being allowed in law enforcement."

His mom followed Deke into the lounge. "What, actually to become cops, you mean?"

"Yeah, Des says they're lazy bastards and he'll never accept one working for him."

Finn tried to tune him out. Deke was like 50 percent of the human population: completely against the enhanced humans being trusted to do any sort of government work whatsoever. Finn never usually rose to anything he said, but keeping the peace didn't matter anymore. He didn't need to shut up and take whatever crap came out of Deke's mouth. Finn was going to shoot him down when his mom spoke up and silenced him.

"You remember Adam, Finlay? If you ask me, his poor mother should have disowned him years ago for all the trouble he brought their poor family." His mom clucked unsympathetically.

Finn's feet froze just as he was about to disappear into his room. "Adam? Adam Mackenzie?" Finn added for clarification, but he knew it wasn't necessary. He knew exactly who his mom meant.

Finn and Adam had been best friends all through elementary school. They pored over the old car magazines Adam's brother got. They played on the same soccer team. Finn found math easy and helped Adam, and Adam explained his English questions to Finn when the words never seemed to be in the right order on the page. He also read to Finn when Finn struggled to do it himself.

Then he went to Adam's house one morning, as he always did to catch the bus together, and heard hysterical screaming before he was halfway up the path. Adam's big sister opened the door, crying, and said Adam was sick and wouldn't be going to school that day. Finn bit his lip in worry. It sounded like something awful was happening inside, and he wanted to make sure Adam was okay. But at eleven years old, there wasn't much he could do, so he spent a miserable day at school and then rushed back to Adam's as soon as he jumped off the school bus and his feet hit the pavement.

Finn arrived to find an ambulance and two black cars parked outside. His heart nearly bounced out of his chest, and he dropped his schoolbag and ran down the path just as the door opened.

Finn screeched to a halt and stared in horror as Adam was led outside with his hands tied. Special zip ties, the sort Finn knew were used on the enhanced because some of them could do clever things with locks and metal. He knew that because Deke's friend Des had just gotten a job at the sheriff's office and told him how they were taught to use them on the vermin, which

Deke had thought funny. Finn didn't understand then who Deke meant by vermin, but everything was crystal clear now, and he spent the next thirteen years remembering that moment.

Adam was crying hysterically and pulling against the two cops leading him away. He was in such a state that he never even saw Finn, and after the cops unsuccessfully tried to make Adam walk, one of them just picked him up, and Finn saw his face and finally understood.

The small jagged mark under his left eye was livid on his skin. That was when Finn started crying as well, because he knew Adam would never be back at school and he'd just lost his best friend.

Finn never saw Adam again. Adam's family moved away shortly after. Finn's mom said they couldn't deal with the stigma, the shame.

"I heard he might get locked up for good, finally. New York. They'll throw away the key. Good riddance, I say."

Finn rounded on his mom in fury. "Good riddance? He was a child when they took him away. Eleven fucking years old and sent to live in a prison for doing nothing wrong other than waking up one morning with a mark on his face. How would you feel if it had been Deke or me? Would you have called the cops on one of us?" It wasn't compulsory. The police only ever got involved if the child's abilities were deemed dangerous and the parents couldn't cope.

His mom started spluttering about Adam turning out no good, in and out of prison for petty crimes after he aged out of the foster system, and how his mom was a saint for still going to visit him.

The horror of his mom's words finally sank in. "You told me you didn't know where they'd moved to. How do you know his mom is so upset?" Finn pressed his lips together in anger as his mom reddened slightly. "You knew," he accused. "All these years you've known where they lived."

He could have gone. Maybe found out where Adam was. Told his best friend a small scar made absolutely no difference to him. That he was important to Finn, even if he was no longer important to anyone else.

"How could you? All those years I begged you to try to find out." Finn swallowed the bitter taste of betrayal.

"You don't want to go near any of their sort," Deke said, unimpressed and uncaring. "They might infect you, give you something."

"Infect me?" Finn repeated incredulously. "It's a genetic condition, not a fucking disease," he shouted. "You really are as fucking stupid as you look."

Deke opened his mouth, but his mom beat him to it. "Finlay Mayer, I won't have such disgusting language in this house. While your brother is providing a roof over your head out of the goodness of his heart, you will show him proper respect."

Finn laughed shortly. That was it. The only upside of the fuckup his life had become. He could leave. He was finally free. He didn't have to worry about any interviews anymore or swallow Deke's daily insults and goading. He didn't even bother to respond to his mom. He just walked toward his room to pack his stuff.

He could feel his phone vibrating in his pocket as he headed to his room and absently answered it. He wasn't really listening to the man on the other end of the call; he was too busy seeing Adam's face in the same nightmare he'd had for thirteen long years.

FINN WAS exhausted. Two days later he was still reeling from the telephone call that threw all his plans for porn sites out the window. Apparently they had made a *mistake*, and should he want to discuss a possible future with the FBI, he should be present at this meeting. He also should tell no one except his next of kin, which was all kinds of weird. He had absolutely no fucking idea why the hell he was currently standing outside the FBI field offices in Tampa, Florida. Since when did new FBI recruits get trained in field offices?

He even challenged the agent he spoke to on the phone, not trusting Deke to have found out and somehow set the whole thing up as an elaborate joke. Agent Gregory, Assistant Special Agent in Charge, as he had introduced himself, just sounded amused and told him to call back on the telephone number he was sending to his phone. After Finn was directed back to the same agent after calling a very official-sounding main switchboard, Finn's apologies were cut off with another laugh, and he was told being cautious was a good attribute to have in a trainee.

His second connecting flight from Des Moines was grounded due to "technical difficulties," which meant he was on standby for over eleven hours because it was spring break, and they wanted him to go to one of the busiest tourist areas in the entire Western Hemisphere.

He left home before either his mom or brother woke up and decided to leave a note just saying he was going to do some traveling. He wouldn't give either of them a chance to jinx this until he found out exactly what *this* was.

Which was why, after over twenty-four hours, he was standing there, sweating in what felt like hundred-degree heat in a very rumpled suit and tie. It was his only suit, the one he got for his dad's funeral. He had no idea what to wear, but the agents he met all through the interview process were dressed in suits, so he copied them.

Finn stared at the huge building in front of him. It looked new. At least four stories high and next to one of the many Florida lakes. The access from the road was dominated by a big gatehouse with guards stopping every vehicle that tried to enter. Finn heaved his bag, which hadn't seemed that heavy yesterday when he started carrying it, but now felt like there was an elephant nesting in there. He blew a breath out and wished he hadn't finished his last bottle of water in the cab. He walked toward the guard, who carried a very respectable-looking MP5 slung over one shoulder. He put his bag down and introduced himself and tried to explain why he was there.

Finn was completely convinced he sounded more and more suspicious until he mentioned Agent Gregory's name and the guard checked the list of expected visitors and immediately waved him forward. Another guy in a suit, looking a lot cooler than Finn, met him at the door.

"Hi, I'm Agent Fielding—Drew Fielding." He seemed pleasant, with reddish brown hair and brown eyes. Clean-shaven and "buttoned up," as his brother would have said—not always a compliment, coming from Deke. Finn grimaced at his sweaty palms and resisted the urge to wipe his hand down the front of his pants before they shook. Agent Fielding didn't seem to notice anything, though, and led Finn through a door past a large reception desk. He waved at a couple of doors as they went past. "I'll give you the proper tour after you've spoken to Agent Gregory."

And eight hours sleep, a shower, and a gallon of water.

Finn licked his dry lips. He debated whether to ask why he was here and not at Quantico, then thought discretion might be in order and he should wait until he saw A-SAC Gregory. Agent Fielding took a turn to the right and started up some steps—some very narrow back stairs he thought no visitors were ever likely to see. In fact, Finn was convinced they were the step version of the service elevator. It was getting weirder and weirder, and he was getting hotter and hotter, despite considering himself physically fit and despite the air blasting out. At least there was no way he was going to take his jacket off, even if it was appropriate. His shirt would be soaked through.

Agent Fielding stopped at what seemed to be the fourth floor, and they entered a plain unmarked door into a small, unmanned reception area. Just a few chairs and a vending machine graced the lobby. Agent Fielding waved toward a chair. "Take a seat."

Finn swallowed and looked at the vending machine. "Do you mind?"

Agent Fielding followed his gaze. "Sure, sorry. I should have asked."

Finn put his hand in his pocket for some change, but Agent Fielding continued. "It's free. It's just a good way of keeping it cold." He smiled and disappeared through another door.

Finn eagerly pressed the button on the machine, and it dropped a bottle of water. He'd gotten the cap unscrewed before he sat, and half the contents drunk before he stretched his legs out. He could feel the water cooling his throat. He stared around him. Not what he imagined a field office would look like. He expected it to be busier somehow. If it weren't for the official phone call he'd made, he would still suspect this was all an elaborate hoax. Finn finished his water and looked again at the closed door Agent Fielding had disappeared through.

He sighed heavily and rubbed a hand over his tired eyes. He was never able to sleep when he was traveling. Not that he'd done much except by car. He'd flown more in the last twenty-four hours than he had in his life. Finn stifled a yawn and got to his feet stiffly. If he wasn't careful, he'd be asleep.

"And what use do you think he's going to be?"

Finn turned and faced the closed door the angry voice could be heard from. Finn's heart sank. He hoped to God they weren't talking about him. A quieter voice he couldn't make out responded briefly. It sounded like a third voice joined in.

Finn was wondering whether to risk sitting down again when the door burst open and Agent Fielding stormed out. Without so much as a look in Finn's direction, he disappeared through the door to the stairs they had come up. Finn swallowed. Now what had he done?

An older man appeared at the doorway. Finn would put him in his fifties, at a guess. About the same height as his own five foot ten. Quite a stocky build, brown eyes, hair graying at the temples. The same ubiquitous suit. He put out a hand to Finn and flashed a tight smile. "Mr. Mayer? Good to meet you, and I'm sorry you have had such a trying journey. Agent Gregory."

Finn stepped forward in relief and shook Agent Gregory's hand firmly. "Pleased to meet you, sir," Finn responded.

Gregory waved Finn in front of him. "Come in, take a seat. There's someone I want you to meet."

Finn walked in, sat, and looked up, a pleasant smile fixed on his face. Two seconds later the smile went, and Finn could barely hear Gregory's words over the pounding of his heart.

A man lounged in the corner of the room. Finn wasn't sure exactly if "man" described the giant he faced. Certainly the office chair, substantial enough for Finn, looked like dollhouse furniture because of the guy who was sitting on it. Pale blond hair was tied back in a leather thong at his nape. He had on a suit, but this one was obviously tailor-made. No suit off the rack would fit the most powerful shoulders Finn had ever seen, and that's when, as far as Finn was concerned, the shit really hit the fan. He couldn't even swallow. He never registered the piercing blue eyes that stared in challenge. He barely noticed the stubble surrounding his jaw or the tightly pressed full lips.

All he'd heard about enhanced humans came flooding back into his mind. The height. The build. The—as if to confirm Finn's thoughts, the man turned to his right—*birthmark*. The small mark under his eye that looked like a lightning bolt.

He fixed his blue eyes on Finn, and Finn felt completely pinned. His arms grew heavy. His legs felt like lead. He strained to inflate his chest to pull oxygen in. Sweat broke out on Finn's brow; he couldn't breathe.

"That's enough, Talon. Dammit," Gregory cursed, and in an instant, the weight crushing him lifted, and Finn took a gasp of oxygen. Then another.

"You see?" The huge man—Talon—lurched to his feet, and Finn couldn't help but wince.

"And how is that test at all fair?" Gregory spluttered. "No regular human can withstand you—you know that."

Finn had had enough. He got shakily to his feet. "Can someone tell me just what the hell is going on?" he demanded.

"You just proved what I have been saying for the last thirty minutes," Talon said in disgust. "That enhanced don't partner with regulars."

Finn looked in astonishment at Gregory.

Gregory sighed. "Finlay Mayer—" He gestured over to Talon. "—meet Talon Valdez. Your new partner."

Finn gazed in horror at Talon. Everything he had spent the last ten years working for had just come crashing down around his ears.

Victoria Sue fell in love with love stories as a child when she would hide away with her mom's library books and dream of the dashing hero coming to rescue her from math homework. She never mastered math but never stopped loving her heroes and decided to give them the happy-ever-afters they fight so hard for.

She loves reading and writing about gorgeous boys loving each other the best—and creating a family for them to adore. Thrilled to hear from her readers, she can be found most days lurking on Facebook where she doesn't need factor 1000 sun-cream to hide her freckles.

Facebook: www.facebook.com/victoriasueauthor
Twitter: @Vickysuewrites
Website: victoriasue.com

ENHANCED
WORLD

WHO WE TRULY ARE

Victoria Sue

Enhanced World: Book Two

Talon's deadly abilities are spiraling out of control. Desperate to keep Finn safe, Talon struggles to protect the man he loves with all his heart and not become the greatest risk to Finn's life.

Finn has no choice but to offer himself as bait for the evil forces kidnapping enhanced children, facing danger he is untrained and unprepared for, and he will have to do it alone.

Does Talon have one last fight in him? Will he slay everyone who wants to destroy Finn and the team, or will he finally discover that to defeat their enemy and the ultimate threat, the biggest battle he has to face is one with himself?

www. dreamspinnerpress.com

Victoria Sue

BENEATH THIS MASK

ENHANCED WORLD

Enhanced World: Book Three

Gael Peterson has spent years hiding behind the enhanced abilities he wears like a mask, even though he is an important, confident member of the FBI's exclusive H.E.R.O. team. The hurt and betrayal of his mom's abandonment and his father's fists are secrets buried deep beneath the ugly scars on his face, and he doesn't trust Jake, his new regular human partner, with any of them. In a world where those with special abilities like Gael's are regarded as freaks and monsters, it won't be easy for him to rely on Jake to have his back, especially when the abilities of a vulnerable nonspeaking enhanced child make that child a murder suspect.

Tempers rise and loyalties are challenged, and when the serial killer targeting the enhanced finally sets his sights on Gael, not only will Gael have to trust Jake with his secrets, he might have to trust him to save his life.

www. dreamspinnerpress.com

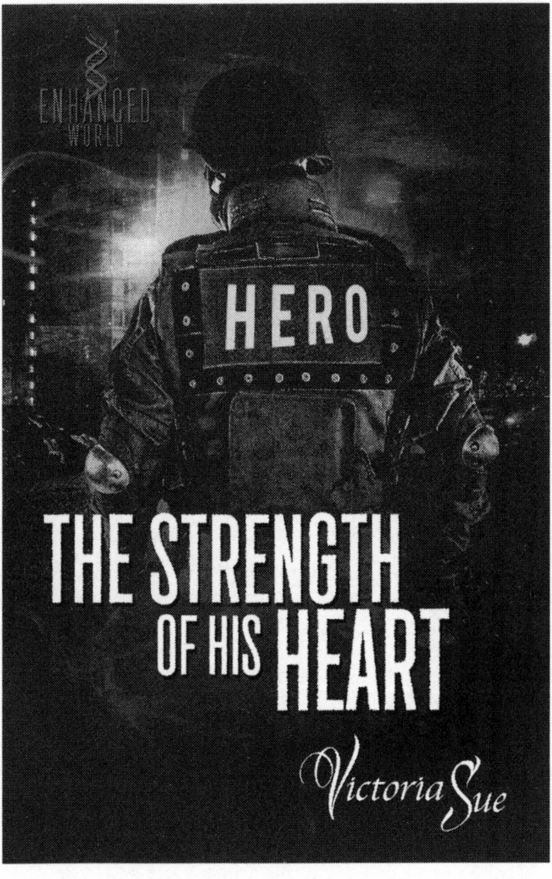
ENHANCED
WORLD
HERO
THE STRENGTH
OF HIS HEART
Victoria Sue

Enhanced World: Book Four

To protect and serve.... All Vance Connelly ever
wanted to do was continue his family's tradition and
join the Tampa Police Department, but his dreams
were crushed the day he woke with the enhanced mark
on his face. After years of struggling to adjust to life as
an enhanced human, by a stroke of luck, he met Talon
Valdez and became a proud member of the FBI's Human Enhanced Rescue Organization.

Samuel "Angel" Piper is eager to leave his DEA
undercover work behind as he joins the HERO team
as Vance's regular human partner. But Sam's painful
past is ever present, just below the surface of the life
he has built for himself as an ambitious young agent.
When the team investigates rumors of a new drug using enhanced blood, the case's mysterious connection
to Sam threatens not just his life but Vance's.

Trust doesn't come easy for Sam, but Vance is
willing to fight to convince his partner that the strength
of his heart might be the salvation they both need.

www. dreamspinnerpress.com

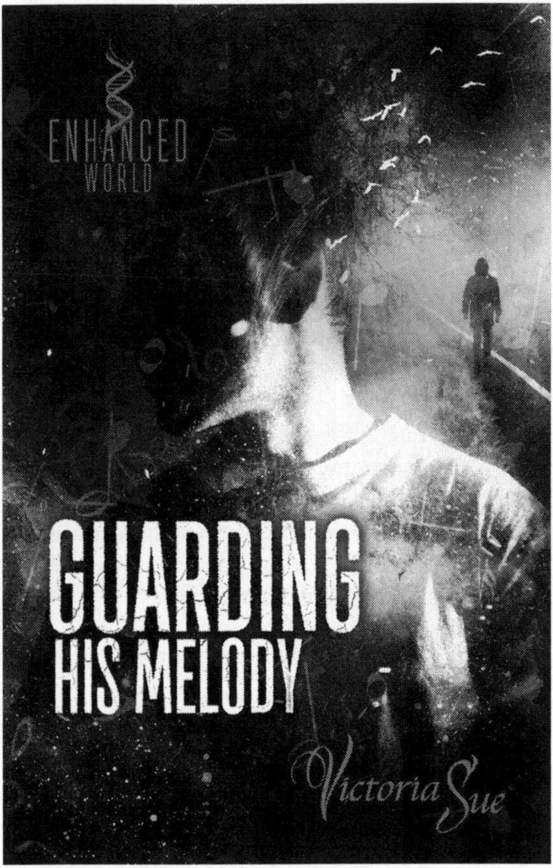
ENHANCED
WORLD
GUARDING
HIS MELODY
Victoria Sue

A Story from the Enhanced World

Deaf since childhood, Sebastian Armitage had a promising musical future until his dreams were shattered when he transformed at twelve years old. In a world where enhanced humans are terrorized and imprisoned, his life shrinks around him even more as he suffers the torment of his father's experimental research to enable him to hear.

Gray Darling—struggling with the scars left by his experience in Afghanistan—agrees to provide short-term personal protection when anonymous threats escalate into assault on those closest to Seb.

As the lines between protection and attraction blur, Gray and Seb can't ignore the intense feelings drawing them together. But secrets and betrayals might prove deadly, unless Gray is willing to risk it all. And Seb must find the strength to make his own future and sing his own song....

www. dreamspinnerpress.com